Powers of the Mind

They were a very special group, indeed.

Each one of the women was blessed—or cursed? —in some particular way with an extra sense, a unique talent, or an unusual ability . . . something which made them seem very frightening to the rest of the world.

Who could feel easy with a mindreader, a precog . . . or with someone who could teleport? Not many people, that was for sure.

And so the Wild Talents banded together out of necessity, both for mutual protection against a hostile world and for some warm human contact.

Then they began to train themselves for even greater power . . .

To Ride Pegasus

by Anne McCaffrey

A Del Rey Book

BALLANTINE BOOKS • NEW YORK

This book is
respectfully dedicated to
Betty Ballantine,
a woman of many talents

Contents

1 To Ride Pegasus   1

2 A Womanly Talent   57

3 Apple   121

4 A Bridle for Pegasus   157

1

To Ride Pegasus

To Ride Pegasus

The slick pavement, oily with rain and motor lubricants that had dripped from the hundreds of ill-repaired vehicles utilizing the major north-south artery into Jerhattan, caused the accident. Henry Darrow had not been exceeding the speed limit when he passed the old two-seater. But he had a date with destiny. And kept it on time.

Had there been no rain that day, or had the lane been closed as scheduled for resurfacing, or had the old two-seater maintained the minimum speed in the left-hand lane, Henry Darrow would not have been exasperated enough to pass, would not have skidded on the slick paving, would not have crashed into the guard rail, would not have fractured his skull so that a bone fragment pressed against the brain pan; had the accident occurred even half a mile further up the arterial road, Henry Darrow would not have been sent to the one hospital in the area equipped with a special electro-encephalograph.

As things came to pass, this was how his accident was to occur: exactly how. In fact, he had jotted down the exact time in his astral notebook: 10:02:50 post meridian. He had also reminded himself that day not to take the arterial route back into Jerhattan but he had not foreseen one slight delay at the gasoline station which caused him to change his mind and take the fateful route, forgetful of his own prognostication.

Of course, since it was a major turning for him as well as millions of other people, he could never have avoided

3

the accident. Which is why his subconscious—or so it is maintained—prevented him from remembering his forecast at the critical moment.

Henry Darrow was therefore injured, seriously, with minor fractures in the left leg as well as the depressed fragment of skull bone. Had Henry been fully conscious during surgery, he would have assured the surgeons that, despite the severity of the wound, he would live. They would have been dubious. Henry Darrow *knew* when he was going to die—from myocardial infarction, some fifteen years, four months, and nine days in the future.

He couldn't tell them since the cranial pressure affected his speech center and he was mercifully unaware of his surroundings. Brain surgery can be a harrowing experience.

The operation was technically successful and Henry was assigned a bed in the intensive care ward, cardiac and encephalographic monitors keeping close track of his vital systems. The Southside General Hospital boasted the very latest technology, including one of the ultra-sensitive electroencephalographs, familiarly known as "Gooseggs." The Goosegg equipment was developed during the Apollo flights in the 70s, to monitor the effects of the mysterious "lights" which periodically afflicted the astronauts, and to record any suspected damage by cosmic radiation to the brain tissue. The ultra sensitive equipment was primarily used now in hospitals to detect brain damage to newborn infants suffering oxygen starvation during birth, or, as in Henry Darrow's case, brain injuries where similar oxygen deprivation, bleeding, and pressure must be ascertained.

The intensive care nurse on duty when Darrow regained his sense after surgery was, as Destiny preordained, Molly Mahony, a rather plain girl who good-naturedly bore a lot of teasing from her colleagues for her avowed dedication to nursing. She was invariably assigned the critical cases because she had a knack of pulling them through the crises.

"Dr. Scherman, would you look at the print-out on

Mr. Darrow's EEG?" she said when the resident checked in at her station. "The alphas are unusually strong for a man as critically injured as he, aren't they?"

Scherman looked obediently at the graphs, nodded sagely and then gave her a wink. "He been conscious at all? Giving you a line?"

Molly shook her head, very serious though she knew he was teasing her. Scherman always did. "He's not regained consciousness, Dr. Scherman. I'm to notify Dr. Wahlman when he does. But should I give him a ring about these readings?"

"Ah, don't bother, Molly. That one's lucky he can print anything out on the Goosegg. You'd've thought he'd've known better."

"Better? About what? He was an accident casualty, wasn't he?"

"Better about going out at all. He's Henry Darrow, the astrologer. Christ, it costs a fortune to consult him about your future." Scherman snorted. "And he couldn't cast his own properly."

Scherman left after a cursory glance at the other i.c. patients. Molly Mahony looked with renewed interest at the brain injury. She knew of Henry Darrow, though she wouldn't have admitted it to many. No more than she would have admitted to anyone that she felt she had the gift of healing. Unlike her grandmother who'd had no medical background and ran into problems with her "healing hands," Molly had professional cachet and knew best how and when to apply her "whammy."

Having a unique talent, Molly was keenly interested in all the paranormal manifestations. In her lexicon, the astrologist merely used the signs of the zodiac to focus a precognitive gift, one fortunately more scientifically based than tea-leaf reading or card-telling. Just as the nursing profession allowed her to focus her healing talent on a scientific basis. So she knew of Henry Darrow and now tiptoed, like an awed sycophant, to the bedside and stared down at a face she hadn't noticed before.

His face had character even in lax-jawed abnormal coma. The eye-sockets were black and blue pits, and here and there a trace of blood had escaped the emergency clean-up. It was unfair of her to look at him in such a condition. She laid the back of her hand gently against his cheek, not liking the color of his skin. She flicked back the sheet, took a fold of the pectoral skin, and gave it a brutal twist. Well, at least he had reactions. She patted the sheet into place and stroked his cheek again.

The cardiograph pulsed slow but regular, though there were traces in the reading that spelled the beginnings of arteriosclerosis. No more than would be apparent in any reading of a forty-two-year-old heart which had lived well and hard.

Now she placed strong, slender fingers on his temples, pressing lightly, trying to "feel" where the real injury was. Not that which the surgeons had corrected when they removed the splinter and released the pressure on the brain. But the psychic injury, the essential blow to the vitalities of the man, which had been shocked by the proximity of death, by the exigency of the operation—that ultimate violation of personal integrity.

So often in her reading of case histories, she'd seen the simple term "heart failure," or the more complex medical annotation of heart stoppage for a variety of physically inexplicable and unnecessary reasons. Shock, they would term it for lack of better explanation, "the patient died of shock." Fright, Molly called it. When a patient of hers retreated from reality in this sort of fright, Molly would draw that violated integrity back again with her Talent.

The response to her healing touch on Henry Darrow's brow was different and puzzling. The cardiogram etched bolder, stronger peaks and the Goosegg made frantic passes on all four recording bands.

Henry Darrow's eyelids flickered, opened, and a faint smile crossed his lips.

"What the hell hit me?" he asked.

"You hit you," Molly replied, "on the center post of your car when you crashed into the guard rails, Mr. Darrow. Head ache?"

"Christ yes!" He moaned and tried to reach upward.

"Don't. You've suffered a severe concussion, head lacerations, your left leg is fractured . . ."

There was mischief in the clear green eyes that met Molly's. "You're not supposed to tell me such things, are you?"

Molly smiled. "You know anyhow. And you really ought to pay more attention to your own predictions, Mr. Darrow."

The Goosegg chattered crazily and Molly whirled to see what was happening. But Henry Darrow was grabbing her arm, his eyes widening with bewildered surprise and incredulity.

"You're a Gemini. What's your name? You're going to marry me."

Love at first sight is a rare enough incident, particularly in a hospital setting, despite what the romances say. But far rarer was the scientific accident that proved a long suspected truth. For what had registered on the Goosegg's chart was indisputable proof that the parapsychic talent exists. Henry Darrow had a precognitive experience when he looked at Molly Mahony as a person, not just the nurse in attendance, and "knew" she would be his wife.

They did marry, as soon as his leg was out of the cast. Marriage was not the only thing Henry foresaw for Molly: he knew, too, her date of death, a fact he never disclosed to her. Talents, he learned very shortly, had to discount such precogs in their own lives if they were to operate efficiently for others. Molly was treasured, loved and cherished all the days of her life by her husband because he knew how little of her time he would enjoy.

The significance of the Goosegg's remarkable activity did not immediately impinge on Henry's awareness. To

Molly Mahony belongs all the credit, therefore, for lifting the parapsychic function from the realm of chicanery to science.

For starters, Molly was fascinated with the unusual strength and pattern of Henry's EEG charts. She couldn't dismiss, as Dr. Scherman had, the variations. In her favor was a natural inclination to place Henry Darrow's mind into an exceptional category. Added to that, she knew Henry'd had the precognition of their marriage at the precise moment the Goosegg went wild. At the very first opportunity she tried an empiric experiment. She attached the electrodes to her own skull the next time she had occasion to exert her own ability in the intensive care ward. A similar variation occurred in her reading; not as intense as Henry's, but significant. She took several more of herself, and copied those portions of Henry's records which showed this curious excitation.

She was rather surprised that Dr. Wahlman, Henry's surgeon, did not cancel the Goosegg monitoring when Henry appeared to have recovered from the worst of the concussion. She wondered if Wahlman was as interested in the EEG variation as she was.

Henry had two more precognitive incidents before she felt she could approach Dr. Wahlman with her private conclusions.

"For my own information, Dr. Wahlman, what is the significance of this activity in an EEG?"

"Well, now," said Wahlman, taking the graphs diffidently and studying them in a manner which told Molly that he hadn't a clue. "To be frank, Mahony, I don't know. This particular sort of print-out usually occurs just prior to death. And Darrow's very much alive." The surgeon looked towards Henry's closed door with some irritation. Henry had insisted on pursuing his avocation of charting horoscopes, had even imported his computer, embarking on a cerebral activity which apparently had no deleterious effects on his rapid recovery but did not strike Wahlman as exactly the sort of occupation suitable to a man recovering from a near-fatal head injury.

"And these?" Molly showed him her own graphs.

"Whose are these? A terminal reading? No, couldn't be. The alpha's too intense. What are you up to, Mahony?"

"I'm not certain, doctor, but I do know that when Mr. Darrow is . . . hardest at work, that's when this sort of variation occurs."

"Jasus help us, the damned Goosegg's queer for astrology?"

Molly smiled and apologized for bothering the surgeon with anomalies.

"Mahony, if you weren't the best post-operative nurse we have, I'd tell you to bug off. But if you have any idea, any unreasonable idea, why that kind of reading occurs, would you please let me in on the secret?"

She let Henry in first.

"The moment you woke up after your accident and asked was I Gemini and then said I was going to marry you, was that a precog?"

"Fact, my love—fact!"

"No, Henry, stop that now. Later. Answer me. Was your precognitive faculty at work?"

"Violently." The modified bandage on his head gave him a slightly rakish look but he stopped caressing her, responding to her serious mood.

"And, for instance, when Mrs. Rellahan was here, you told me that you had an intense prevision . . ."

"Hmmmm." Henry's mouth tightened slightly with dislike.

"This is what the Goosegg printed out. See, here the rapid needle, strong strokes, the length of the pattern . . . And, in these . . ."

"That's not my pattern, too, is it? Quite a difference."

"No, that's my brain waves. And this is what happens when I'm healing."

Henry looked slowly up at Molly, an incredulous joy

brightening his eyes, a light suffusing his face that re-
warded Molly for her efforts and intuition.

"Molly, my own heart's darling, do you know what we
have here?"

The world in general remained skeptical. Fortunately
Henry Darrow cared very little for the world's thoughts
but he was able to produce proof to a powerful, wealthy
few that the parapsychic faculty existed in certain individuals and could be manifested at will.

A whole new line of research was instigated by those
private persons and concerns which had long hoped for
scientific recognition of the paranormal abilities.

"I've always had a presentiment of Destiny, of being
on the threshold of some vast important breakthrough,"
Henry told Molly during the early hectic days shortly before they formed the first Parapsychic Center. "Most
megalomaniacs do, too, and your psychotic paranoids like
Nero, Napoleon, Hitler and Kyudu. That's why I had that
team of psychiatrists examine my mental health with fine
Freudian tongs. Nonetheless it's a prejudicial admission.
D'you know, I've been afraid to forecast my own future
too far in advance now? Some details are unwise for any
man to know . . ." He looked with unfocused eyes at the
blank wall in front of them for a moment before he
smiled reassuringly at her. "I've been a dilettante up till
now and my critics can say either that I gained my wits
in that accident, or lost the few I had, but *that* event was
the threshold of my . . . of our destiny."

"Damn the torpedoes and full steam ahead," Molly replied, gesturing theatrically.

"And torpedoes there will be," Henry agreed grimly.

"I thought you said you didn't see far in advance . . ."

"For myself, I meant. Not for what we must do." He
was silent again for a moment. "God, it's going to be fun."

Molly looked at the amusement in his eyes, the antici-
patory gleam of malice. "For whom?" she asked.

His eyes sparkled as he turned his gaze back to her.

"For us," he said, hugging her affectionately, "for all of us," and he meant the newly recruited Talents. "We may perceive the outcome, but half the fun, most of the fun in life, is getting there. And I've got just enough time."

As soon as he was sufficiently recovered to argue with his surgeons (and because Molly assured Wahlman that Henry couldn't get around *her* vigilance), he was allowed to go back to work full time. Not, as previously, in his capacity as a dilettante astrologer, but as the manager, organizer, fund-raiser, and recruiter par excellence for the Parapsychic Center.

"Mary-Molly luv, it's going to be accomplished in steps, this establishment of the Talented in the scheme of things. Not society, mind you, for we're the original nonconformists," and he tapped his forehead just below the pink flesh of the newly healed head wound. "And Society will never permit us to integrate. That's okay!" He consigned Society to insignificance with a flick of his fingers. "The Talented form their own society and that's as it should be: birds of a feather. No, not birds. Winged horses! Ha! Yes, indeed. Pegasus . . . the poetic winged horse of flights of fancy. A bloody good symbol for us. You'd see a lot from the back of a winged horse . . ."

"Yes, an airplane has blind spots. Where would you put a saddle?" Molly had her practical side.

He laughed and hugged her. Henry's frequent demonstrations of affection were a source of great delight to Molly, whose own strength was in tactile contacts.

"Don't know. Lord, how would you bridle a winged horse?"

"With the heart?"

"Indubitably!" The notion pleased him. "Yes, with the heart and the head because Pegasus is too strong a steed to control or subdue by any ordinary method."

"You couldn't break our sort of Pegasus anyhow," Molly said firmly. "Wouldn't want to even when he flies so high . . ." She burrowed into Henry's arms, suddenly frightened by the analogy.

"Yes, luv. When you ride the winged horse, you can't dismount. Anymore than you can suppress the Talent you've been given. We'll find our bridle, I think, with time and training and more practice at riding.

"That Goosegg was the really important break. Now we can prove parapsychic powers exist and who has them. We can discredit the charlatans and clowns who've given the rest of us a bad name. The real Talents will be registered with the Center, and we'll have graphs to prove they've had valid Incidents. The Center will supply them with the specialized jobs that utilize their Talents. From just a sampling of validly Talented people we've already attracted, I can think of hundreds of top jobs."

"Even Titter Beyley and Charity McGillicuddy?" Molly Mahony Darrow's eyes danced with mischief because Titter drank continuously and Charity pursued an old profession diligently.

"Takes a thief to catch a thief and Titter's been stealing for years to support his habit. Remember that Charity's heart of gold beats in a true telepath's breast."

"Size 42-C."

"Molly!"

"Go on with our future, Henry."

"I want Watson Claire as our PR man because I know damned well he's a receiving telepath: he must be to handle clients the way he does. He's got a positive genius for presenting *the* campaign a client'll buy. Claire's the sort of person we've got to enlist, for his sake as well as ours. Ours, because we've got the biggest goddamn public relations program on our hands, and the public can make or break us. His sake, because he's not happy pushing products he despises."

Molly nodded sympathetically.

"We get an intensive information program going and that will help recruiting. Then we've got to start rescue operations for those hidden Talents and especially those poor misfits in institutions because they heard voices . . . which they did . . . or they imagined impossible things, which they didn't. Or their empathy with the world around them was too great to be endured and they abandoned reality. And we've got to figure out the best way to train these Talents once we've got them verified.

"*Then* we've got to get exactly the right place to live in."

"To live? But this apartment is . . ."

"Okay for us, for the time being. But not for the rest of us. No, now don't worry, Molly luv. I know where we're going."

Molly regarded him steadily for a second. "But you don't know exactly how we'll get there, is that it?"

Henry laughed, nodding.

"That's the challenge, luv."

"And then what's on the agenda? I'd better know the worst."

Henry chuckled to give himself time to evade. "Then comes one of the harder jobs . . ."

Molly's eyes grew round. "You've outlined a lifetime's work and then tell me one of the harder jobs . . ."

"Will be to establish professional immunity for the Talents so we don't get sued out of our eyeball sockets because we said something would happen which didn't because we said it would. Oh, we'll get it sooner or later, but I'd rather sooner than later when you consider the money that'll be tied up in suits. But that won't be my headache."

"It won't be?"

"I can't live forever, luv."

She clung to him and he gave her only a quick embrace.

"I'll live long enough, Mary-Molly luv, and so will

you." He put her away from him then, for he had to keep his desire in check with the pressures of his destiny.

"Now, gentlemen, the subject all wired up to the electroencephalograph, familiarly known as the Goosegg, is a telekinetic Talent. That means, gentleman, that he can move objects without any other agency than his mind. Ralph, would you be good enough to demonstrate?"

Ralph, who used to be known as Rat Wilson, was not the most prepossessing of individuals, being skinny to the point of emaciation, with a rodent-like face and a mouth that remained slightly open due to untended tonsils and adenoids; but his rather large grey eyes were dancing with mischief and interest. That he had perfected his art in the variety of correctional institutions which had attempted to remold him to society's requirements was irrelevant—now.

He sat under the electrode net of the Goosegg at one end of a large hall, a small TV camera throwing a picture of the print-out on the big screen above him. Forty-seven scientists and businessmen were seated around the room, in the center of which sat a table with a variety of objects: a hammer, nails and a plank of wood; a coffee tray with an urn, cups, cream and sugar; a guitar; and a training set of waldoes, limp and grotesque without hands to fill the gloves.

Henry Darrow walked to the other end of the room, as far from both Ralph and the table as possible.

There was a significant silence in the room, with the audience casting glances from table to Ralph to Henry. Suddenly a cup rattled, rose, was joined to a saucer and aligned itself under the spout of the urn which was tapped almost simultaneously to pour coffee into the cup. Belatedly, a spoon clattered into the saucer.

"Who takes it black?" asked Ralph as cup and saucer veered to the nearest watchers.

"I do," said one cool businessman, lifting his hand.

"Hang on to it then, mac," replied Ralph. "Got it?"

"Hey!" The man closed his fingers around the lip of the saucer but when Ralph released it, he was unprepared and the black coffee sloshed over the saucer rim onto his hand.

There was a slight wave of amusement, shattered by the crash of a hammer driving a nail into a block of wood.

"I'll make the next one white. Who's for it?"

A second cup was delivered to its receiver as the hammer drove the nail smartly into the wood. At the same time, the waldoes jerked alive and began to assemble the objects in the tray. The guitar twanged with a bawdy ballad.

With cups sailing around the room, the crack of the hammer to the tempo of the song, the industry of the waldoes leaving everyone gaping, Henry returned to the stage, taking a pointer and starting the sales pitch.

"As you will notice, if you can take your eyes from the flying saucers, Ralph's use of his Talent results in the hard variations of the alpha waves, here and here. The beta fluctuation is rapid, deep. Note the difference at the beginning of the graph before Ralph started. Notice the increase as he stepped up the output of the parapsychic faculty. Has anyone any doubts about the authenticity of this demonstration? Will you accept this print-out as valid, and that the graph represents Ralph's paranormal ability?"

"Stop him!"

Henry signalled to Ralph and coffee cups crashed to the floor. The hammer bounced and fell to the table and the waldoes went limp to a discordant twang on the guitar.

"For chrissake," and the man on whom a cup of coffee had fallen sprang to his feet, wiping at soaked pants and dancing from the hot bath. Instantly the cup righted itself and incredibly refilled with the just-emptied coffee.

"Sorry about that, mac, but someone said stop!"

The abrupt surcease of the parapsychic was recorded on the graph, as was the minor activity of mopping up the spill.

"Hey, my pants are dry!"

"Are there any other questions?" asked Henry, winking surreptitiously to the grinning Ralph.

"Yes," and a heavy set man towards the rear of the room stood slowly to his feet. "Coffee vending machines handle this sort of service, an idiot can drive a nail; granted a waldo is used for delicate sterile operations, any long hair plays guitar . . . not all at once, admittedly, but how would someone like Ralph be employed? And incidentally, I know his background."

"You might say," Henry said with a smile, "that Ralph is a real product of his background of reform school and correctional institution. That's how he acquired his Talent. Society wasn't ready for Ralph or his Talent. We are.

"We've demonstrated here that Ralph can do a variety of things simultaneously; tasks requiring multiple action such as assembling coffee implements and teleporting them to the proper destination, as well as exercises requiring a certain strength and/or precision.

"However, Ralph has a limited range. We've duplicated today's fun and games over a distance of half a mile, but not further with any precision or strength. Ralph is not a superman. That's the first point I wish to impress on you. He has a Talent but it's a finite one, suitable for certain, rather limited use. He would be a profitable investment for someone like yourself, Mr. Gregory, for precision assembly under vacuum, sterile or radiation conditions.

"I don't say that Ralph is a totally reformed character at all," and Henry grinned at Ralph, "but he is now able to purchase legally the things he used to heist. He is subject, and he knows it, to the mental examination of a strong telepath. He also thoroughly enjoys his present occupation."

"You bet, mac." And the scathing look Ralph bent on the audience left no doubts that the little man delighted in disconcerting the men of distinction, rank and position.

"If you can't cure 'em, recruit 'em," Henry added.

"Are you implying, Mr. Darrow, that half the population of jails and mental institutions are peopled by your misunderstood parapsychics?"

"Not at all. I admit we're testing many so-called misfits to see if thwarted or yes, misunderstood, paranormal Talents are not partly responsible for their maladjustment. But that does not mean they are all graduates of institutions.

"Talent, gentlemen, can include something as simple as being a born mechanic. We've all known or heard of the guy who just listens to the sound of an engine and knows what's wrong with it. Or the plumber who can dowse the exact location of a break in water pipes. Or the pyromaniac who "knows" when and where a fire will break out and has so often been accused of starting it; the woman whose hands ease a fever or soothe a pain, the worker who knows instinctively what the boss needs, the person who can always find what's been mislaid or lost. These are everyday, but *valid,* evidences of the parapsychic Talent. These are the people we want to include in our Centers—not just the more dramatic mind-readers and clairvoyants. The Talented are rarely supermen and women, just people who operate on a different wavelength. Employ them in the proper capacity and utilize their Talents to your advantage."

"Besides money, what do you want from us, Darrow?"

"Doctor Abbey, isn't it? From you and your colleagues all over the world, I want the public admission that Talent has left the tearoom and entered the laboratory. We have scientific evidence that the parapsychic faculty exists and can be used, at will, with predictable result. Science, gentlemen, by definition, is any skill that reflects a precise application of principles. The principle in Ralph's case is moving objects without artificial aid."

"I might buy the teleportation, Darrow," replied Doctor Abbey, slightly contemptuous, "but go back to the tearoom a minute. Give me an example of the science behind precognition."

"I knew you'd ask that, Doctor Abbey. And I predict

that you will receive a favorable answer to your latest inquiry into the problem—" Henry raised his hand to suppress Abbey's exclamation, "I'm discreet enough, Doctor
Abbey—into the problem you're investigating with Doctors
Schwarz, Vosogin and Clasmire. That, Doctor Abbey, is
predictable, scientific and accurate enough—since your
correspondence with the three men is a closely guarded
secret—to be convincing. Right?

From the stunned expression on Dr. Abbey's face as he
sank into his chair, Darrow knew he was right and Abbey
was convinced.

"Now," Henry asked the audience in general, "all of
you have had problems which I believe some of our
Talents can solve. What am I offered?"

"Why, after fourteen years and nine rent increases—
which I didn't protest by the way—will you not renew my
lease?"

"Mister Darrow, I've been told that your lease is not
renewable and that's what I've been told to tell you."

"How come the 'Mister Darrow,' Frank? Now look, I've
paid my rent right on the button for fourteen years. I've
had no more than legitimate redecorating, why am I not
able to renew my lease?" Henry knew the problem, had
foreseen this situation, but he was human enough to like
to see people squirm. Particularly if it might let in a little
wisdom and understanding of Talent.

Frank Hummel looked very uncomfortable.

"C'mon, Frank. You know. Don't try to kid *me* you
don't."

Frank looked up with a miserable expression in his
eyes. "And that's it, Hank. That's just it. You do know.
You know too goddamned much and the other tenants
are scared."

Henry threw back his head and roared with laughter.
"No one's conscience is clear? My God, Frank, do they

really think I *know* or care, for that matter, about their petty intrigues and affairs?" Then he saw he'd offended Frank and wished he were a telepath, not a precog. "Frank, I 'see' no more than I did when I used astrology to focus my Talent. No one was afraid of me when I was just a star-gazer."

Frank did squirm at Henry's choice of phrase because that's how the man thought of Henry.

"I can't read minds," Henry went on, "and come to that, Frank, I don't really know what's going on under my nose. My Talent is not for individuals: it's for mass futures. Oh, yes, important individuals who will affect the lives of millions. But not if Mrs. Walters in 4-C is going to have a baby . . . not unless I have cast her individual horoscope . . . and she's too scared of her husband to come to me for that." Henry sighed for even that piece of common sense insight was now being misconstrued by the apprehensive real estate agent. "Look, everyone in the building knows Walters's opinion of me, and how scared she is of him. That takes no Talent at all, Frank. And it takes no Talent either to know that Walters is probably one of the prime instigators in getting me evicted."

"You're not being evicted, Mr. Darrow."

"Oh no?"

"No! It's just that your lease is not being renewed."

"How much of an extension can I have to find new quarters? You know how tight the housing situation is in Jerhattan."

Frank looked everywhere but at Henry.

"Frank . . . Frank? Frank, look at me," and reluctantly, hesitantly, the man obeyed. "Frank, you've known me for fourteen years. Why, suddenly, are you afraid of me?" Henry knew the answer but he wanted Frank to admit it. One man, one Frank Hummel, wouldn't change the struggle of the Talented for acceptance but it might change one other mind now, three next week. Every ally was valuable. And to have allies one had to admit to enemies.

"It's just that . . . that . . . hell, you're *not* a star-gazer anymore, Mister Darrow. You're for real." The apprehension in Frank Hummel's face was equally real.

"Frank, thank you. This isn't easy for you and I will make it less easy but I want you to remember fourteen years of a very pleasant relationship. I knew you'd be here today. I knew it four months ago when Molly and I had that series of graffiti painted on the door and the so-called burglary attempts. I've a lease on new quarters. We're moving tomorrow."

Frank already had too much to think about. "You mean, you *knew*? Already? But I just got the orders yesterday and you *told* me that you didn't see individual . . . and you're—"

"I'm not lying about what I can see, Frank, but I'd certainly better see what affects myself, or a fine star-gazer I'd be. Right?"

Hummel was slowly backing out of the apartment, less and less convinced. Once again Henry wished he were a telepath—or at least empathic—and could know what was running through Frank's mind and counter it.

"Do me one favor, Frank," Henry said. "On the 18th of next month, in the fourth race at Belmont, bet every credit you've been saving on a horse named Mibimi. Only don't place your bet until the last minute before the race. Will you do that for me? And then when Mibimi wins, remember Talent is useful."

Frank had retreated to the elevator and Henry wondered if the confused man had taken in his tip. He didn't often give them but for a friend you can do a favor . . . if it'll cement his friendship.

Henry shrugged as he closed the door. The scene just played in his living room had been repeated over and over, with acknowledged Talents as reluctant dramatis personae.

Just another of those paradoxes which assailed them from all sides now that Talent was respectable. By removing the onus of haphazard performance, by having Talents registered with the Center, they could contract for premium wages. But suddenly the Talents were also elevated into the genus "pariah," found themselves untouchables, unwelcome and feared, all through misunderstanding.

Watson Claire was mounting a massive soft-sell public information program, abetted by his contacts in the media profession who were delighted at something newsworthy. Judiciously applied blackmail kept the worst newsmongers at bay. But it would take time, Claire said (and Henry understood), for the program to seep down to the level where it was most required . . . in the housing developments which were now ousting anyone suspected of possessing Talent.

Well, the immense warehouse Henry had leased in the dock area would suffice until he'd figured out how to appeal to George Henner. That financial wizard had an accounting to make and Henry was vastly amused by recent findings. It was going to be fun watching Henner's reactions.

He picked up the comunit to call the warehouse: the shielding had been in place a week ago so there had been just the finishing of the living quarters. Maybe he should have used telekinetics to move his furnishings? No, that would be a bad scene, however personally satisfying it might be. Some things even Talents had better do the usual way.

"My name is Henry Darrow, Commissioner Mailer. This is my wife, Molly; Barbara Holland is our finder, and Jerry comes along to lug the Goosegg. I believe this is your list of most wanteds?"

"Just what is this?" The Commissioner for Law Enforcement and Order had risen in indignation from his paperfree desk. "My appointment was with James Marshall, not you, Darrow."

"I know. Jim got it for us because you've refused to see . . ."

"A bunch of tearoom crackpots!"

"Well, we're here and you're going to listen . . ."

"Not if I have any say . . ." The Commissioner was fumbling with his desk set and swore when the telltale lights did not wink on at his touch.

"It won't work, Commissioner Mailer," Henry told him. "I forgot to mention that Jerry's telekinetic and keeps closing the switches as soon as you press. Sorry. You're incommunicado until you listen. And watch. Barbara, if you would, please? Here's the list. Just sit here. Ready, Molly?"

The Commissioner's raging did him no good since his office was soundproofed. He continued to fumble futilely with his comunit, unable to believe that it wouldn't function because some nondescript young man stared at it. He didn't notice that Molly was quietly placing the electrode net on Barbara's head. The girl adjusted it into the scalped spots in her hair and nodded to Henry.

"I gather these are in order of preference?" Henry asked the Commissioner. Henry perched on the desk, unperturbed by the Commissioner's belligerence and profanity.

"Preference? What'n'hell are you talking about, Darrow? Get your circus out of here. This is a law enforcement and order . . ."

"Neither of which you are able to maintain with the current restrictions on your men," said Henry, interrupting with such a forceful tone that the Commissioner's sputtering died and he stared at Darrow in amazement. Few people had addressed the LEO man in that tone of voice. "That's why I'm here, to render assistance you can't get from any other agency. Now sit down, shut up, and listen. Who do you want us to find for you first?"

"Find?"

"Find!"

The two men locked eyes and there was a quality in Henry's that wrought a sudden change in the Commissioner.

"All right," Mailer said in a tight hard voice, "find me the man they call Joe Blow."

"The Joy Pill man?"

"That's him."

Henry flicked out the second IBM card and handed it to Barbara Holland.

"Enough for you, Babs?"

The girl studied the sketch drawn by police artists from verbal descriptions of victims of the elusive Joe Blow. She read the notations on his most frequented locations, his general modus operandi. Then she looked up at Henry with a grin.

"This isn't a really fair test, Henry," she said.

"Ha!" exclaimed the Commissioner, an unholy delight in his eyes.

"No," said Barbara, "because I've encountered him so it's easy to track him down." She closed her eyes, clasping the card between her hands. The needles on the Goosegg began to whip across the graph paper. Her smile widened and she opened her eyes. "He's on the corner of 4th Avenue New East and 197th Street. He's wearing a long blue duty mac, with waterproofed shoulders, and a long blond wig. No moustaches today. He's carrying nothing illegal but he has a great deal of money on him and some folded papers."

The Commissioner was fumbling with his comunit. "For God's sake release it or whatever. I've got to get . . ."

"Why?" asked Barbara. "You want him with dust or acid or the Brown Joy, don't you?"

"I want him in any way."

"Can you charge him?"

"I've only got to get him . . ."

Suddenly the comunit came alive on every previously pressed band, but the Commissioner got it sorted out and had a squad vehicle dispatched to the coordinates, to apprehend a man answering Barbara's description. Then he turned back, smiling sourly at the four people. "We'll see

what we'll see. *If* such a man is there, we'll have him in
three minutes. My people are quick and efficient."

"So are mine," said Henry and looked expectantly at
Barbara, who nodded.

"What's that all about?" demanded the Commissioner.

"I'm keeping track of him," Barbara replied, and suddenly the third band began to show activity.

"That is the Goosegg at work, Commissioner Mailer,"
said Henry.

"Are you reading my mind?" Mailer looked alarmed
and angrier.

"Not at all," Henry replied. "I'm not a telepath. I'm a
tea leaf reader on a grandiose scale . . ."

The Commissioner pursed his lips to hear his own
description of Henry Darrow thrown back at him.

"All right, then, tell me now if my men'll succeed?"

"Barbara can tell you better than I. I don't deal generally with individuals. My specialty is mass movement.
But Barbara can find Joe Blow for you now and any time
you want to check on his whereabouts . . ."

"They have him," Barbara said, and held out her hand
for another card.

The Commissioner stared at her suspiciously.

"Oh, let's let his men tell him, Babs."

She shrugged and settled back in her chair. Then
brightened and smiled sweetly at Mailer. "You left your
pipe in your ski jacket, Commissioner, the blue one
which you don't usually wear. If you call home right
now, you'll find your wife there. And remind her the
coat is under your red dressing robe in the first closet."

Mailer regarded her with narrowed eyes. "I thought
you said you weren't a mind reader."

"I never said that," Barbara replied, then pointed to
Henry. "He did. And I can only get impressions of lost
articles. You did lose the pipe and were just now thinking
where had you put it. And the only reason I know about
your wife is because you say you can never find her when

you need her." Barbara kept her face very straight but
Henry knew her to be possessed of a sense of devilment,
very much in evidence under that air of innocent helpful-
ness.

This "finding" was making far more impression on
the Commissioner than her location of Joe Blow.

The comunit buzzed.

"They picked up a man, answering that description.
What do they do with him? He's demanding rights."

Mailer was unprepared for only one moment. "Search
him. There's been a local robbery and a man answering
his description was seen nearby. You're supposed to find
a wad of credits and papers. Invoke citizen search prerogative."

"He's carrying roughly 8000 credits, sir," said Barbara.

"The heist was 8000."

There was a second long tense silence.

"He's got it, sir."

"Book him!"

The fleeting expressions on Mailer's face now told of intense mental conflict. He was a man to whom a miracle
had been offered and he was too scared to accept it.

"Barbara is parapsychic, Commissioner. We brought
Goosegg in to prove to you on a scientific basis as reliable
as ballistics, without a tea leaf in sight, that her mind
generates a specific type of electrical impulse when she
uses her parapsychic Talent. She can't read your mind except when you, or anyone, are worrying about something
lost, strayed or stolen . . ."

"Stolen—" The Commissioner pounced on the word.

"If you mean that hijacked shipment of crowd gas,
Commissioner," said Barbara, "it's in a warehouse, with
a southside feel. It's very dark inside, which hampers me:
I can't see in shadows. I can make out some white air-
freight containers, they've a plastic feel, rather than wood
or steel. There's a geometric design in dark paint in the
lower left hand side." She frowned and the Goosegg chat-

tered rapidly for a moment and then toned down to a mild, normal swing. "I'm sorry. There simply isn't enough light there."

The Commissioner snorted but her information had obviously given him something to work on. "South side . . . air freight . . . white . . ." His fist slapped down an end key. "Jack . . . what air freight companies use white containers with geometric designs in lower left hand . . . Oh, they do. Now, what air freight companies use southside depots . . . Oh. Hmmm. Well, check your contacts like right now." He turned a cold dispassionate look on Barbara. "You can't be more specific?"

Barbara gave Henry a quick glance before answering. "I've already narrowed the search to a small section of the city with as many specifics as I can see. There can't be *that* many warehouses for air freight! I've done more than you've been able to, Mr. Mailer."

"Now, just a minute, young lady . . ."

"You've had more than a minute, Commissioner, and my time is valuable." Barbara was on her feet, the electrode net in her hand. "We're wasting time with this one, Henry. And I don't like him. Miserable vibes from him, just miserable!"

She left the room. Molly quietly began to pack up the Goosegg while the Commissioner stared first at the open door and then at Henry.

"She operates more efficiently with an occasional word or two of thanks, Mailer. Most people do." Henry gathered Molly into the curve of his arm, motioned courteously to Jerry to take the Goosegg and wishing Mailer a pleasant good-day, left.

"Hey, just a minute . . ."

Henry turned at the door. "As Babs said, Mailer, you've had more than a minute and our time is valuable."

"Does Charity have to be sedated again, Gus?" Henry asked the Center's physician. "We've got her a temporary contract to find out the troublemaker in the Arrow Shirt Company."

Gus ducked his head, his face twisted into a grimace, wanting to say no and having to say yes. He leaned against the now flagged door to Charity McGillicuddy's two roomed accommodation on the living floor of the Center's warehouse building.

"Even with the shielding we've got, Hank, it's not enough privacy for the empaths and telepaths. Not enough physical distance. No way to get out and away from ourselves, if you get what I mean. We're sort of all crammed into this warren despite the conveniences and amenities. You might say, it's too much of a good thing . . . too close a buddy-buddy act. Like an overdose of euphorics. Everyone's high here on sheer good fellowship. And it's much too much for Charity."

Henry looked towards the corridor window with the projection of sunlight on the grass, a huge spreading beech tree, russet against an autumnally blue sky. Though it was so realistic that the leaves moved gently and the angle of sunlight altered slowly, Henry knew it to be only a projection and his mind would not accept the fantasy that deluded millions of warren dwellers.

"Talent requires certain realities not obtainable in this age," Gus went on. "And one of the most important is physical freedom and elbow room." He snorted, aware of the impossibility of fulfilling that requirement in Jerhattan's overcrowded boundaries.

"We've been offered that old game preserve in . . ."

"Too goddamned far to commute and most of us gotta." Molnar was head neurologist at the Midtown Hospital Center although he spent more time as the Center's physician.

"Okay," Henry said, "I'll do what I can."

"Henry?" Gus eyed his friend suspiciously. "What are you up to now?"

"Me? Nothing." Then Henry Darrow assumed a crouched stance and rubbed his hands together, chuckling evilly. "But Destiny . . . haha HA! I know when we twain shall meet. Soon!"

Gus rolled his eyes heavenward to deal with Henry Darrow in this whimsical mood.

"Oh, don't worry, Gus," Henry said in a normal voice. "I usually call 'em, you know."

Gus nodded sourly.

"Content yourself," Henry continued, "with the enticing thoughts of dissecting my brain when I die, and trying to figure out just how I do it."

"Ha!"

"You can't subpoena Barbara Holland, not on those grounds, Commissioner Mailer," Henry Darrow said. "But you can hire her services from the Center . . ."

"What Center?" demanded Mailer, looking scornfully around the minuscule space that served as Henry's office.

"The Center we'll shortly acquire with the wages you'll be paying Talents like Barbara, and Titter Beyley and Gil Gracie and . . ."

"Titter Beyley?" The Commissioner hovered on the verge of apoplexy.

"Yes, Titter. He drank to stop finding things. Alcohol affects the parapsychic faculty, sometimes it inhibits, as in Titter's case; sometimes it sharpens."

"Now, just a minute, Darrow . . ."

"My minutes are valuable, Mailer. I only have so many. You want things and people found: Barbara has that faculty and so does Titter Beyley. Actually Titter's much better for inanimate objects than Barbara. He doesn't like people. And the day you find out he's been drunk on duty, *then* complain."

"And you mean to stand there, young man, and tell me that I'm going to get shot at Saturday? Again!" Governor Lawson tipped his chair back and roared with laughter: an exercise he broke off abruptly to glare with an intensity akin to hatred at Darrow and the wraith-like Steve Hawkins. "So what else is new?"

"The predictive Incident says that a .38 slug will penetrate the right ventricle." Steve's voice shook slightly. Henry wondered if he'd made a mistake in bringing Steve, who was very new to his gifts and the Center's staff. "The man will approach from the left . . ."

"What does it matter where he comes from?" The Governor said, sharply, hostilely. "Oh, I don't disbelieve you, Darrow. Or you, Hawkins. I've heard too much about you people to be skeptical anymore. But, if I don't appear . . ."

"You have to appear," Henry replied. "We ran the alternates through a probability computation and find that your appearance at that Forum Meeting must take place to sway a currently uncommitted 8% of the popular vote to your party. Without that 8%, you fail to receive the critical majority and if you fail, the Laborites can obtain the plurality they need to effect a counter-measure that would have disastrous consequences on the economy."

Governor Lawson began a chuckle, his belly shaking first before the amusement was shunted up the rotund abdomen to the chest and finally became audible in the head cavity. Finally Lawson's lips parted to emit a rich, juicy laugh.

"So, that's the way it'll be, huh?"

"Yes, if your eloquence doesn't falter with foreknowledge."

"Huh? How's that?"

"You have been given a prescience of the immediate future. Such knowledge could, in itself, alter the circumstances of the future. We do not always have either the personnel or the foresight to modify the future. In your case, we make an exception. A Laborite Majority is not a good thing for the Talented."

Governor Lawson nodded in appreciation of that expediency.

"Your man will intercept the bullet?"

Henry nodded.

"And the nut will be put away? That's better than leaving him free for another shot. Good! How many political figures does your group protect?"

"Those who need it. And we'd appreciate a kindly word for the Center when Steve diverts that bullet."

Lawson nodded agreement. "Those who need protection? Or those whom you need, Darrow? No, don't answer that one. Answer this . . . will I win this election?"

Henry smiled slowly. "You know the answer to that one, Governor, but the *fun* lies in making certain you've played the game right."

"How far do you guys play fun and games?"

"Just far enough!"

"Now, Mr. Rambley, what seems to be your problem?"

"Not my problem, Mr. Darrow. Yours!" The Internal Revenue Department man smiled a thin smug smile and began to pull IBM cards from his neat fake-pig case.

"Really?"

"We have here WT forms from the Department of Law Enforcement and Order, from Johns Hopkins, Bethel General, Midtown, from Dupont, Merck Pharmaceuticals . . . need I go on?"

"Just as you please."

"These salary chits represent the earnings of Barbara Holland, Titter Beyley, Charity McGillicuddy, Gil Gracie, Frank Negelsco, Augustus Molnar . . ." Again the IRD representative regarded Henry Darrow with a cute expression on his fleshless face. "I could continue . . ."

"Just as you please. I give every government official the courtesy due his office." Henry inclined his head towards Mr. Rambley who, for the first time since he'd minced into Henry's tiny lair, looked nonplussed. "After all, some of my best people are employed by the government."

With an irritated sigh, Rambley closed the stack of cards and tapped them in an admonitory fashion on the desk.

"Come now, Mr. Darrow. These people," and he brandished the cards, "earn tremendous salaries and yet there is no record of a single tax deduction, no returns . . ."

"They donate their salaries *in toto* to the Parapsychic Center. They lease their services contractually to the various employers. The Parapsychic Center files a corporate form to cover them. Under Corporation Law. . . ."

"No one in their right minds would . . ." Rambley bounced on the end of his chair with indignation and disbelief.

"I never said any of the parapsychic Talents were in a right mind. In fact," Henry went on with gentle amusement, "there is every reason to believe that the core of the parapsychic is, if anywhere, in the left hand part of the brain."

"Mr. Darrow," Mr. Rambley was on his feet. "You did say that you gave government officials the courtesy due their office?"

"Yes, didn't I? Consequently, you're wasting time, your government's and mine, Mr. Rambley. The individuals represented by those neatly slotted cards do donate their total income to the Parapsychic Center. Our accountant will be glad to show you the appropriate records and contractual agreements . . ."

"But . . . but I *know* that that Titter Beyley creature is driving a four passenger 350 horsepower vehicle!" Such an incongruity shocked Mr. Rambley.

"Yes, Titter's always wanted to drive a big one. The car belongs to the Center. You can check the registration papers."

"And that . . . that Charity McGillicuddy has a blue ranch mink coat."

"Indeed she has. She requisitioned it from Stores about four months ago."

"She requisitioned . . . from Stores?"

"She has a position to maintain now and her appearance is of great concern to the LEO office. Think how embarassing it would be for someone employed by the LEO Commission to be arrested for wearing stolen furs. Of course, Charity says that now she can buy 'em instead of 'lifting' 'em, half the fun's gone. But it gives her a great moral boost to wear blue ranch mink in the LEO Block. We try to keep our workers happy."

Rambley had stared at Henry Darrow through this ingenuous explanation but his indignation rose with every gently spoken word.

"This won't be the last you'll hear from me, Mr. Darrow. You do not mock the Internal Revenue Department, Mr. Darrow." He slammed the file cards into his case, hands trembling with outraged dignity. "You'll hear from us."

"That's fine by me. Just call ahead for an appointment. Only consider the fact that Senators Maxwell, Abrahams, Montello and Gratz approved our corporate structure."

Rambley's eyes widened.

"And the presidential advisor, Mr. Killiney, acted as our financial assistant. Don't you have *his* card in that file?"

Rambley exited, reduced to mutterings.

"Do you often trick your way into a private home, Mr. Darrow?"

"When I've been unable to secure an appointment any other way, yes, Mr. Henner." Henry smiled pleasantly, trying not to glance with obvious envy at the spaciousness of the magnificently furnished living room. Such accommodation was almost archaic.

George Henner appeared more amused than irritated by Henry Darrow's impertinence as he leaned back in his Italian brocade armchair.

"If it's money for your palm-reading, table-tilting crystal-gazing tricks, forget it."

"On the contrary, sir. I've affirmation that I can ask you to join our happy band." Henry smiled at the surprise in Henner's yellowed eyes.

"Join you?" Henner burst out laughing. His head went back showing a veritable gold field of fillings in his upper teeth. "By God, Darrow, you've made my day! If you can't lick 'em, recruit 'em?"

"Actually," Henry went on smoothly, seating himself and crossing his legs, counterfeiting an ease he didn't feel. He noted the flicker of irritation in Henner's face but the financier had a reputation of letting a man have enough rope to hang himself. "Actually, Mr. Henner, your abilities in the financial world are as solidly derived from the parapsychic as my own. Incidentally, you're the crystal ball reader . . . although I see you've got a modern computer for stock market print-out instead of the old glass case."

Henner gave an amused grunt but said nothing, his silence a subtle prod to keep Henry talking.

"You're known," Henry continued obediently, because that was the way the interview ought to proceed, "to have a genius, a second sight into what stocks are going to rise, which will fall, what bond issues will pay the keenest long-term profit. And I can prove that you're parapsychic."

Henner cocked his head slightly to one side, his amusement deepening, as he tacitly encouraged Henry to produce his proof. Darrow spread the graph out on the table. "I know you've followed the newsmedia coverage on us, so you're familiar with this sort of graph. What you may not immediately appreciate is the fact that this is your graph."

Henner became immobile with attention.

"When you had your last routine physical a month ago, your physician employed a Goosegg. He didn't realize that it wasn't his own office model so he's blameless. You did, however, experience what we call an Incident and it is recorded on this graph, here and here. I believe the Incident was in connection with the Allied Metals and Mining merger in which you managed quite a 'killing.' "

"You don't read thought from an EEG graph, Darrow."

"Hardly. But you placed a phone call directly you were through your physical to your office and within the next few hours the merger was announced . . . but not before you had acquired a tidy pile of Allied stock. Are my *facts* correct?"

Henner nodded slowly, his eyes, narrowed to intense slits, watching Henry Darrow's face.

"That's proof," Henry said, rustling the graph paper, "that you're parapsychic, Mr. Henner."

The silence which ensued, designed to make Darrow exceedingly uncomfortable, did not. For a long space, Henry returned George Henner's stare, then folded his arms and gazed around the beautiful room. Finally he turned back to Henner and smiled.

"Blackmail?" asked Henner.

Darrow shook his head.

"No. You'd be far too clever for that. No, I'd hazard the guess that you want to borrow my Talent, as you call it, to make your fortunes? That would still be essentially blackmail, wouldn't it, Darrow?"

Henry pursed his lips a little, expressing dubiety.

"Well, then what is it you want from me? It's something."

"Actually, it's the twelve acre tract of land on the Palisades."

Once again Henry wished he were a telepath to read the emotions swiftly passing through George Henner's mind. He had startled the financier, he had touched the most vulnerable point of the shrewd man's life: his intense love, and need for, the beautiful estate of Beechwoods. It had been in Henner's family for a hundred and forty years, was a showplace which few saw. And Henner's need of Beechwoods was as great and for the same reasons as Henry Darrow's.

"How could you know?" demanded Henner in a hoarse whisper.

"That the State intends to confiscate all privately held lands within a hundred mile radius of the Jerhattan city limits? I know because it is as important to me as it is to you to know these things."

Henner was on his feet, pacing to release the energy of his anger. In a barely audible monotone he inventively assigned destinations to the State en masse, the needs of the unhoused, unwashed multitudes in general and those particular officials who had failed to keep Henner's ancestral home inviolate.

"If, however, the property is already owned by a religious, medical, educational or charitable institution which will accommodate a sufficient number of our ever-expanding population, they cannot confiscate your property even under the terms of Section 91, Paragraph 12 of the Housing Act of 1998."

"This is 1997, man. That Act isn't passed yet. I can still defeat it."

"No. It will be passed."

Henner tried to stare that knowledge out of Henry's mind.

"And you know the inevitability, Mr. Henner. None of your contacts can hold out any hope of defeating that measure, nor of defending your Beechwoods."

"And it's your table-tilting tea-leaf readers who'll infest my home?"

"Your physical condition is poor, Mr. Henner, and your nerves damned near the breaking point. The solitude and privacy of this house and its grounds are vital to your life. It would be to any parapsychic mind forced to tune in on the emotional chaos that haunts the very air we breathe. You know you've been living on borrowed time for the past year. You know what alternative dwelling accommodations will do to you."

"Do you happen to know," asked Henner casually for he'd got control of himself again, "the exact date of my death?"

"As I know the exact time of mine, Mr. Henner. You will die of a heart attack, the aorta will be closed by a globule of the arteriosclerotic matter coating your veins, at nine-twenty-one PM, exactly one year, nine months and fourteen days from now."

A gleam of challenge livened the deadly intent of Henner's gaze. "And if I don't?"

"If you don't, then revoke the grant of Beechwoods to the Center. In the meantime, you'll have secured your last days in the ancestral home, which is your prime concern at the moment."

"I could have a heart transplant . . ." Henner was clearly enjoying this.

"Not with a diseased liver and the condition of your arteries."

"And that's your prophecy, Darrow?"

"A medical certainty," Henry said. "I've toyed with the notion of a transplant myself since my death will also occur from myocardial infarction on a certain May twelfth, at ten-fifty-two PM. But by May twelfth of that year, I intend to have accomplished the major part of what needs to be done to establish a viable, self-sufficient Parapsychic Center in North America . . ."

"On the Beechwoods estate?"

"On the Beechwoods estate. By May twelfth, I shall be grateful for the peace and tranquillity of my grave."

Henner's eyes flicked from Darrow's to some inner middle distance, the harsh cynical lines of the financier's face softened.

" 'Ease after war, death after life does greatly please'?" The words were softly spoken but there was no quarter in the hard look Henner then turned on Henry Darrow.

"In your scheming where does this house end up?"

"As an integral part of the Center."

Henner's expression was ironic. "And my money? I've no next of kin."

Darrow laughed. "You keep harping on your money, Mr. Henner. We don't *need* your money. Check our books on that. But only the Center can offer one of its own members what his money hasn't been able to secure for him."

For a long time Henner gazed out the French windows that gave on the flagged terrace, towards the sweep of magnificent lawn and the superb beech trees. When Henner finally turned back to Henry, his hand was extended. The two men shook three times in the ancient custom of binding a bargain.

"Answer me one thing, Darrow! Did you foresee winning?"

"I knew that we would eventually secure Beechwoods, Mr. Henner," he said, permitting regret to tinge his voice. "But I wanted your cooperation."

"Cooperation? You goddamn well know I had no choice!"

"Didn't you?"

George Henner had wandered into the Graph room just as the first of the three Incidents was recorded. He had the habit of appearing in the various departments, taking what he called a perverse interest in the eventual eviction of the Center from Beechwoods. In point of fact, Henner had admitted to Molly Darrow that the Center had given him something to live for. He'd been feeling much better since Henry'd conned him out of Beechwoods. Despite his professed intention of harassing Henry, George Henner's passing suggestions were usually solid advice. And despite his crotchety and often irascible manner, the Talents became fond of him.

"Got a strong Incident," Ben Avedon, the duty officer,

told Henry on the intercom just as George Henner wandered into the Graph room. "Patsy Tucker."

In moments, Henry and Molly arrived in time for Patsy's phone call of such details as she'd "seen."

"I'm on the water again," she said, breathless in an attempt to verbalize before details escaped her. "And there're boats. Four. Sun's at a late afternoon angle, on my left so I must be looking north. There's land beyond the boats, pines, a bluff. And oil on the water. I can see it all rainbowy. The oil scares me. It's going to ignite, and then the water's covered with flames and the boats are eaten up and . . . oh, it's going to be wicked, Ben. Can you locate? Have I given you enough? I can't remember anymore and the flames cover any details."

"It is a sooner?"

"Awful soon. Today. I'm sure of it. But it's morning, and I saw late afternoon . . . is there time enough?"

"Sure. Plenty of time. I'm feeding the computer with the data right now. Old didactic will pin the place down, Pat. But have you a notion about the size of the boats involved?"

"Oh, yes, of course. How stupid of me. I forget you haven't seen. One's small, a pleasure craft . . . a power boat . . . no sails. That's the one that goes on fire. Two long low boats . . . I guess they'd be tankers. And a higher boat . . . I mean, one higher above the water . . . And they're all much too close together. That's the problem because they'll all catch fire."

"A pleasure boat, two tankers and a freighter in the late afternoon. That's fine, Pat. And the pines and bluff and being close together indicate a channel of some description. Now . . . think hard again, Pat. Did you see any markings on the boats, funnel markings, ensigns, names?"

After a silence Pat mournfully admitted "seeing" nothing because the fire and smoke occluded.

"Get one of the pyros on it," Henry told Ben. "Patsy, Henry here. That's a good job, lass. Now take it easy.

We'll buzz you back with confirmation. Grand work, Pat." Henry disconnected her line, shaking his head, knowing how worried the girl would be until she heard they'd prevented the collision. If only there'd been markings to speed up identification, and then if the participants could be dissuaded from arriving on the previewed scene. . . . He moved deliberately to the computer panel and began tapping out queries. "Undoubtedly a seaway. Could be Sheepshead Bay area, East River . . . no, not there. Or one of the canals . . ."

"St. Lawrence, with tankers *and* freighters . . ." suggested Ben.

"Or the Great Lakes . . ." said Molly.

Before there'd been a print-out on possible locations or what traffic was already in the St. Lawrence Seaway, a second graph began to chatter.

"Right on time," said Ben. "Here's Terry, our local friendly reliable pyro."

"How come you don't *know*, Hank?" George Henner asked, settling himself on a stool in the corner.

"Not enough people involved, George, and too close a range for me. That's Patsy's specialty—cliff-hangers. Besides, don't you agree that the good executive makes all the long-range decisions and leaves ·the picayune nitty-gritty details to keep his staff occupied?"

George grinned but he said nothing more, listening as intently as the others to Terry Cle's verbalization of his "sight." The broad outline correlated with Patsy's although he "saw" the event from a different perspective. He had sufficient detail on one tanker and the small craft to result in exact IDs for both from Ship Registration. And there was a tanker of the Iricoil Line proceeding down the Seaway en route for Toronto, ETA 7:48 PM at that port. The small craft, the Aitch Bee, was registered to an A. Frascati, and was at that moment moored in a small boat basin on the American side of the Seaway.

Probability figured the cost of the collision and fire at several millions and a thirty-six hour tie-up of Seaway traffic, plus delayed cargoes which would complicate schedules and routines for ninety-two companies, involving work-loss of some eighteen thousand people.

"Okay, Ben, get out the usual warning format. See if Iricoil will listen to us."

"And if Iricoil doesn't want to believe?"

"We get after this Frascati. In fact, he'd be easier to bully than Iricoil but we've got to warn them, too."

Iricoil was suspicious and uncooperative and, in phrases just short of insult, refused to consider diverting the tanker. Its supplies were urgently required in Toronto by late evening. Frascati was not at his home nor in his business office. Urgent messages were left for the man to contact the Center before taking out his pleasure craft. Henry was dialing the Seaway Authority Control when George cut the connection.

"I've got an idea, Hank," George said. "I've watched this routine so often and seen you insulted, ignored, and calumniated. No one trusts the altruist anymore, whether he's Talented or not. You've warned Iricoil, tried to do them a favor. They aren't buying. Well, like the puppy who leaves too many messages, let's rub their nose in it."

"You mean, let the accident occur?"

"More or less. Considering what's involved in terms of credit and work-loss, and considering that I have shares in four of the companies to be effected by the snarl-up, will you play it my way, this once?"

Henry began to relax. "What have you in mind, George?"

"You did leave timed messages at Iricoil and for Frascati, didn't you?"

Ben Avedon tapped the computer panel. "All time-sealed, George."

"Fine. Now, issue a telex warning to Seaway Authority. Then give me a few comlines to work from and Molly to help me. Irenee was telling me about their new oil-pollutant at Dupont. This would be good PR for him. Always like to oblige friends. Which reminds me, you get on to

Jim Lawson . . . our revered Governor owes you a favor or two for that bullet Steve stopped. And ask him for a few more VTOLs and a couple of frogmen."

"Why?"

"You don't know?"

Henry grinned. "Would you believe an educated guess?"

Henner chuckled. "My, my, how the mighty have fallen . . . Guessing!"

"Run the show your way, George."

"Yes, let a pro show you how, Henry Darrow. You're too damned soft. You talk too much. Action speaks louder than a hundred of your Talented words."

At exactly 16:32 hours of a bright spring afternoon, an Iricoil tanker proceeding down the St. Lawrence Seaway fouled its propellor on a tangle of steel cables, origin unknown. The tanker drifted athwart the current as a United Line freighter entered the narrow channel from the opposite direction. A second tanker, also United Line, making speed enough to reach Toronto port by dark, cruised into the danger zone, although it was apparent that the Iricoil boat was in distress. Both United Line ships continued, evidently hoping to pass the injured vessel, one on the port, the other on the starboard. Likely they would have succeeded but the Aitch Bee, also impatient to reach port, came bucketing down the searoute. It swung rather close to the distressed vessel. As Frascati ever after maintained, he wanted to see if he could be of any assistance in getting a message ashore: a ridiculous alibi since the tanker was well equipped by radio and ship-shore telephone. Frascati's propellor became fouled on the same villain cable. The freighter began to pass the disabled pair and her wash slammed the small craft into the Iricoil tanker. The United Line tanker was broadside of the Iricoil when her bow swung out. Tanker #2 swung to starboard to avoid a collision and her stern banged into

Iricoil, splitting a seam in the aft oil hold just as the small craft was ground between the two bigger hulls. Its galley fires caught old grease and spread in the cabin as the yacht's gasoline tank was breached. Oil pouring from the Iricoil vessel would shortly ignite from that flame.

At this point the hovering rescue copters intervened as newsmedia cameras recorded the event from every angle. Foam quickly doused the yacht fire, the oil-pollution material gobbled up the spilt petroleum and kinetics held back additional oil loss by pressure until the teleports could get the conveniently handy plates into position. Other kinetics and the frogmen worked loose the steel cable and it was hoisted out of the way. "Captain" Frascati and the two crew members (his sons) of the damaged yacht were lifted up and another team of kinetics kept the little ship floating until the belatedly arriving coast guard cutter could tow it into port.

The Seaway was not blocked since all four vessels were cleared out of the narrow channel before others made the passage. There was no loss of life and no long-term pollution of the water. The Parapsychic teams were volubly and embarassingly thanked for preventing a major disaster, and by cocktail time everyone was pleased by the denouement, especially Patsy Tucker and Terry Cle.

The congratulatory euphoria lasted twelve hours, at which point the Seaway Authority began to realize that matters had come to near-disaster in an unprecedented way.

"What was the meaning of sending us only a telex to announce a major disaster?" the Seaway Commissioner demanded in such stentorian tones that George Henner need not have listened in on the second comunit in Henry's office.

"You were informed by telex, as usual," Henry replied in a mild tone of voice.

"By telex! When countless millions of credits were at stake? And blockage of the most important waterway in North America? And do you realize that we have only just balanced the sealife ecology in that strip of waterway? That oil . . ."

"You were informed . . ."

"Well, I'm informing you that you're in for a suit of criminal negligence . . ."

"Negligence of what, Commissioner? You were informed nine hours and thirty-eight minutes prior to the accident by this ex-officio group, which is not a government sponsored or accredited agency. We act for and in the public interest. But we are understaffed and overworked. You could have queried this office for more particulars, although all we had were included in that telex. Your Authority could have held back any one of the four vessels involved, thus preventing the . . ."

"Are *you* accusing the Seaway Authority of negligence?"

Henry held the receiver away from his ear, shook his head, and replied in his mildest manner, "Forewarned is forearmed, sir." He caught George Henner giving the high sign of approval.

"You'll hear from us, Darrow. You people can't get away with irresponsible behavior like this."

The connection was rudely and noisily broken.

"Did you figure a lawsuit in your calculations, George?" asked Henry.

Henner rubbed his hands together in glee. "*If* they sue, we'd win."

Henry couldn't exactly share in Henner's gleeful anticipation. The precog knew of the multitude of lawsuits which would be served on Talents in the next decades and the sheer cost of inspired defense made him shudder. The money would be available but it was credit that could be used to better advantage in training and identifying Talent, not defending against misunderstanding and greed. By late afternoon, Henry's premonitions of immediate disaster were borne out by additional suits of negligence which arrived from United Line, Iricoil Tankers and A. Frascati.

"Let me handle this," George Henner told Henry and his hastily convened executive staff. "I don't need any crystal ball or anerodic graph needle to tell me how to manage this sort of crap."

Before he had Henry's voiced approval, he was on the wires to the major media networks, chatting familiarly with presidents and commissioners. By the time the films of the Parapsychic Center's assistance had been widely aired, with a few choice comments on how the Center operated to forestall major disasters, the threatened legal action against the Talents was withdrawn. Suits were entered against the Seaway for criminal negligence. Then the Center, on George Henner's advice ("Make 'em pay for it, when they don't listen to you."), sent bills for the rescue operations to Frascati, United Line and Iricoil Tankers.

"And from now on, Henry," George said, "don't ever follow up your telex warnings with personal phone calls. Don't be the supplicant, damn it. Be the prelate!"

Henry watched with inner amusement as George Henner paced up and down the floor, his eyes flashing, even his stride firm and aggressive so that Henry could see traces of the strengths which had amassed George Henner his considerable fortune and which had overwhelmed less determined adversaries in the business world.

"There's no point in you bruising your larynx with persuasion. You've proved your worth over and over again and this Seaway bollix ought to make a validated Parapsychic warning worth the paper it's printed on, even at the dreadful price of paper these days."

"A sound argument, George, and I appreciate your help . . ."

George stopped midstride, glaring at Henry through narrowed lids.

"Yes, I am helping you, aren't I? Shouldn't do that, should I?"

"My friendly enemy," replied Henry with a laugh.

"Ha! Tell me that when my executors snatch the rug of Beechwoods from under your telepathetic feet . . ."

"And we need you, George," Henry raised his voice to overwhelm Henner's snide remarks. "If I can convince a skeptic like you, I'm well away to swaying John Q. Public to my side. He's more variable than you, and he will be the hardest to win over."

John Q. Public, however, quixotically decided the Seaway Authority had been foolish to ignore the Parapsychic warning. Criticism was heaped on the Seaway from every quarter. Later the Authority was somewhat exonerated of primary guilt since the Court felt that good judgment on the part of any one of the other three skippers would have prevented the accident and no costs were awarded the claimants. The official records cited and credited the Parapsychic Center with averting a major calamity, and loss of life and property. All Transport Authorities were severely enjoined to heed any warnings from the Center which involved public transport.

For the next few weeks all precogs of traffic problems, possible fire, storm or spring floods throughout the world were instantly acted upon. The Center was besieged with anxious calls about whether Mr. S could undertake that long distance flight, or Mrs. J could safely make her annual pilgrimage from Florida to Wisconsin, and if there had been any precog about the transfer of cyanide cylinders to the authorized Atlantic Trench dump. Thousands of hopeful people applied for the simple tests which would indicate if they possessed some useful Talent.

"It's an ill wind that blows no good," Henry remarked to Molly after another hectic day answering urgent calls and dealing with anxious queries.

"I suppose so," she said, sinking wearily into the armchair of their private suite in the main house. "But I wish we had more Gooseggs or a surer way of spotting the live ones."

"Any today?" Henry fixed Molly a stiff drink.

"Yes," and she brightened as if she'd temporarily forgotten the event. "One very strong receiving telepath out of forty-five aspirants." She accepted the drink, turning the glass in her hand as if the amber liquid held some other answer. "Henry, they come in so hopeful . . . and some of them leave so angry and disappointed. As if *we* ought to be able to find what doesn't exist . . ."

"Not your fault, love. Everyone wants to be, in some way, unique, and can't realize that being unique is a responsibility as well as a privilege. You can't cure that. How strong's the telepath?"

Molly brightened. "I think he's very strong, but he's been blocking thoughts, the way they all do. Out of fear. He may need a lot of training."

"No, not too much," Henry said easily, pulling his chair close to Molly and clasping her free hand. "Young fellow, isn't he? Welsh extraction, Welsh name. Right?"

"I just sent the report in . . ." Molly began, startled, and stopped mid-sentence, arrested by Henry's knowing look. "Not another one, Henry?"

"They do seem to appear right on schedule," Henry grinned at her but there was a shadow in his eyes. "Right on schedule. One day I'll be wrong."

"Don't, Henry." She clasped his hand tightly, reassuringly, knowing the strain of his unfortunate infallibility, knowing that some of the events he foresaw he'd rather not have seen. "And, he is, as you predicted, Welsh," she went on in a light voice, "by name, Daffyd op Owen. Very likeable chap. He's important?"

Henry nodded. "He won't need more than some basic pointers and a few quiet weeks here to wash the 'noise' out of his mind and learn to project as well as receive."

"Well, that's one on the plus side of the ledger." She rotated her shoulders to ease the day's strains but Henry's disclosure about young op Owen made her feel much better about her labors.

"When is he moving in?"

"Don't you know?" she asked in a bantering fashion.

"What I know I wish I didn't. What I'd give anything to know, I have to wait and see."

She smiled at him lovingly. "You mean, if we retain Beechwoods?" When he nodded, she chided him gently. "How often have you been wrong in the merest detail?"

"It's not how often I'm right, Molly luv, it's will I be wrong *this* time, this once? This important, crucial, critical once? Such a terrible gift, luv. Terrible when your knowledge means the loss of a friend . . ."

"Henry, your recognition, the very challenge of the Center," and her arm gesture encompassed all of Beechwoods, "have kept George Henner alive . . . and kicking." She peered into Henry's face, reassuring him by touch, word and look. "He's determined to do you out of Beechwoods, if only by a minute. That determination alone has strengthened his hold on life. I've seen his medical reports, Henry. I know." She leaned back in her chair. "You've done him quite a favor and he knows it. I shouldn't be surprised if he hasn't left the Center Beechwoods anyway."

"He hasn't. He showed me the will."

Molly opened her mouth to say something then thought better of it.

"All right," Henry went on, catching her look of mischief, "so he could write a second one in secret . . . No, we've a wager on and . . ."

"I know what you mean, hoping to win the wager loses a friend."

"I can see horizons wider than mortality but I cannot always see the sparrow fall."

"So young op Owen will be your successor?" George Henner was in a very testy mood that morning.

"Yes, but of course, not for some time yet . . ."

"You've got it all foreseen, have you?"

"Certainly the basic problems . . ."

"Ha! I thought you'd already solved the basic problems . . ."

"By no means, my friend," and Henry's laugh was mirthless. "I've had the easy part. No, really. The establishment of the Center—and others in time in strategic parts of the globe . . . is only the first bit: scarcely the worst.

"Once we'd elevated parapsychic Talents to a demonstrable, scientific basis, it was only a question of some decent organizational effort to make us self-sufficient and independent. We did dodge the governmental attempt to take control because we operate more efficiently as a private agency and because you could imagine the tax payers' shrieks about funding tea-leaf readers? Funding was no real problem once we could prove Talent. Training, now . . . that is a long term program. We've got to develop more efficient techniques in recognizing and training Talent and that takes Talented personnel. Getting industry and the government to accept our workers was child's play with what we can offer." Then Henry sighed. "The suspicions of the general public can't be totally allayed but with the help of a discreet PR program, people can become accustomed to the Talented.

"No, George, some of our biggest problems are yet to be solved. The knottiest one is establishing legal protection for Talent. Without that, all we've carefully built could be wiped away in legal fees, damages and law suits . . . particularly against the precogs. Oh, I see that we'll get professional immunity sooner or later. I'm greedy. I want it sooner. And that's why a telepath like Dai op Owen is required as Director. He's more sensitive to the immediate situation. By God, the times I've wished I were a telepath . . ."

George snorted.

"It's easier for a man who can delve into thoughts, not the future. That's assured."

"Ha!" Light flittered from George Henner's sunken eyes. "Not yet. You've three days, four hours and five minutes to go."

"No," Henry replied gently, "no, old friend, *you've* three days, four hours and five minutes to go. And I shall miss you."

"Ha to that as well! See any new signs of decay?" George jerked his head this way and that.

Henry shook his head slowly. "I will miss you, you old bastard."

"Will you? Will you when I defy your prediction and you and your Talents are thrown out into the mass noise again?"

Henry summoned a laugh. "Then why haven't you died long ago?"

George glared at him. "I intend to make you sweat, Henry Darrow. Sweat. Bleed. Die a little."

"And you wonder I want a telepath as a Director?" He gripped George firmly by the shoulder and gave him an affectionate shake. "Play the enemy if it pleases you: if the choler makes the blood continue to run in your veins. You're more our friend than enemy. And I know it."

"Ha! You are nervous. You're worried that you're wrong. That this time you're wrong! I'll prove you wrong if it's the last thing I do."

Henry cocked his head at George, grinning ironically. "You may at that, you old bastard. I've never claimed infallibility, George. And you've heard me state time and again that fore-knowledge of the future can alter it . . ."

"Cop out! Rationalization!" Henner shook with triumph. "You're admitting defeat! Ha!"

"Have I made your day, George? Fair enough! I've got to go placate that tax man again. See you later."

"Don't waste your time with him. He's stupid. No way they can tax the Talents with the structure *I* helped you build. And don't miss the party! The Death Party!"

"Christ, Hank," Gus Molnar complained to Darrow, "he's had me checking him over on the hour all day! And then that gaggle of 'impartial physician witnesses' check on me." Molnar ran his hand nervously through his long fair hair, his eyes restless with anxiety and irritation. "And suddenly he won't let Molly out of his sight. Said her healing hands would turn the trick. Give him the minute he needs. Goddamn old bastard!"

"Cool it, Gus. It's what he needed to keep him alive." Henry chuckled and straightened his tunic jacket, poked at his softly tied scarf.

Gus made a disgusted noise in his throat. "You're so damned sure?"

"Not at all. Unfortunately."

"Unfortunately? With the future of the Center at stake on one man's heart beat?"

"I've seen that we do get the property. I regret that it has to be validated by the death of an old and valued friend. I could almost wish that he does live past the appointed minute . . ."

"Minute . . ." Molnar corrected him. "Bastard's got a huge alarm clock rigged, to the Greenwich-mean-time minute!"

"C'mon, Gus. Let's go to the wake and cheer the corpse on!"

"My God, Darrow, how do you do it?"

The Death Party was assembling, reluctantly, in the vault-roofed lounge of the Beechwoods mansion. George had invited a select few to be "in at the death."

Indeed, as he said himself, he had outlasted most of his contemporaries and those three represented today were more enemies than friends. George quipped that business enemies had a reputation of being in at the death. He was dressed in his Vietnam campaign battle dress, remarking that he'd cheated Him then as a twenty-year old, so it behooved him to keep the appointment now suitably attired. Most of those present were Talents or connected with the Center. Young Daffyd op Owen was present. So were LEO Commissioner Mailer, trying hard not to look uncomfortable, Governor Lawson, several Senators, representatives from four charitable organizations (probably benefiting under the will, Henry decided when he saw the guest list), and the four physicians who'd been chosen at random from the AMA directory by George and flown into Jerhattan for the event. That was George's way of solving any medical question. With a touch of ghoulish humor, George had decreed—not that he didn't trust the Talents implicitly, but one had to protect oneself—that the autopsy would be performed on his corpse immediately after death had been assumed.

The party consequently generated little joviality despite the abundance of liquor and exotic foods on the sideboard. George ate sparingly, drank slowly. Anything he consumed these days, he complained, tasted sour or flat or insipid and caused heartburn.

Conversations were conducted in sepulchral tones and languished easily. The occasional laugh was quickly suppressed. Only Henry Darrow contrived to look at ease though Molly knew, by the way he rubbed his thumb and index finger together constantly, that he was in a highly nervous condition. She didn't dare touch him since she was not a whit less distraught herself, and would only double Henry's tension. The person who was suffering most was young Daffyd op Owen. She had become very fond of the sensitive young man and wished that he didn't have to be present. He'd not had time to learn to shield himself, certainly not in such an emotionally loaded situation as this. Daffyd was visibly sweating, yet gamely trying to simulate proper party behavior as he chatted with another young Talent, a precog named Mara Canning.

As the appointed time drew nearer, any semblance of normality dwindled: efforts to keep party talk going faltered. Everyone had one eye on the clock and the other on George Henner.

"You're supposed to be happy," George Henner complained when the current silence remained unbroken for sixty-four seconds. "My death means you're all safely ensconced here." His scowl was ambiguous. Then he pointed a finger at Henry. "So tell me, Hank, if you lose the wager, where will you go? I . . ." and he laughed hollowly, "or my executors expect you to vacate the premises . . . immediately."

"And we will. I've assembled every telekinetic we've got . . . and a flock of physical muscle men. We can clear the premises in an hour, I'm told. You will grant us that much time?"

Henner grunted, then brightly asked where the new Center would be located.

"I've a site upstate seventy miles: woods, a small lake, very pastoral. The disadvantage being the distance to commute. You know what copter traffic is like over the City and the Talents are contracted to be at work on time . . . no matter what."

Henner's chair had been wired to monitor his life-systems, and the results were broadcast on a screen visible anywhere in the room. George glanced up at it incuriously.

"All systems still go?" he asked, swinging around to the nearest medical man who, startled, nodded. "Three minutes and counting, Henry?"

"George, may I remind you that this excitement is bad for you?" Henry said.

"Excitement bad for me? Goddamn you, Darrow, it's kept me alive months past the estimate those jokers gave me. You've kept me alive, damn your eyes."

"Damn 'em?" Henry laughed. "That was the point, George, and you've admitted it before impartial witnesses, too."

Henner pursed his thin, bloodless lips, glaring at various people in the room, unsatisfied with his present victim's reactions and unable to vent his feelings on anyone better suited than Henry. His restless, probing glance fell briefly on Molly.

"Having to leave here will put your program back, won't it?"

Henry shrugged. "For this decade, perhaps yes. The new location will be too far for prospective Talents in the subbie class to come for the test. We can have mobile units . . . once we have the personnel. Trouble is the units have to be especially constructed . . ."

"Yes, yes, you've told me all that." George flounced around in his chair, seeking a new or comfortable position as well as another victim. But he returned to Henry. "You'll be sorry you've kept me alive. In exactly two minutes and four seconds . . ."

"No, George, I won't ever be sorry for your life. Only sorry for your death."

"I can believe that!"

"Indeed you can!" cried Molly, unable to bear George's taunting acrimony.

"Molly . . ." George's voice entreated her and she instinctively stepped toward him, her hands outstretched to give the comfort which had often eased him. But he leaned away, suddenly suspicious even of her. Her hands flew to her mouth as the rebuff wounded her. But his reaction broke Henry's tight control.

"Damn it, George, she only wants to help."

"Help me? Live? Or die!?"

Molly began to cry, turning towards the wall. But Henry took her in his arms, for once the comforter.

"Molly didn't deserve that from you, George. The wager was with me!"

"He didn't mean it that way, Henry," said young op Owen, the words bursting from his lips, as if he'd been holding back for some time the desire to speak out.

Henner nodded, his face flushed with what Dai op Owen afterwards said was remorse. But the monitors began flashing warning signals.

"Hell, Molly," George began in a choked voice, "I don't distrust *you*." Then the death alarm went off. "Ha! The appointed minute . . . And I'm alive! You're wrong, Henry Darrow. You and all your tea-leaf, table-tipping crystal-gazing . . ."

At precisely 9:00:30, George Henner's heart gave a massive contraction and stopped. Cameras on the dead man recorded that his hand raised slightly, towards Henry and Molly before the dead body collapsed.

Accustomed as they were to the death processes, the physicians in attendance were held motionless by the dramatic circumstances. Gus Molnar reacted first, hand moving towards the adrenalin syringe.

"No!" cried Dai op Owen, stepping forward, his hand outstretched. "He wants to die. He doesn't want to win the wager."

"My God," cried one of the physicians, pointing to the screen. "Look at the Goosegg. It's gone wild. The mind's still alive . . . No. Consciousness has gone. But God, look at the graph."

"Let him go. He wants to go," Daffyd op Owen was saying.

Molnar looked first towards Henry whose face was expressionless, then at the other physicians staring at the monitor readings.

"That means the brain's dead, doesn't it?" asked LEO Commissioner Mailer, pointing to the Goosegg graph now scribing straight lifeless lines.

Two of the medical men nodded.

"Then he's dead," said Mailer, glancing towards the Governor who nodded accord. "I'd say you won the bet, Darrow."

"The wager said 'minute', I trust, not second?" asked one of the Senators.

"He shouldn't've excited himself like that," a doctor muttered. "This party was a mistake. Of course we weren't consulted on that. But it set up circumstances which would obviously result in overstimulation, certain death for a man in Henner's condition."

"Or, there's the voodoo element in this," another physician said without rancor. "Tell a victim often enough that he'll be dead at such and such a time and the subconscious takes over and kills the man."

"Not in this instance," said Gus Molnar, loudly and belligerently. "And there's ample medical substantiation, including your own remarks," he added, pointing at the voodoo adherent, "that the stimulation provided by the original bet kept George Henner alive long past his own medical men's estimate. The bet did not cause his death, it caused his life."

No one ventured to refute that statement.

"I believe," spoke up one of the attorneys present, "that the autopsy was to be performed immediately?"

As if on cue, two men appeared from the hallway, wheeling a stretcher. Silently they approached, their passage unimpeded as guests stepped aside hastily. The body was laid on the stretcher in silence. But, as the men took their positions to leave, Molly broke from Henry's embrace. With gentle fingers, she closed the dead man's eyes. The tears streamed down her face as she kissed George on the forehead. The stretcher glided out of the room. No one spoke until the last sound of footsteps in the hall was gone.

"Mr. Darrow," said the attorney, his voice sounding abnormally loud after the requiem silence, "I was enjoined by Mr. Henner to make a few announcements at this time usually reserved until several days hence. I was to tell you that this was one wager he didn't wish to win and hoped he wouldn't: no matter what indication he gave to the contrary. He said that you were sportsman enough, Mr. Darrow, to appreciate the fact that he had to try to win." The attorney turned to the physician who had brought up the voodoo insinuation. "He also ordered me to counteract any attempt to bring charges resulting from a misinterpretation of today's sad occasion. He empowered me to say that he had implicit trust in the integrity of all members of the Parapsychic Center. We," and he gestured towards his colleagues, "are to be the executors of Mr. Henner's estate, the bulk of which, excluding a few behests and excluding these grounds now the irrevocable property of the North American Center for Parapsychic Talents, is to go into a Trust Fund, providing legal assistance to anyone registered with the Center who may be imprisoned or charged with damages or lawsuits following the professional use of their Talent, until such time as specific laws are promulgated to give the Talents professional immunity." The lawyer gave Henry a wry grin. "He said, and I quote, 'If you ride a winged horse, you'd better have a wide net when you fall. And that takes money!'

"He also said that after he was dead," and the lawyer faltered, embarrassed by the inadvertent rhyme, "he said the party was to begin. That this was to be considered a joyous occasion . . ."

"He *was* glad," Daffyd op Owen said, and his rather homely face lit with happiness. "That was so astonishing. His mind, the thoughts were happy, so happy at the moment of death. He was happy, I tell you. *I know* he was glad!"

"Thank God!" was Henry Darrow's fervent prayer. He raised his untouched drink. "A toast, ladies and gentlemen." Glasses obediently were lifted. "To those who ride the winged horse!"

One after another the glasses followed Henry's into the fireplace of Beechwoods to preserve the tribute to George Henner's memory.

2

*A Womanly
Talent*

A Womanly Talent

"If you were one whit less honorable, Daffyd op Owen," exclaimed Joel Andres heatedly, "you and your whole Center could go . . . go fly a kinetic kite."

The passionate senator was one of those restlessly energetic men who gave the appearance of continuous motion even in rare moments of stasis. Joel Andres was rigid now —with aggravation. The object of his frustration, Daffyd op Owen, Director of the East American Parapsychological Research and Training Center, was his antithesis, physically and emotionally. Both men, however, had the same indefinable strength and purposefulness, qualities which set them apart from lesser men.

"I can't win support for my Bill," Andres continued, trying another tack and pacing the thick-piled green carpeting of op Owen's office, "if you consistently play into Mansfield Zeusman's hands with this irrational compulsion to tell everything you know. If only on the grounds that what you 'know' is not generally acceptable as reliable 'knowledge.'

"And don't tell me that familiarity breeds contempt, Dave. The unTalented are never going to be contemptuous of the psychic abilities, they're going to continue being scared stiff. It's human nature to fear—and distrust—what is different. Surely," and Andres flung his arms wide, "you've studied enough behavioral psychology to understand that basic fact."

"My Talent permits me to look below the surface rationalizations and uncover the . . ."

"But you can*not* read the minds of every single one of the men who must vote on this Bill, Dave. Nor can you alter their thinking. Not with your thinking and your ethics!" Joel was almost derisive as he pointed a nicotined finger accusingly at his friend. "And don't give me that wheeze about lawmakers being intelligent, thoughtful men!"

Op Owen smiled tolerantly at his friend, unaffected by the younger man's histrionics. "Not even when Senator Zeusman steals a march on us with that so apt quotation from Pope?"

Andres made a startled noise of exasperation, then caught the look in the other's eyes and laughed.

"Yeah, he sure caught me flatfooted there." He deepened his voice somewhat to mimic the affected bass of Mansfield Zeusman:

" 'Who sees with equal eye, as God of all,
A hero perish or a sparrow fall . . .'

"What a rallying cry that is! Why didn't *I* think of it first? Mind you," and Andres was deadly serious again, "that quote is pure genius . . . for the opposition. Spikes our pitch in a dozen places. The irony is that it would be just as powerful for us if we'd only thought of it first. Dave, won't you reconsider," Joel asked, leaning across the table to the telepath, "eliminating the precogs from the Bill? That's what's hanging it up now in Committee. I'm sure I could get it put on . . ."

"The precogs need the legal protection most of all," op Owen replied with unusual vehemence, a momentary flash of alarm crossing his face.

"I know, I know," and Andres tossed a hand ceilingward in resignation. "But that's the facet of the parapsychic that scares—and fascinates—people most."

"And that is exactly why I insist we be as candid as possible on all phases of the extrasensory perception Talents. Then people will become as used to them as to 'finders,' 'ports' and 'paths.' Henry Darrow was so right about that."

Joel Andres whirled back to the desk, gripping the edges fiercely. "The prophet Darrow notwithstanding, you don't tell suspicious, frightened people everything. They automatically assume you're holding something back because *they* would. *No* one dares to be so honest anymore. Therefore they are sure that what you're withholding is far worse than what you've readily admitted." He caught the adamant gleam in Daffyd's eye and unexpectedly capitulated. "All right. All *right*. But I insist that we continue to emphasize what the *other* Talents are already able to do . . . *in their narrow specialized ways.* Once people can stomach the idea that there *are* limits on individual psionic Talents, that all Talents are not mind readers cum weight throwers cum fire dowsers cum crystal-ball-seers, all rolled up into one frightening package, they'll start treating them as you want Talents treated: as professional specialists, trained in one area of a varied profession and entitled to professional immunity in that area *if* they are licensed and registered with the Centers. *Don't*," and the hand went up again as Daffyd tried to interrupt, "tell them you're experimenting to find out how to broaden every Talented mind. *Don't* ask for the whole piece of bread with jam on it, Dave! You won't get it, but you will get protection for your people in the practice of their speciality, even your precogs. I'll bear down heavily on the scientific corroboration of authentic foresights," and Andres began to pace a tight rectangle in front of op Owen's desk, his dark head down, his gestures incisive, "the use of computers to correlate details and estimate reliablity of data, the fact that sometimes three and four precogs come up with the same incident, seen from different angles. And most importantly—that the Center never issues an official warning unless the computer agrees that sufficient data coincides between Incident and reality . . ."

"Please emphasize that we admit to human fallibility and use computers to limit *human* error."

Joel frowned at op Owen's droll interjection. "Then I'll show how the foresight prevented or averted the worst of the Incidents. That Monterey Quake is a heaven-sent example. No heroes perished, even if a few sparrows did fall from gas discharges."

"I thought it was the meddling with the sparrow's fall that perturbs Senator Zeusman" Daffyd remarked wryly. "For want of that seed, the grain won't sprout . . ."

"Hmmm, yes, it does! 'What will be, will be,' " and Andres mimicked Zeusman's voice again.

"Since he initiated Pope," said op Owen, "I'd reply 'Whatever is, is right.' "

"You want me to turn Papist now, huh?" Joel grinned wickedly.

Daffyd chuckled as he continued, "Pope also advises, 'Be candid where we can but vindicate the ways of God to man!' "

The gently delivered quote had an instant effect on the senator, comparable to touching a match to a one-second fuse. Midway to explosion, Andres snapped his mouth shut, sighed extravagantly and rolled his slightly yellowed eyes heavenwards.

"You are the most difficult man to help, Daffyd op Owen!"

"That's only because I'm aware how carefully we must move in the promulgation of this Bill, Joel. I don't want it backfiring at the wrong time, when some of the basic research now in progress becomes demonstrable. The Talents can't be hamstrung by obsolete statutes imperfectly realized on a scrabbling compromise basis."

"Dave, you want to run before you can walk?"

"No, but trouble has been foreseen."

"Darrow again, huh? Or are you hoist on your own petard?" Joel waggled a finger triumphantly. "Trouble stemming from current non-protection. Go cast up a precog *after* the Bill is passed."

"Ah-ha" and Daffyd mimicked Joel now, "but we don't see the Bill passing!"

That rendered Andres speechless.

"And we are hoist on our own petard," the telepath continued with a hint of sorrowful resignation in his voice, "because all our preventive methods *are* affecting the future, unfortunately, much as Senator Zeusman presented the syndrome in his Sparrow's Fall peroration. That was such a masterful speech," op Owen said with rueful envy. "Valid, too, for as surely as the Center issues a warning, allowing people a chance to avert or prevent tragedy, they have already prejudiced the events from happening as they were foreseen. That's the paradox. Yet how, *how* can ethical man stand aside and let a hero perish, or even a sparrow fall, when he *knows* that he can prevent unnecessary or premature loss."

"The Monterey Quake could *not* have been prevented," Joel reminded him, then blinked in amazement. "You're not holding out on *me,* are you? You haven't found a kinetic strong enough to hold the earth's surface together?"

Dave's laughter was a spontaneous outburst of delight at his friend's discomposure.

"No, no. At least . . . not yet," he said just to watch the outraged expression on Andres's mobile face.

There were few people with whom Daffyd op Owen could relax or indulge in his flights of humor and hyperbole. "Seriously, Joel, the Monterey Quake is a spectacular Incident and a prime example of the concerted use of Talent, minimizing the loss of life or property. We have never had so many precogs stimulated in their separate affinities. And it's the most concrete example of why precogs need legal protection. Do you realize that the Western Center was deluged with damage suits for the tsunami that followed?"

"*That* was predictable."

"But *we* issued no warnings. And it's against such irrational attitudes that precogs need legal protection more than any other Talent. Theirs is stimulated by mental perceptions as erratic as a smell in the morning air, a glance at a photo, the sound of a name. In a sense, precog is tremendously unreliable because it cannot be used as consciously as telepathy, teleportation and tele-kinesis. And to protect the Talent as well as the Center, we insist on computer corroboration when details are co-herently specific. We never issue a public warning until the computer admits reliability . . . and we get damned because we have 'heard' and not spoken. Of course, a num-ber of our precogs have become absorbed into business where peculiar affinities place them. For instance," and Daffyd held up a tape-file, "this young man, who's apply-ing for progeny approval, is a fire-conscious. But he's one reason this city has such low fire-insurance rates: his Talent prevents them—a blessing indirectly passed on to every resident . . ."

"Hmmm, but scarcely spectacular enough to register with the average egocentric Joe Citizen," said Andres sour-ly. He was restless with Daffyd's earnest review of facts he knew well. "However, every little bit helps, Dave, and the public moves a lot faster pro bona pocketbook."

"True, exactly true, and they get rather nasty when we try to save them money and will not understand that a legitimate forewarning automatically alters the future, even to the point of preventing the foreseen Incident which will have cost old publican money, or time, or effort he *then* feels was unnecessary."

"And there we are, right back at square one," said Joel in flat disgust. "That is what Mansfield calls 'med-dling' and what makes him fight this Bill with every ounce of his outraged moralistic, neo-religious, mock-ethical fibre. Remember, he's backed by the transport lobbies, and every time one of your precogs hits that jolly little brotherhood, causing delays, hurried inspections, the whole jazz—you got a number-one headache. Because, when the predictions don't happen as predicted, Transport swears your meddling is superstitious interference, uncalled for, unnecessary and nothing would have happened anyway."

Daffyd sighed wearily. "How many times have we found bombs? Fuel leaks? Averted hijacks? Metal fatigue . . . mechanical justifications?"

"Doesn't signify, Dave, not if it touches the pocketbook of the Transport Companies. Remember, every precog implies fault: human or mechanical, since the Companies will not recognize Providence as a force. And human or mechanical, the public loses faith in the Company thus stigmatized. When Company profits are hit, Company gets mad, sues the precog for defamation of character, interference, et cetera."

"Then we are to allow the traveling public to fry in their own juice or be spread across the fields because a precog has seen a crash but doesn't want to offend a Company? For want of a screw the nail was lost!" op Owen's usually soothing voice was rough with asperity. "Damn it, Joel, we have to preserve impartiality, and warn any one or anything that is touched by the precognitive Talent, or we do usurp the position of the Almighty by withholding that evidence. I don't care if the transportation companies then decide to disregard the warning— that's their problem. But I want my people protected when, in good faith and based on computer-accepted detail, they issue that warning. We have no ax to grind, commercially, thanks to the Darrow endowment and member support, but we must continue to be impartial."

"I hope your altruism is not going to be your downfall," said Joel, his manner unusually grave.

"There's been no warning that it will," Daffyd replied. A hint of irritation in his voice.

"You're too honest to be up against us crook politicians," Joel said, grinning, then glanced at his watch. "Wup. Gotta go."

"You push yourself too hard, Joel. You don't look well."

"A bit liverish, that's all, and no snooping."

"Not without permission and you know it."

"Hah! Among friends, I don't trust telepaths. Say, how's the recruiting program?" Joel asked as he swooped up his travel cape and case.

"We get hopefuls every week," the director replied as he escorted the senator to the elevator. "Sometimes we even catch a few young ones, before they learn to suppress a perfectly normal ability."

"That's another phrase you should delete around Zeusman," Joel said. "He will not buy your premise that every mind has psionic Talent."

"But, Joel, *that* is scientifically valid. We know that those who possess Talent have strong, healthy twenty-first chromosome pairs. It is certainly admissible evidence that when the twenty-first is blurred or damaged to any degree, brain function is inhibited. And, with the Downs's Syndrome, you have mental retardation."

"Don't beleaguer me," Joel said with widened eyes of innocence, "I believe!" He laid a hand on his heart. "I couldn't doubt—not after that 'finder' located my brother in the mine shaft before he bled to death. If we could only subject Mansfield Zeusman to such an experience, he wouldn't be so skeptical. Can't one of your pet Talents do something about that? I thought they always keep an eye on controversial men to prevent assassination and stuff."

Op Owen gave a snort. "Would Senator Zeusman honor a precog foreseeing his own demise?"

"Hmmm. Probably not. Say, you're not funded on the Government Research Program, are you?"

"No, thank God. The Henner Bequest was reserved for that. Why?"

"Hmmm. Just that Zeusman is extending this argument against the Bill to all 'specious'—as he terms it—forms of research, government funded. And spring is appropriations time, you know."

"Fortunately, we've never had that kind of pressure."

"Talented of you," Joel said with a grin.

Behind him the elevator door slid open and a young woman, obviously in a hurry, ran out, right into the muscular frame of the young Senator.

She blurted out an apology, flushing with embarrassment as Andres reached out to steady her. Then her eyes opened wider as she saw op Owen and one hand flew to her mouth. "I'm awfully sorry, sir."

Just as Daffyd recognized Ruth Horvath, he also identified the combined emotions of shame at her precipitous arrival into a distinguished champion of the Talented, regret for her impulsiveness in coming to the Tower at this hour, and the underlying hope and apprehension that had compelled her to come. Instinctively, Daffyd touched her with soothing reassurances: but Joel Andres's amiable and admiring glance was the tonic the pretty woman needed.

"No harm done, I assure you, Miss . . . ?"

"*Mrs.* Horvath . . . Senator Andres," Daffyd said and watched Joel's expression change from delighted interest to flattering chagrin.

"I do apologize, Senator," Ruth repeated, her cheeks blush-stained again.

"And I apologize for being in the wrong place at the wrong time and . . ." an extravagant sigh " . . . too late." He bowed deeply to Ruth, reluctantly stepping aside to let her pass.

Instead she fumbled with the elevator button.

"I'm on my lunch break," she said with a stammer. "I've got to get back."

The panel slid open and Andres stepped in beside her, one finger jamming the "hold" button.

"Me, too," he said, grinning down at her.

"Your file is on my desk right now, Ruth," Daffyd said, suddenly comprehending the reason for her visit and her hesitancy in mentioning the subject in Andres's presence. "I'll call you tomorrow."

Her face lit up, her eyes became eager and, as she glanced away, Daffyd thought he saw the shine of tears.

"Take care of yourself, Joel. You're working too hard."

"A pleasure, I assure you." Joel's laugh was cut off by the closing door.

Daffyd op Owen stood looking at the indicator panel for a few moments before he turned slowly back to his isolated tower office. He had much to think about. Not that he would deflect one centimeter from his course of action. Only his firm beliefs sustained him for it didn't require precog, only intelligent extrapolation—which some uninformed people insisted was the essence of precog—to determine the difficulties still faced by the Talented all over the world. The Bill was so vital a forward step, raising the Talents from the onerous category of "mental chiropractors," (Senator Zeusman's phrase, though chiropractic treatment had long been an accredited branch of medicine), to a creditable position among professional abilities. Mansfield Zeusman had already stalled the Bill in Committee for months, was capable of stalling it through the summer, and keeping it off the agenda next year. The senator was hoping to find some discrediting Incident that would forever banish hope of legal protection for the Talented.

The sheer genius of that Pope quotation was a measure of their opponent's worth, op Owen mused as he turned to the mass of administrative files awaiting him. The pity of it was that the quote would have been much more applicable to the Talent side of the argument. Come to think of it, much of Pope's "Essay on Man" was to the point.

Other pertinent lines came easily out of mental storage. Not much that Daffyd op Owen had once seen could elude his recall. . . . a blessing as well as a handicap.

> With too much knowledge for the Skeptic side,
> With too much weakness for the Stoic's pride,
> He hangs between, in doubt to act or rest:
> In doubt to deem himself a God or Beast:
> In doubt his mind or body to prefer
> Born but to die and reasn'ning but to err . . .

"Enough!" and op Owen roused from introspection to direction. He flipped open the nearest tape case and slapped it into the playback. It seemed somehow meet that it was the Horvaths's progeny application. Were op Owen a superstitious man he could have accounted it a good omen: a favorable auspice for the work he and his fellow directors around the world were inaugurating. Breed like to like, strengthen strong genetic Talent traits and develop, not the super race of omniscient, omnipotent superpeople Zeusman basically feared, but people trained and conditioned from childhood to use their Talents for the benefit of man. And, by such service, force the World to recognize the treasure that can be unlocked in the unused, untapped portion of the human brain.

A flaming, shattering precog caught Lajos Horvath at the moment when REM sleep was over and his unconscious mind was rousing from that phase of rest.

His groan of anguish awakened his wife instantly. With the reflex of training. Ruth flipped the recorder and pulled the retractable electrode Goosegg net to his head, expertly clamping the metal discs on the circles of his scalp that had been permanently depilated.

Blinking her eyes to see the reading in the dawn-dim room, Ruth watched the definite pattern of an Incident emerge. Center was already picking it up for authentication. The Incident lasted a scant eleven seconds before the brain waves settled back to a calm reading. She lay back, going through the discipline that would relax her and prevent her from imposing her haste-urgency reaction on Lajos. As soon as he roused, she must be composed enough to question him for a verbal report.

She achieved the proper repose quickly, suppressing the thrill of satisfaction at her success. She was no longer as troubled by flashes of envy that Lajos possessed a valid Talent while hers was so nebulous as to elude identification. Now it was enough for her to know that,

by the exercise of the deep empathy which existed between them, by her womanliness, she made his development more certain. Lajos needed her as a buffer, a source
of solace from the sharp edges of Talent. Even the
strongest personality could succumb to the Cassandra
complex that destroyed the sanity of the unwary precog. Why was it, Ruth mused in a quiet inner voice,
that tragedy has such a vicious way of reaching out of the
mists of the future: like a falling man, blindly grabbing
at anything to restore balance and avert his fall?

Again the needle rushed across the graph, a slight
whoosh barely audible in the quiet room. Ruth glanced
over to make sure the Incident was being beamed to
the Center and noticed the smile on her husband's face.
A smile? A happy premonition? She forced herself to relax, unaccountably assailed by a raving curiosity. Lajos
so rarely had happy foresights, and fleetingly she regretted
that he was a precog.

Lajos stirred restlessly. He was waking now. She
turned on the voice recorder and leaned towards him.

"What is it? What do you see?" she asked in the soft
persuasive voice the Center had taught her to use at these
times. Her ability to stimulate his verbal accounts was
highly praised, for it was sometimes difficult for the precog
to articulate the semi-real into sufficient detail for preventive or supportive action.

"Flames!" Lajos groaned. "Must it always be flames?"
He sat bolt upright in bed then, his brown eyes wide as
he stared straight ahead at the retinal image of his pre-
monitory vision. The electrodes were jerked from his
skull, retracting with a metallic clink into the case. "The
ship's burning, exploding. Throwing flaming debris across
the harbor into the suburbs. Damp it! Deflect! Shield
those passengers. Watch out! The propellant will spray.
It's exploding. Contain it!"

"Markings on the liner?" a gentle but insistent voice
whispered from the intercom.

Lajos shook his head, blinking furiously in an attempt to

hold the fading sight. "It's awash with flame. I think I see an eight, a four, a three—or is it another eight? It's a Reynarder. It must be. They're the only ones who use that class."

"Which class?" the inexorable whisper wanted to know.

Suddenly Lajos sagged, panting with shock, cold sweat breaking out on his forehead. He lay back exhausted.

"It's gone," he moaned. "It's gone."

"You had a second one," Ruth said. "What was that about?"

Lajos's brows drew together in a half frown as he brushed his straight black hair out of his face. He kept it overlong to hide the depilated circles where the electrodes fit. His lips curved in a half-sided smile. "Something good?" he asked hopefully.

Ruth suppressed her sigh. Lajos rarely detailed the felicitous ones.

"Incident validated, a strong reading, Lajos," the intercom voice said. "Report in as soon as you're able."

"They'll check it out, won't they?" Lajos asked needlessly.

"Action already initiated."

Lajos lay so still that Ruth knew it was not passive quiescence but rigid strain. Another thorn in the Talented's side was the harsh realization that their warnings were often disregarded and they were forced to see their predictions come horribly true. Ruth wiped the sweat from Lajos's forehead and began to massage his neck and shoulders. After a moment he grinned weakly up at her.

"What a way to start the day, huh?"

"At least you ended on a happy note. Maybe that means they'll prevent?"

"If they can correlate enough data, in enough time," he said gloomily. "*And* Reynarder bothers to listen!" He flopped onto his stomach, pounding the mattress with impotent fists.

Ruth transferred her attention to his muscular back. She loved the line of him, the broad double plateau of his shoulder blades with the small mounds of hard muscle, the graceful curve that swept down to the narrow waist, the hollow of his spine, the Grecian beauty of his buttocks. She quickly suppressed a flare of desire. This was not the time to intrude sex on his personal anguish. And she knew that her intense sexual hunger for him stemmed from a yearning for the child of his seed. A daughter, tall and fair, with Lajos's dimples in her cheek. A son, strong-backed and arrogant, with thick black straight hair.

This hunger for his child was so primal, it paralyzed the sophistication overlaid by education and social reflexes. Nowadays a woman was expected to assume more than the ancient duties required of her. Nowadays, and Ruth smiled to herself, the sophists called those womanly talents, Maintenance, Repair and Replacement, instead of housekeeping, cooking, nursing and having babies, but the titles didn't alter the duties nor curb the resurgent desires. And, when you got down to it, men still explored new ground, even if it were alien lands, and defended their homes and families. You could call Lajos's precog a kind of an early-warning defense system. Well, then, she'd added the chore of being Cerebral-Recording Secretary to Maintenance and Repair but they'd better let her Replace soon or. . . .

She concentrated on more soothing thoughts, using her latent empathy to ease his remorse. When he began to take deep long breaths, she knew he was conquering the aftermath of the Incident, dispelling its destructive despondency. He had done everything he could. He could *not* change the course of every fated life. Some events had to come to their dire conclusions, for out of present tragedy so often rose future triumph; the result of sorrowful recriminations was often the catalyst of progress. A specious rationale in the Silver-lined Cloud Approach but true enough to save the sanity of the Talented.

It was a bitter thing, Ruth understood, to be Talented: bitter and wonderful. But it was worse to have evidence of Talent and never know what it was. Nonsense, she told herself sternly, discarding these reflections, you can't be what you can't be.

"Ahh, you've got the right spot," Lajos said gratefully and she doubled her efforts across the heavy shoulder muscles.

And yet, when she anticipated his desires and needs, sometimes the words from his mouth, she wondered just how she had tapped that need; just what might awaken the occluded Talent within her.

The Center believed that psionic abilities were latent human characteristics: their absence due to malfunction of the necessary brain synapses or, even more basically, underdevelopment due to a protein lack in the gene. When chromosomes in the twenty-first pair were damaged or blurred, no Talent was detected. There was no aberration in Ruth's chromosomes, and although she tested as Talented, her ability was unidentifiable. She had never been able to stimulate an Incident involving any of the known abilities. She'd met Lajos during her testing: they'd been approached by the Eastern American Center after finishing their secondary schooling and had qualified for the six-months' training designed to stimulate latent Talent. Their genetic history had been taped back to the fourth generation. They had endured hours of cerebral recording on the Goosegg under a variety of stimuli. Ruth was finally labeled "indeterminate"; Lajos showed strong precog tendencies.

Ruth still secretly hoped that her Talent would develop. She'd been assured that this was a possibility: they cited her high empathy rating, her ability to anticipate attitudes and actions of those nearest and dearest to her. True, she might be no more than a receptive telempath, one unable to broadcast but receptive. Ruth therefore alternated between hope and despair: being a practical creature, she dwelt mostly on the pessimistic side of the pendulum, refusing to believe anything but the most conclusive evidence. This attitude was reinforced during Lajos's worst Incidents, when she wanted no part of the cruel gift.

Lajos Horvath was one of several thousand Talented people, licensed and registered with the Center; devoted to its precepts and ideals, contributing all of his salary to it. The Center was not paternalistic, nor did it require any recompense. But the Talented preferred to live together, if possible, on or near, the Center's grounds at Beechwoods, among their peers: reassured and reinforced. As the Center "policed" its own members, it also protected them.

Ruth had no specific objections to their situation: she had willingly taken the course orienting unTalented partners to their gifted spouses. She would have undergone a far more arduous requirement, so deep was her love of Lajos. But lately, obedience to E.A.C. had begun to gall Ruth and it was not due to any fault of the Center's. She recognized that.

The muted buzz of the intercom roused both of them. Lajos propped himself up on his elbows, his profile towards her so that she observed the thin bitter line of his mouth and knew that he was steeling himself.

"Lajos," it was Daffyd op Owen, "you were correct. A class 7 Reynarder had a propellant leak at Buffalo jetport."

Something in the director's slow deep voice told them that Lajos's information had not averted.

"And?" Lajos's question was a firm demand for the truth.

"We had to compute the variable details with the possible airports near water, flights landing or departing on the Reynarder line. We got only one other personal precog involving the Incident but your data alone—particularly the registry—was sufficient. The loss would have been catastrophic without your warning. Teleports on the Rescue Squad deflected most of the flaming wreckage into the Lake before it could land in the suburbs. Kinetics managed to shield the passenger deck until the propellant could be foamed. The passengers and crew suffered massive heat prostration but all will live. Ruth, does he need a tranquilizer?"

"No!" the negative exploded from Lajos's lips.

"Good lad!" op Owen's voice was warm with approval. "We've authenticated the Incident. It averted a major tragedy: one more pound of evidence on our side of the scales for the Bill. And the passengers and jetport personnel *know* who gave the warning."

Lajos went limp with relief as the Director signed off with expressions of gratitude. Lajos half-turned his face and Ruth didn't know for a moment whether to comfort him or not. She waited. Finally he gave a long shuddering sigh and relaxed, one hand slipping over the side of the bed, fingers limp, the veins in his forearm bulging, blue under his unusually fair skin.

"Then what I saw—didn't happen, Ruth. The jet didn't turn into a flaming hull, exploding all over the suburbs. So what did I see? Which didn't happen because I saw it? Because my seeing it was sufficient to alter the future?" He shook his head, his beard stubble rasping against the tightly drawn bedsheet, but his voice was no longer hoarse with recrimination; it was calm: his philosophy was asserting itself.

Ruth felt the muscles in her shoulders unknot and only then realized how tense she had become, waiting for his reaction.

" 'A paradox, a paradox, a most ingenious paradox,' " she chanted lightly, stroking his back with her fingertips. "My darling pirate," and she kissed his cheek.

Lajos bounced out of bed and stretched, his sleep-pants falling off his narrow hips. He grabbed them back up, not out of modesty but to keep from tripping over them on the way to the bathroom.

"Maybe the good precog you had . . . it followed a bare sixty seconds after the first, you know," Ruth remarked later as she served his breakfast, "was the realization that you had averted."

Lajos considered that, then shook his head. "No. The two were definitely non-related."

"Why is it," Ruth asked with mock shrewishness, "that you can detail the horrors but not the happies?"

He didn't know and began to eat heartily, his appetite indicative of restored equilibrium.

"Got to run, honey. Be a busy day. And that's no precog. It's a sure thing." He grinned then kissed her soundly. "Annual review of contracts, and Zeusman notwithstanding, the Firm handles the government's insurances in this city."

Ruth would have to hurry as well. She disliked being late although her job was not essential. She fitted filaments to fractional feeders, an intricate, delicate operation which required deft hands even with waldo-aids, and a certain tenacious patience with micro-movements. Her employers never objected to her occasional delays as they employed teleports and telekinetics for the transportation of delicate equipment and to assemble by remote control the "hot" components of instrumentation to be used in the Jupiter probes. Ruth did not need to work, for Lajos was highly paid, but she preferred to keep busy until their request for progeny was approved. She wanted so to be a full-time mother.

There was unlikely to be a problem in receiving approval—eventually—but anyone was liable to pick up a dose of accidental radiation that could blur or damage chromosomes. They knew their genetic patterns were sound and they had completed the three years' probation to establish the compatibility and stability of their marriage. For the last six months they had undergone continual egg and sperm cell check for possible aberrations. It was time-consuming, but who wanted a handicapped child? It had taken years to weed out the psychedelic damages that had resulted in the freaks of the late Seventies and early Eighties. There were still occasional mutants as a result of the heavy Solar Winds in the first decade of the twenty-first century. It was only common sense to check every variable.

But Ruth found it hard to be patient. She asked for very little of what her heritage had once seemed to offer. She didn't mind being an unidentifiable Talent, she had adjusted to it. She didn't really mind the often worrisome role of a passive observer to the mental agonies of Lajos's perceptions: she loved him and she helped him. She did mind the growing sense of futility. Nowadays, with shelter and food assured one, with the excitement of space explorations to capture the imagination, with leisure to develop interests and hobbies, everyone had the opportunity to use their full capabilities, yet she was constantly frustrated. If only she could be a full woman to Lajos, not just caring for him, but raising his children, preferably his Talented children! She would do everything in her power to make sure they would succeed where she had failed.

On his firm's table of organization, Lajos Horvath was listed as a "Contract Analyst and Underwriter" of the Eastern Headquarters of the Insurance Company. Conservative in so many areas, the insurance field had been one of the first major industries to see the advantages of staff 'precogs'; particularly one such as Lajos whose accuracy in fire-hazard control had been established beyond question.

Most of his precognitive Incidents dealt with flaming substances, as other precogs seemed to have reliable affinities for water, autos, metals or certain types of personalities. There was a friendly debate within the Center whether "finders" were precogs or clairvoyants, but they had affinity for "lost items," organic and inorganic. There were four in Lajos' Firm, and they represented huge annual savings for their employers.

Once Lajos's precogs would have been ascribed to astuteness or hunches or shrewd extrapolations. Indeed, he himself was perfectly willing to put the vaguer apprehensions under that generality. But training and sensitivity had sharpened many "hunches" into definitive perceptions: Check the cellar of that building for dangerous refuse, the janitor is lazy and has not discarded all possible combustibles. The wiring in that attic is frayed and the owners tend to overload their circuits with heavy-draw appliances. Sometimes the Incident was sustained: This building will be vandalized, fire is involved. The police were then requested to keep that building under surveillance. The surveillance was sufficient to prevent the breaking and entering which Lajos had predicted, but the Company had long ago learned not to protest the measures suggested by their perceptives. Insurers are accustomed to statistics, and Talents saved them too much in claims. Sometimes, as that morning, Lajos would experience a general alarm, touched off by the imminence of a violent fire, or a sudden flaring of fire-danger resulting from a vehicular crash. There were days when nothing activated his Talent. And days, of which this was one, when everything seemed to smell vaguely of smoke or be wreathed in ghostly flames. He had to censor half a dozen false impressions by checking them against the small office Goosegg. He had learned to differentiate the valid precogs: that was why he was licensed and registered by the Center.

He finished the pile of contracts, noting those about which he experienced twinge-hesitations that indicated a future review would be wise. On his way home, he suddenly felt a lightness of spirit, an ebullience quite unaccountable after his strenuous day. He didn't try to analyze it, too delighted with the relief to want to question the source. But, as he opened his door, Ruth raced into his arms.

"We've been approved as parents," she cried, clasping him tightly to her in an excess of elation. "Director op Owen himself called me just a few minutes ago. *You* ought to have been home when he called."

"Which proves that op Owen is no precog," Lajos said with a chuckle as he pressed her soft slenderness to him. He buried his lips into the curve of her neck. "That's an anodyne for this morning."

"Why for this morning?" she asked, pulling back and searching his face with worried eyes.

"Oh, it's all right, sweetie, but he knew I'd hear all the details. Reynarder Inc. was warned the instant my Incident identified the ship but they refused to issue a blanket halt on all outgoing and incoming vessels with those numerals. Reynarder's money is back of the Transport Lobby and they support Zeusman, you know. They *can't* admit that Incidents, backed by cerebral variations, computer-sorted, validated by the Center are NOT superstitious nonsense. But a lot of people check out their flights nowadays with a licensed precog."

"Then I say that companies like Reynarder deserve what they get!"

"Hey, we can afford not to be petty. And besides, I want to talk about us: about our child. What'll we have first? Boy or girl?"

Ruth stiffened in his arms and pulled back to look her husband straight in the eye.

"Do we have to specify? Does it have to be predetermined?" she asked in a small voice, aware even as the words popped out that she sounded resentful. "Oh, I don't mean it that way. It's just that when you predetermine, it takes away all the mystery that's left to motherhood."

"Ruthie," and Lajos's tender teasing voice thrilled her. "You're a real recessive. O.K., we'll just let nature take its course."

"Can't we eat first?"

Lajos threw back his head and laughed boyishly at her deliberate coquetry. He hugged her until he heard her ribs crack and her dinner sizzling.

It was a magical night. Ruth responded to lovemaking with an ardor that astounded her husband: a surrender that left him breathless and not a little awed: as if, sloughing off the onus of contraceptive interference, she could allow herself to be touched to the depths of her being.

If the quality of their loving had anything to do with the final product, their child ought to be a perfect human, Lajos thought as they finally fell asleep in each other's arms. There was no guarantee that conception occurred that night. In fact, Lajos hoped that it hadn't if Ruth would react like this until she did conceive.

Shortly, however, it was apparent that conception had occurred. Ruth developed a luminous beauty that touched everything around her with harmony. Jerry Frames, the Center's resident physician, with a healing talent, privately told op Owen that the foetus was female and that Ruth was healthy enough to experience no problems.

The girl weighed seven pounds and three ounces at birth and was immediately christened the Little Princess by the nursery staff in the Center's hospital. Her parents called her Dorotea and were utterly besotted with her miniature perfection, her pink-and-gold beauty. They were oblivious to the curious stares and whispered comments of the staff. It was Ruth, preternaturally sensitive to anything regarding her daughter, who began to notice the surreptitious glances, the cluster of people constantly near her daughter's crib.

"You're hiding something from me," she told Jerry Frames accusingly. "There's something wrong with Dorotea."

"There's not a thing wrong with her, Ruth," Jerry replied sharply and thrust the baby's chart at her. "You've enough pediatrics to read the medical notations. Go ahead."

Ruth scanned the sheets quickly, then reread word and graph, checking the laboratory reports of body function, the cerebral and cardiac readings, even the nourishment intake and eliminations. There was definitely nothing abnormal about Dorotea. Even her chromosome mapping was XX/healthy/normal. Reassured, Ruth passed the clipboard back, and smiling confidently, continued to nurse her child.

Frames later said that he'd had a moment of pure panic because he couldn't remember how much genetic training Ruth had had or might remember. Op Owen assured him that his instinctive impulse had been the only possible course under the circumstances.

"It's exceedingly fortunate, though, Jerry," the director said, his eyes active with speculation, "that they are already under the Center's protection. That child must have every safeguard we can provide. I want equipment installed in her nursery, tuned to her pattern day and night. If what we suspect is correct, it may manifest itself in her first six months. Can you imagine the strides we can make in formulating an early childhood program with such a superb example?"

"A pure case of doing what comes naturally."

"Nothing must interfere with that child's development."

"I still don't see why we've kept it from the parents. Are you stepping down from your 'know-all, tell-all' pedestal after all?"

Op Owen returned the physician's sardonic look.

"I'm not a precog, but I felt a strong reluctance to inform Lajos."

"Why? He'd be walking nine feet tall to think he produced such a Talented child."

"Haven't we changed sides, Jerry?"

"It's one thing to withhold information from the unwashed public, but another to clam up on one of the gang."

"We don't know positively that Dorotea Horvath is . . ."

"Come off it, Dave. Cecily King is a strong TP and she *heard* that child protest birth. Oh, I know that some of 'em can cry out in the womb but this was no physical cry or it would have been audible to the rest of the delivery room personnel. Is your stumbling block Ruth Horvath?"

Op Owen nodded slowly.

"Well, that makes a little more sense, although I'd say she'd welcome her daughter's Talent. A kind of vindication that she's never been identified. Unless you call the transmission of strong genetic traits a Talent."

Op Owen shook his head, his lips pursed in thought. "She has wanted a child desperately. As a mother wants a child: not as a Talented person wants evidence of succession." He spoke slowly, the words dragged out of his mouth as if he were sorting the thoughts. "Lajos says that although Ruth is a great help and very understanding, sometimes his Incidents bother her more than she admits. Let's just let things take their course. We'll keep an eye on them."

"What they don't know won't hurt them, huh?" Frames sighed. "Wish you'd let that attitude spill over into other areas, Dave."

Op Owen regarded the doctor intently. "I can conceivably bend a little privately, for the benefit of those under my care, but I cannot as easily rationalize the broader issue which I cannot oversee or control."

"All right, Dave, but I feel, and Joel Andres feels, that private reactions are a strong basis for predicting public ones. You're reluctant to tell Ruth Horvath, a girl conditioned and trained to accept Talent, that her child shows exceedingly strong telepathic Talent. You willingly want to broadcast information that even frightens me, and I'm Talented, to a public that is in no way conditioned to accept a fragment of that knowledge. The two attitudes cannot be reconciled."

"The ethical position of the Talented must never be questioned."

"Dave," and there was entreaty in Jerry Frames's voice and manner, "*you* are unable to be unethical. The withholding of prejudicial knowledge is not unethical, it's plain good ol' common sense. Which you are sensibly applying to Ruth Horvath's case. How many times I have considered telling a patient he's bought it and how few times have

I actually come clean. Very few people can stand the whole, complete, unvarnished truth."

"I hang between, in doubt to act or rest," op Owen said, resigned as well as frustrated.

"What's that?"

"I apologize, Jerry. Your point is well taken. I've erred—on the side of the angels, I hope—but this attitude of mine towards Ruth Horvath *is* a curious vacillation from my tendency to be forthright. Yet I know that there is a reason to be slightly devious."

"Then you'll ease back on this all-open-and-above-board routine?"

"Yes, I'll ease back as you put it."

"Still," and Jerry frowned slightly, "it isn't as if they won't find out soon enough." He meant the Horvaths.

"They need time to get used to the idea." Op Owen was thinking about humanity.

"Where on earth did she get those blue eyes?" Lajos asked as he sat entranced by his three-month-old daugher's attempts to capture her toes. She flopped over, gurgling cheerfully to herself.

"Heavens, it's possible," Ruth replied, beaming fatuously as she caught her daughter's eye. "I may be grey-eyed, and you brown, but we both have ancesters with blue eyes—four generations back."

"I always said you were recessive, hon."

"Humph. I don't mind in the least, not if it produces a blue-eyed blonde daughter with dimples. And I've got her, haven't I, love? You're all mine."

"Except for the twenty-three chromosomes from me."

Dorotea twisted her head backwards over her shoulder and burbled moistly at her mother.

"Love at first bite," Lajos said in a mutter of mock surliness. "There's a conspiracy of females against this poor lone male."

Dorotea impartially gurgled at him, her eyes bright and wide and happy.

"You never had it so good," said Ruth.

And Lajos privately admitted the truth of that. Ruth was so enthralled with her daughter, their apartment had a noticeable atmosphere of benevolence. He was more relaxed than ever, and despite an increase in Incidents, extending beyond his usual affinity, he suffered less from the depressions and exhaustions that were the inevitable postlude.

The day Dorotea's Talent blossomed, Daffyd op Owen was reviewing the records obtained overtly and covertly from the Horvath apartment. He'd had Lester Welch, his electronic chief, rig a buried web in Ruth's mattress, in case the baby instinctively contacted her mother first. However, Lester had pointed out the slight variation in Ruth's readings. It was more as if the needle had snagged itself on an imperfection in the graph paper. There was no such variation on the baby's recordings. Welch had been about to discredit the occurrences until he checked them against Lajos's and discovered that the minute variations in Ruth's chart always occurred exactly at the onset of Lajos' Incidents.

"She might well be a latent 'receiver,'" op Owen said to Welch, "only now beginning to develop from continued proximity to her husband and the advent of the child. I can't present another explanation."

"That'd be nice, Dave. Ruth's a good little person: cheerful, intelligent and crazy for her husband and child. Just the sort of well-balanced, understanding parent to have for a . . ."

Lester was abruptly staring at op Owen's retreating back. The man had leaped to his feet and raced down the hall to the recording room. Lester Welch was not Talented, although his electronic engineering was often sheer inventive genius, but op Owen didn't react like that without good cause. When Welch reached the doorway, he saw that Charlie Moorfield, the day engineer, was hunched over the console, unconcious, but op Owen's attention was for a graph.

"Take a close look at Dorotea's graph," op Owen said, grinning fit to pop his jaw, and then he passed his associate on his way out.

Common sense told op Owen that, despite the urgency of the summons, there could be no danger threatening the baby. Yet he could not disregard that call. What could have happened, he wondered as he ran down the front steps. Suddenly he noticed that there seemed to be a mass exodus from all parts of the building. And everyone was headed in the same direction. As abruptly as the call had been issued, it ceased. People slowed down, stopped, looking around, grinning foolishly.

"What was that?" "Who called?" "Wot hoppened?"

"It's all right," op Owen found himself reassuring them. "A new technique improperly shielded," he said to the telepaths. And grinned at his own dissembling as he continued towards the Horvath's apartment.

There was a crowd in the hall before their apartment. Op Owen politely pushed his way through the disturbed residents. Dorotea, her baby face still tear-streaked, was held high in her mother's arms, cooing and chortling at the smiling faces around her. Op Owen's arrival signaled the crowd's discreet dispersal and shortly, he was alone with the mortified mother.

"I'm so embarassed, sir," Ruth said, jiggling her baby as she walked nervously up and down her living room. "I fell asleep with the tape recorder blaring away. And I just . . . didn't hear Dorotea wake up . . . I've never done such a thing before and we've never permitted her to cry long . . ."

"No one is remotely suggesting that you mistreat Dorotea." Op Owen smiled as the baby flirted delightfully with him. "In fact a little honest frustration is very useful. It certainly placed her Talent."

"Ooooooooh," and Ruth collapsed on the sofa, staring wide-eyed at Daffyd op Owen as she absorbed the implication, which she had been too preoccupied with calming Dorotea to see.

"She broadcast a *very* loud signal. I shouldn't be at all surprised if every Talent in the city heard her."

No sooner were the words out of his mouth than Lajos charged through the door.

"What happened to her? How did she get hurt? My head is splitting!" Lajos snatched Dorotea from her mother's lap to examine her firsthand. She began to whimper, catching his anxiety.

"Only her feelings were hurt," Ruth replied, suddenly very calm. Op Owen noticed that with approval: she was dampening her own distress to soothe the others. "I'd fallen asleep with the tape recorder blasting away and just didn't hear her when she woke up hungry and all damp." She took her daughter back, rocking her until the baby began to beam again. "She was hurt because she felt she was being ignored, isn't that right, sweetie?"

"Well, good god!" Lajos sank onto the couch, mopping his forehead. "I never heard anything like it before. Sir," and he turned to op Owen, "look, this can't . . . I mean, can this sort of thing happen every time my daughter's upset?"

"Oh, I'm sure she's likely to protest many assumed indignities, Lajos. Babies have to suffer some frustrations to grow. We'll just move you all to a shielded apartment and dampen down that lovely loud young voice."

"You're not surprised about Dorotea at all," Ruth said, regarding op Owen with round, suspicious eyes. "So that's why everyone was so excited about her in the nursery."

"Well, yes," the Director agreed slowly. "She was heard by the TP nurse at birth."

"But I thought psionic Talents don't usually show up until adolescence . . ."

"Conscious Talent," op Owen said, correcting her.

Ruth looked down at the drooling baby in her arms. A strained look crossed her pretty face. "But I want Dorotea to have a normal, happy childhood!"

"And she won't because she's Talented? Is that it, my dear?" Op Owen knew, sadly, that his instinct about not telling Ruth at once had been all too well-founded. "Except for this ability, which might as well be drawing freehand, she *is* a normal, healthy child, totally unaware that she is in any way remarkable . . ."

"But I know you'll want to test her, and all that, with stimuli . . ." Ruth's distress was so acute that she couldn't go on.

"Ruth!" Lajos bent to comfort her, surprised by her reaction. She clutched her daughter tightly to her.

"My dear Ruth!" op Owen said gently, "testing and stimuli are for people who come to us after they have subverted and suppressed their Talents. We know what Dorotea is already, a very strong telepath. And we've been 'testing' her, as you call it, already. As for stimuli, I assure you," and there was nothing forced in op Owen's chuckle, *"she's* applying the only stimuli . . . to us."

Lajos laughed, brushing his hair back from his forehead as he remembered his frantic homeward flight. Beneath his arm, he could feel Ruth relaxing. A slight smile touched her lips.

"Dorotea will have an unusual opportunity, my dear. One denied you and Lajos, and myself, and so many other potential Talents. She has the chance to grow up in her Talent, learning to use it as naturally as she learns to walk and talk. We will all help her to understand it . . . as much as we do ourselves," he added with a wry smile. "To be candid, Ruth, we are in much the same position as your daughter. We are all learning to act in a publicly acceptable fashion with this new facet of human evolution. Psionic Talents are in their infancy, too, you know.

"You might even extend the analogy a little to include the Andres Bill, which we hope will afford all Talents professional status and legal protection. We, in effect, must prove to the public, our parent-body, if you wish, that we are not 'bad,' 'naughty' or 'capricious' children. Dorotea has already contributed something to that end," and op Owen caught himself before he explained his own revelation. "Dorotea needs love and reassurance, discipline and understanding. She'll pick that up from you, Ruth, with your warmth and sweetness. I want her, possibly more than you do, to have a normal, happy childhood so that she will be a normal, happy adult."

He rose, smiling at the baby's infectious gaiety.

"See, she knows how pleased we are with her right now, the little rascal."

Op Owen left, assuring them new quarters within the week. Ruth was so quiet and thoughtful that Lajos remained home the rest of the day. He found the revelation of Dorotea's Talent as much a shock as Ruth apparently did. However, by morning, he was consumed with a paternal pride and, in the succeeding days, discovered an overweening tendency to maunder on about his daughter's prowess. By the time they moved to the larger, shielded apartment, he was accustomed to the notion and, since Dorotea made no more frantic summonses, succeeded in ignoring it. Until he noticed the gradual change in Ruth. At first, it was no more than a sudden frown, quickly erased, or a nervous look towards the baby's room if she slept longer than usual. Then he caught Ruth looking at her child with that wary expression he had once privately called 'the Freak Look,' which un-Talented people occasionally directed at him when they discovered his affiliation with the Center.

"You've got to stop that, honey," he blurted out. "You've got to keep thinking . . . strongly . . . that Dorotea is just like other kids. Or you'll prejudice her. Which is the one thing we have to avoid."

Ruth vehemently denied the accusation but she turned so white around the lips that Lajos gathered her quickly into his arms.

"Ah, sweetie, she hasn't changed just because we've found out she's Talented. But she *is* perceptive and she can sense your feelings towards her. You start suppressing that 'freak-feeling' right now. You think positively that she's our beautiful baby girl, sweet and loving, kind and thoughtful. She'll have that opinion of herself and it won't matter that she's a strong TP as well. She'll merely consider that part of the whole bit. It's when she senses criticism and restraint and hypocrisy that we'll be in trouble. I had to get used to it, too, Ruthie. Say," and he tilted her chin up and grinned down at her reassuringly, "why don't we get a little help from op Owen? Talk this over with him. He can put a block on if you need one."

The very suggestion that she couldn't love and understand her own child made Ruth indignant. She'd had years of parent training. She understood every phase of early childhood development. She adored Dorotea and she certainly wouldn't do a thing that might jeopardize her daughter's happiness. They both felt better after such a candid discussion and the problem was shelved.

"Sir, I thought you ought to see the Horvath charts," Lester Welch told op Owen. "A variation keeps appearing in Ruth Horvath's. See?" and Welch unrolled the paper, pointing here and there to the almost imperceptible alteration in Ruth's normal pattern. "See, here and here, it's a couple of microseconds longer and broader. It begins to broaden minutely until it hits this frame which has remained constant. Now, compare her time-sequence to Lajos's . . . and remember we're picking up her pattern anywhere in the new apartment just as we pick up his from the office."

Op Owen saw the correlation immediately.

"He's finished no precog in six weeks?"

Welch contented himself with a nod as op Owen studied the graphs.

"If I didn't think it was impossible, I'd say Ruth was suppressing him. But how?"

"Don't you mean why?"

"That, too, of course, but 'how' is the bigger question."

"If you mean the type of pattern, Dave, I can't give you that. There isn't enough to identify it as a known variation."

"That wasn't exactly what I meant, although I would like a magnification of this to study. Can you put on a more sensitive gauge, or a faster needle, to lengthen the stroke?"

"Hmmm." Welch considered the suggestion. "I'll rig up something, I guess."

Op Owen chuckled. "One of the comforting things about you, Les, is your unfailing rise to the challenge. I don't believe you know what failure is."

Welch regarded his superior with some surprise. "Failure is an inability to consider what is not presently known. Like Ruth Horvath's variation?" Then he added, "Or Senator Zeusman's strategy?"

Op Owen dismissed that with a wave of his hand and continued to scan the Horvaths' readings. "Dorotea's first Incident rocked him, didn't it?"

"Yes, it shows up in his sleep pattern as unusual restlessness the first nights, but see, he's calming down by the third."

"It's from that date that his precogs begin to dwindle."

"By God, you're right. I thought he'd be too stable for a deviation like that."

"Yes, he's been too consistent a precog. I think I'll call him in and drop a few leading questions to see what reaction I get." Op Owen initiated the call then and there.

"There's nothing wrong with Dorotea, is there, sir?" Lajos asked as soon as he entered the office.

"Good heavens, no," Daffyd op Owen said, gesturing Lajos to a chair.

"It's about my drop in Incidents, then, isn't it?"

Op Owen eyed his young colleague for a moment, savoring the peripheral emotions the man was generating.

It took no Talent to recognize the defensive nervousness in Lajos's attitude.

"Not exactly. There are always periods of rest for precogs, caused by any number of valid reasons, including the absence of fires. However, your graphs show an onset of Incidents, broken off just as they begin."

"Once or twice in the office, I've felt as if something was preventing me . . ."

"Preventing you . . ?" Op Owen prompted Lajos gently as he had broken off, startled by his own phrasing.

"Yes, sir," Lajos went on slowly, "it's as if something's preventing me from previewing. Sort of like . . . glancing into a strange room and having the door slammed in your face."

"Aptly put. Could you suggest why . . . or perhaps what . . . is preventing you?"

"You think it's a psychological suppression, don't you?"

"That's my first thought"

Indignation and disbelief were Lajos's instant reaction. "Why would I want to suppress suddenly?"

"Something you yourself don't *want* to see. Precog is not the easiest of Talents, Lajos," op Owen replied. "Often the precog imposes his own block, as a relief from the psychological pressures."

"If you think there's a chance that I'm developing the Cassandra complex . . ." Lajos was heatedly provoked now.

"No, that follows an entirely different pattern."

"Dorotea's preventing me?"

"If this occurred only in your home environment, we'd have to seriously consider the possibility. But it's improbable for a variety of reasons: the prime one being that her room is shielded to protect her from overtones of your precogs as much as to protect us from her blatant calls."

"Ruth?" Lajos's hushed question had the power of a shout. "She is Talented after all. But why suppress me? She loves me. I know she does. She's always helped with

Incidents. It made her feel a part . . ." Lajos stared at op Owen. Then shook his head, violently disagreeing with the natural conclusion. "No! I don't see why suppressing me would . . . do her any good."

"Has something else upset her? The suppression starts not long after Dorotea's first Incident."

Lajos covered his eyes, groaning deeply. He collected himself almost immediately and, looking up at op Owen, recounted Ruth's curious uncertainty about Dorotea.

"Yes, I see now what has possibly happened. She's made you her whipping boy."

"Now wait a minute, sir. Ruth's not petty or vindictive."

"I'm not for a moment implying that she is, Lajos. Let us both try to see her conflicts. She's had to make so many adjustments. She had such hopes when she entered the training program. I remember her cheerfulness and vivacity so well. It was difficult to have to disillusion her. You two married and she has exhibited skill in assisting you. But even the most generous soul experiences twinges of envy. She looked forward to maternity as an outlet for her natural inclination and the assuagement of her failures. Suddenly she finds herself with the extraordinary daughter who makes even the Director of the Center jump at her whim." Lajos weakly returned op Owen's smile. "I thought at the time she was very much distressed at the thought of relinquishing any of Dorotea's care to our impersonal toils. I don't believe we entirely relieved her fear that the Center will usurp her role in her daughter's upbringing. Can you see why she may be *indirectly* punishing you for circumstances that threaten her happiness?"

"Yes, I can." Lajos's admission was dejected.

"Now, it's not as bad as that," op Owen said firmly. "In fact, stop feeling guilty and look at the very positive side —Ruth actually has been able to suppress your strong Talent."

"And that's positive?"

"Yes. The underlying problem is Ruth's lack of Talent.

We now can prove conclusively that she has one. She has demonstrated it superbly. Severe frustration often breaks down blocks. And she's had that."

"Of course." Lajos's face began to light up. "Whoa. You said she doesn't know she's doing it?"

"I've proof for her. And the further proof will be the renewal of your precogs. I'll have a talk with her and straighten this out today."

He made the call as Lajos left. There was more to the problem of Ruth Horvath than touched the little family. *If you don't tell all you know, how much is enough?* op Owen wondered.

"All right, I'm forced to believe you," Ruth said, her defensiveness waning under op Owen's gentle redirection, because she also could not deny the evidence of the graphs: of that remarkable, infinitesimal variation that had to be an Incident.

Daffyd op Owen felt himself begin to relax with her admission. He had known it would be a stormy confrontation: one reason why he had not delayed it. Ruth had been appalled by the knowledge that she had subconsciously blocked Lajos. She finally admitted that Dorotea scared her: that she had lost all joy in her daughter and was terrified of predisposing the child towards her.

"Yes, I have to believe you," she repeated, not bothering to stifle resentment, "but it's a pretty poor excuse of a Talent," she added bitterly, "if all I can do is block my husband's, and not even know I'm doing that."

"On the contrary," op Owen replied with a laugh, "it's exactly the one you need the most . . . applied properly."

Ruth glared at him, waiting pointedly for an explanation.

"You've a strong moral code, Ruth. You would not permit yourself to act against your daughter, though her Talent frightened you. But you will have to waive that most laudable principle. Until Dorotea has developed sufficient discretion to handle her mental gift, you are going to *have* to block it."

Ruth blinked in surprise and then her eyes brightened, her mouth formed an "O" of astonishment as she began to understand.

"Of course. Of course, I understand." Tears of relief welled in her eyes. "Oh, of course."

Op Owen smiled at her. "Yes, Dorotea cannot be permitted to dip into any mind she chooses. You must restrict her by your ability to block. You won't need much pressure to dissuade her from broadcasting or eavesdropping."

"But won't Dorotea resent it? I mean, she'll feel me doing it, won't she?"

"All children require limits. Want them. As long as those limits are consistent and reasonable, a child as aware as Dorotea of her parents' approval and affection won't resist. In any event, by the time she could, or would, we shall have been able to instill discretion *and* your moral code. Right now, Ruth, you have all that's required to keep Dorotea from becoming a nuisance and a brat."

Ruth instantly reacted with indignation to his calculated insult and then laughed as she recognized the bait. She left his office considerably reassured, once again at harmony with her situation.

Op Owen envied her that carefree assurance. He still didn't know what to call what she'd done. Yes, she had suppressed Lajos's precog over the last six weeks, but in the four months prior to that Lajos's abilities had increased in strength and efficiency and, except for duration and width, by a similar application of psionic effort on Ruth's part. What did her Talent actually affect? And would it, as he had so blithely assured her, be able to "block" Dorotea?

Well, if she thinks she can, she will. At least she is no longer afraid of her precocious child, he thought. He swung his chair round, gazing out at the peaceful view of the grounds of Beechwoods, seeing the city beyond with its spires, towers and living blocks.

Was I right in my analogy that Talent is in its infancy, and the public is the parent? With the duty to block the undisciplined child? The Talents are more disciplined than the average citizen we often have to search out and rebuke, protect and cherish. It would be catastrophic for the parent to fear the child. How much of the whole truth would reassure, as it had Ruth?

Those who truly understand psionic powers need no explanation. Those who need explanation will never understand.

Two mornings later, while reviewing contracts covering institutions holding government research grants, Lajos experienced one of his strongest Incidents. So powerful was the flame-fear that it was all he could do to pull the Goosegg recording web to his skull and depress the key that would relay the reading back to the Center.

"Flames!" he said, gasping; his mind reeled with the panoramic intense preview.

"Where?" he was prompted.

"A sheet, in front of a huge window, overlooking . . . the grounds. Rhododendrons. Red ones. The clock in the church tower . . . nearly twelve. Too much heat! The converter is flawed. It'll blow. There are so many people watching. They don't belong there." Lajos was abstractedly curious at the sound of indignation in his voice. "They caused the fire. Meddling. I know *him!*" Lajos struggled to get a clear picture of that face.

"You don't like him. Who is he?"

"Ahhh. . . the flames. Obscuring everything." Lajos fell back in his chair, shaken and sweating.

"Can you make it to the Center? I'll send transport," the duty officer said.

By the time Lajos reached the computer room in the Center, the system was already chuckling away at the details, locating which laboratories had scheduled visitors in the a.m.: laboratories using heat converters. The church clock tower suggested a college so that data was added as well as the planting of red rhododendrons.

Op Owen greeted Lajos with a grin of approval. "That was the most intense pattern you've ever projected. Have you any idea why that premonition should affect you so?"

"None, sir," Lajos replied, taking the seat op Owen indicated. He was still shaken.

"The man you knew: he was someone you obviously dislike. Do you have the impression that you've met him personally?"

"No. I recognized his face, that's all. Then the flames leaped up."

"We don't have much time," and op Owen's eyes glanced towards the wall clock, registering quarter to eleven. "Your precog came at 10:12. Unfortunately this appears to be appropriation time and every lab in the country is having its share of visitations. I want to play back your answer, Lajos. I was struck by two things and if you can pinpoint them also, we'll have the 'where' at least."

"Anything." Lajos could see the vivid overprint of the flames in his mind and tried to see beyond their obscuring curtain. "And one day, figure out why I have a pyro-affinity."

"Keeps insurance rates low, Horvath," Welch said drily as he rewound the tape. "Don't knock small favors."

Lajos listened as objectively as he could, appalled at the odd wooden quality of his voice, the fear when he mentioned the flames.

"I've got it, sir," he said. "The converter, the lab, the church tower. Knowing that the people didn't belong there. Wherever it is, is familiar to *me*."

"Charlie," Welch spoke over his shoulder to the pro-grammer, "add Horvath's place and travel card."

Almost immediately a print-out appeared.

"Sir, it's North East University. Checks out, clock in church tower, visible from research laboratory which uses a heat converter."

"Any visitors scheduled today?"

"No report on that yet, sir, but they do have a government funded research project in neo-protein and sub-cellular engineering."

"Check the university direct," Welch said after a nod from op Owen.

"Only limit it to a request about visitors," op Owen added. "There was something else I want to check first."

"Excuse me, sir," Charles broke in as op Owen lifted his desk phone. "Several parties are expected during the course of the day. Dr. Rizor wishes to speak to you."

"When your office puts in a guarded call, Daffyd op Owen, I'm curious. Come clean."

"Henry, we are not alarmists . . ."

"Precisely. So. . . ?"

"We've had a valid Incident that appears placed at North East. Several of the details have not coincided, however. We are fallible, you know."

Rizor's snort was derogatory. "What's the rest of the precog?"

"It centers around the heat converter in the lab building opposite the church tower."

"And? God, it's like pulling nails from you, Dave."

"The heat converter may be faulty. The precog was that it will blow due to a sudden hot lab fire, just before noon, while visitors are on the premises."

"I'd hate for something to happen there now, Dave. We're on the verge of a breakthrough in the neo-proteins. Running tests that are awfully good. But no visitors are expected there."

"Then a variable has already altered the precog."

"That's too glib a dismissal, Dave. Why would a lab fire stimulate your precog? I didn't think they usually worked out of their own area."

"Our precog recognized one of the visitors."

Welch signaled urgently to op Owen.

"Look, Dave," Rizor was saying, "I'm taking no chances. I'll have that converter checked and the building cleared. That'll alter circumstances, too. Besides I don't want visitors in that building until we complete the program. A breakthrough will warrant government funding all next year. I appreciate your calling, Dave. Let me know when I can help again."

Welch was practically apoplectic before op Owen hung up.

"Washington sent in an urgent personal precog for Mansfield Zeusman!"

"That's who I saw," Lajos cried, jumping to his feet.

"Get Senator Zeusman's office on the phone, Charlie, and don't indicate the origin," op Owen said.

"Dave," and Les Welch had a peculiar expression on his long face, "he's the last person to warn. One, he won't believe you. Two, he's our principal antagonist. Let that damned hero perish."

"Les, you have a dry sense of misplaced humor."

"I'm practical as all hell, too," Welch added.

"Can you tell me if Senator Zeusman is expected in the office this morning?" Charlie's voice carried clearly in the tense silence. "Oh, I see. Can you tell me where he plans to be in the morning hours? But surely, he left an itinerary? Thank you." Charlie's voice was wooden and his face expressionless. "He is not in the office. The assistant is a very rude, uncouth bumptious twit."

"If he's not in the office," op Owen said, "he's college hopping—him and that Research Appropriations Committee of his. He's the sly kind is Zeusman, loves to arrive unannounced."

"He could be on his way to North East then," Lajos said.

Op Owen told Charlie to get Rizor back on the line.

"Sir," Charlie reported, concerned, "Dr. Rizor has left his office. Is there a message?"

Op Owen picked up an extension phone. "Miss Galt? Daffyd op Owen here. We have reason to believe that Senator Mansfield Zeusman will pay an unscheduled visit to your campus before noon. Will you please inform Dr. Rizor immediately? Good. Thank you. I can be reached at the Center on a priority call basis. Yes, the situation could be considered critical."

Lajos felt himself unwind a trifle but his apprehension did not completely abate. He smiled weakly at op Owen.

"Paradox time."

"How so, lad?"

"Dr. Rizor believes. He is already altering the circumstances I foresaw. We may have undone ourselves!"

Op Owen's eyes flashed. "At the risk of Zeusman's life, and that of how many others you saw in the precog?"

"No, sir, I didn't mean it that way," Lajos replied, stung by op Owen's scorn. "I meant, that fire can't happen now because Rizor will prevent Zeusman from entering the lab."

"I'd still prefer to see that sparrow fall!" Welch's mutter was clearly audible.

Op Owen swung his chair in idle half-arcs but his eyes remained on his dissident engineer.

"I am not in the least tempted, gentlemen," he said in his usual easy voice. "We are not God. Nor are we trying to replace God. The psionic arts are preventive, not miraculous. We are fallible, and because of that fallibility we have to be scrupulously impartial, and try to help any man our senses touch, whoever he may be, whenever we can. Lajos is right. We have already . . ."

"Sir," Charlie's interruption was apologetic but determined, "two more danger precogs involving Mansfield Zeusman. One from Delta and one in Quebec. Neither could get through to Zeusman and are applying to us."

Op Owen looked as if he might be swearing silently. He glanced up at the clock, its hands inexorably halfway past eleven.

"We haven't altered the future enough," Lajos said with a groan.

"Charlie, alert all rescue teams in the North East area," op Owen said, his words crisp but calm. "I'll try for Rizor. Les, get Lajos a sedative. Henry, I'm glad I could reach you . . ."

"Don't worry about a thing," Dr. Rizor replied cheer-ily. "I've a crew checking the converter and the building is completely off limits. What's this Miss Galt says about Zeusman paying us an unexpected visit?"

"Evidence points in that direction, and we've new pre-cogs of danger for him."

"Look, we're all set here, Dave," Rizor told him in an easy drawl. "No one can pass the gate without checking through my office and . . . Oh, no! *No!*"

The connection went dead. Op Owen looked around at the others.

"That's known as locking the barn when the horse is gone," said Welch in a flat voice. "Lay you two to one and no previewing, Rizor just discovered that Zeusman uses a heli-jet for these jaunts of his."

"Charlie, get me through to one of the mobile rescue team trucks."

"Sir, they're converging on the campus. Only they've been delayed at the gate," Charlie said in a quiet sad voice after a moment of urgent cross-wire phoning.

Welch scratched his head, smoothing his hair back over his ears, trying not to stare at op Owen's expressionless face. Lajos wondered how the Director could sit so calmly, but suddenly, not the tranquilizer but an inner natural composure settled Lajos's tensions.

"Sir," he said to op Owen, "I think it came out all right."

Everyone glanced up at the clock which now ticked over to high noon. The secondhand moved forward again, and again, the sweep-second duly circumscribing its segments of time. The phone's buzz startled everyone. Op Owen de-pressed Receive and Broadcast.

"I want to speak to the Director of this so-called Center," a bass voice demanded authoritatively.

"Op Owen speaking, Senator Zeusman."

"Well, didn't expect to get *you*."

"You asked to speak to the Director; I am he." Op Owen hadn't switched on his visual.

The composed answer appeared to confound the Senator briefly. He had not activated the screen at his end either.

"You've outsmarted yourself, Owen, with this morning's exhibition of crystal-balling. I thought you'd have better sense than to set one up and try to fool me into believing in your psionic arts bunk." The senator's voice was rich with ridicule and self-satisfaction. "Heat converter's blowing, indeed! They're constructed not to blow. Safest, most economical way of heating large institutional buildings. A *scientific* way, I might add."

"I tell you, Senator," Rizor interrupted, "there *is* a flaw in the bleed-off of that converter. My engineers reported it."

"Get off the extension, Rizor. I'll settle your hash later. Applying for funds to run a research program which you arbitrarily interrupt at a vital stage on the say-so of crackpots and witch doctors? Your university is unfit to handle any further public monies over which I have any control." Zeusman was almost snarling.

"I won't get off the extension, Zeusman. This is my college, in what is reputedly still a free country, and I don't regret in any way having listened to Dr. op Owen. There was a flaw which would have exploded under conditions foreseen . . ."

"Don't defend Owen, Rizor," Zeusman said. "His meddling costs his defenders too damned much. How's Joel Andres feeling these days, Owen? How's his amyloidosis progressing? Just remember when you predict his death that the research your scheme interrupted here might have saved his life."

There was a loud clack as Zeusman broke the connection.

"Dave?" Rizor sounded defeated.

"I'm still here," op Owen replied. "What's this about Joel Andres?"

"You've had nothing? I thought you always kept a check on important men . . . like Zeusman." The name was grated out.

"Nothing's been reported on Joel. Precog is highly unpredictable, as you've just witnessed."

"That damned converter *was* faulty," Rizor was angry now and defiant. "It would have blown in the next overload. You saved Zeusman—and you've also saved other people."

"And Joel? Is it true about his liver?"

"So I understand," Rizor said in a heavy voice. "And our research was for a neo-protein to replace the faulty endogenous protein and restore a normal metabolism. Don't worry. The experiments can be reinitiated."

"With Zeusman withholding funds?"

"There are other sources of funds and I intend to use your so-called 'meddling' to advantage. Damn it, the converter would have blown!" Rizor was muttering as he ended the call.

Lajos was utterly spent when he returned to his apartment. Ruth took one look at his face and fixed him a stiff drink. He took it down, and with a weary smile flopped onto the bed.

"Dorotea asleep?" he asked hopefully. He was too disturbed not to generate emotional imbalance and too tired to suppress it.

"Fast asleep. Good for a couple of hours, honey," Ruth replied, her strong fingers already at work on his tense muscles. She did not question his depression and weariness. Slowly she felt him relax as her massage and the stiff drink combined to bring surcease.

He woke in time for dinner and seemed in control again, laughing at Dorotea's antics, playing with her on the floor until her bedtime. Only when the baby was safely asleep in her shielded room did he tell Ruth all that had happened.

"Oh, no, not Mr. Andres," she said when he finished. Lajos didn't notice her quick flush as she recalled her one personal encounter with the magnetic Senator Andres. He'd been . . . so kind to her and she'd been so embarrassed.

"How could I guess that he'd be involved? It was the flames. And how could I know that Zeusman would be saved at Andres's expense?"

"Why, you couldn't, darling," Ruth cried, alarmed at his self-castigation. "You couldn't! You mustn't blame yourself. You saved lots of lives today! Lots!"

Lajos groaned, miserable. "But why, Ruthie . . . *why* does it have to ricochet off Andres? If Rizor hadn't ordered the converter off, the experiment would have been concluded. All they had to do was keep visitors out."

"No, that's not quite true," Ruth told him in stern contradiction. "You said yourself that the heat-converter proved to be flawed. That flaw would not have been discovered without your precog. It would have exploded during the next lab fire. Who knows who might have been killed then?"

"But Andres is the one who needed the neo-protein!"

"They'll come up with a neo-protein somewhere else, then," Ruth said, very positively to distract Lajos. "They've made so many strides in organ replacement . . ."

"Except livers! That neo-protein was supposed to correct some kind of abnormal protein growth . . . faulty endogenous protein metabolism . . . that's what's killing Senator Andres . . . stuff is cramming into his liver and spleen, enlarging them and there's no known way to clear the amyloids. And when the liver doesn't work, that's it, honey. Ticket out!"

Ruth went on stroking Lajos' forehead gently, knowing that he must find his own way out of this. He burrowed his face into her neck, entreating the comfort that she never denied him. Later her mind returned to the terrible paradox, the tragic linkage of circumstance and the sorrow of the well-intentioned Good Samaritan.

God gives man stewardship of his gifts and the free will to use or deny them. Why must it be, that a man acting in good faith, finds himself reviled?

As sleep finally claimed her in the early morning hours, she wondered if she ought now to use her Talent to prevent Lajos from precogs like this. No, she drowsily realized, she had no right to take negative action. One must always think positively. One is one's brother's keeper, not his warder!

"I rather expected a call from you, Dave," Joel Andres said, his grin on the vidscreen slightly waving from atmospheric disturbance. "And that's no precog. No indeed," he rattled on, without permitting op Owen to speak. "The good senator from that great midwestern state called especially to warn me that I'm the next sparrow to fall because my pet witch doctor read the wrong crystal ball. Hey, that rhymes. Now, I don't believe that for a moment, Dave, on account of I don't think that that stupid mockprotein goop would have been jelled or curdled or what have you, in time to save my misspent life anyhow." The words were lightly said but there was an edge to Andres's voice that ruined the jovial effect.

"How long, Joel?"

"Probably long enough to get that Bill out of Committee, Dave, and I'll count the time well spent. Zeusman can't put down the mass of evidence in favor of psionics, the tremendous saving of loss and life already effected by validated precogs. By the way, Welch told me that the precog came in at 10:12. Do you know the time when Zeusman gave his pilot orders to fly to North East?"

"10:12?"

"Right, man. And that's in the record! Right in his flight log and a friend of mine impounded it because the pilot isn't so contemptuous of the circumstances as Zeusman. That pilot was scared silly by the coincidence. And don't think I'm not going to ram that down Zeusman's double-chins."

"He'll never admit our warning saved his life, Joel," Daffyd said.

"Hell, he doesn't have to admit it. The facts prove it. But I must say, Dave, you made one mistake." Joel's chuckle was rich.

"Had I known what I know now, I do believe that this once I'd've sat back and twiddled my thumbs."

"Ha! *I* don't believe that for a minute . . . no, maybe you would have," and the lawmaker's voice rippled with amusement. "If this has buckled your altruistic armor, it's worth it. Worth dying for, because there's nothing trickier to tie down than an honest man gone bad! Now let me go to work."

"Joel, let me know . . ."

"Hang loose, man. Don't rob me of my cool. Not now!"

The senator signed off but Daffyd op Owen sat staring moodily at the wall opposite his desk, unable for the first time in his life to divert his train of thought. His mind writhed in recrimination as bitter as an ancient inquisitional penance.

"Dave?" Welch's brisk voice broke through his introspection. "There's an anomaly on . . . Oh, I'll come back later. . . ."

"No, Lester, come in."

Welch gave his friend a speculative look but he unrolled the graphs without comment.

"Ruth Horvath!" Op Owen was surprised, almost irritated that she should be the subject of the intrusion.

"Couple of things. Here . . . on the baby's chart . . . Incident after Incident . . . compare it with Ruth's. No pattern. Not even an inky hiccup. I thought you said she could block that baby."

Curious now, op Owen scanned the charts. "What's this?" he asked, pointing to a sustained emphatic variation.

"That's the anomaly. Happened last night. It's a spontaneous variation. All her others have been triggered, usually by Lajos. And, if you'll look at the peaks and valleys in last night's records, you'll see that the pattern is kinetic."

"That's too tight for a true kinetic touch."

"Well, it's not TP, it's not 'finding' and what'n'hell would she be trying to do, fast asleep? 'Finding' is a conscious application, anyway. No, this is a kinetic pattern."

"For what reason? Against what?"

"Who knows? The point is, while she has stopped suppressing her husband, she hasn't started blocking her daughter. And that's going to be serious. I mean, we don't need a teething telepath broadcasting discomfort."

"Teething?"

"I forget you're not a parent," Welch said with tolerant condescension, "to *small* babies, that is."

Op Owen was engrossed in the patterns and it was obvious that Ruth was not responding and seemed unable to use a conscious block. And that was too bad. He frowned at the unusual kinetic display of the previous night.

"She's got it. She used it."

"Not consciously."

"I hate to resort to therapeutic interference. It might jeopardize her ever using it consciously."

"It's therapy for Ruth, or that baby'll tyrannize both parents. And that's bad. A kid that strong has got to have limits, right now, before she can develop precocious resistance."

Op Owen examined the charts one last time, shaking his head as he noticed the telepathic patterns on Dorotea's chart, saw the impingement on the mother's and no block.

"These could be legitimate calls . . ."

"Don't evade, Dave. I know you hate interfering with Talent; that it should be spontaneous. Admit Ruth Horvath is one of those who cannot use Talent consciously. Meddle a little!"

Op Owen rose, his face drawn. "I'll drop over to see them today. Let's hope she responds well to hypnosis."

"She does. I looked up her training record."

Two days later Welch came back in triumph, trailing two sheets of graphing tissue like victory streamers.

"You did it, Boss. Look, pass blocked, time and again, with a minimum of effort on Ruth's part. But damn it, she's not a pure kinetic. What could she be moving with such an infinitesimal touch? How does she apply the block?"

"Unconsciously," op Owen replied with a sly grin. "However, it may be because that touch is so delicate, she can't do it consciously. I didn't *look* very deeply. But so many kinds of Talent are fairly heavy-handed, violent. Like using awls in place of microneedles." He winced a little, remembering how his mental touch had uncovered Ruth's pitiful lack of self-confidence in her Talent. All her Incidents occurred without her awareness, deep in the subconscious levels of her mind into which Daffyd saw no need to trespass. She was a nice womanly person: her surface thoughts revolving around her husband, her daughter: all her anxieties were needless guilts over minor details. It was, therefore, relatively easy to block her notions that she would inadvertently harm Dorotea, or try to suppress Lajos. It was easy to erase conscious knowledge of her Talent, replacing it with a feeling of accomplishment and well-being: the post-hypnotic command to respond to Dorotea's telepathic demands and channel them firmly into speech centers. He also displaced her reluctance to have other Talented children because she felt inadequate. Ruth must have great resources of self-assurance. He planted them.

Now op Owen turned to Welch. "Ask Jerry Frames how soon Ruth Horvath can bear another child. I'd like her first two fairly close together before she gets cold feet."

"Cold feet he calls it!" was Welch's parting crack.

"I'm sorry, Daffyd," the Washington precog said, "I've stared at Joel Andres's picture for hours. I've read his House speeches, I've read his memoirs. I've sat in his outer office until the Senate police asked to have a word with me. Then *he* came in, and recognized me, of course. And gave me a scarf to hold." Mara Helm paused. "As a memento, he said. But I don't see it."

"You've had no stimulation about him at all?"

"Nothing dire."

"What do you mean, nothing dire?"

"That's what I mean and all I mean, Dai. Nothing conclusive, in that his life concludes. And, as you know, my accuracy is unfortunately high."

"I don't understand this, Mara."

"No more do I when I hear the gossip around town."

"Which is?"

"That Senator Andres is spending his last moment helping a minority group that not only has predicted his imminent demise but destroyed his one chance of a cure." Her voice held no inflection as she uttered these quick sentences, but her dislike of imparting the gossip was obvious to her listener. Mara cleared her throat suddenly. "I do have a precog though," she added, mildly amused.

"A good one, if I recognize that tone of voice. I could stand some pleasant tidings."

"I'll be seeing you shortly," and she laughed mischievously. "In the flesh, I mean. Here!"

"In Washington?" Daffyd op Owen was startled. He rarely left the Center and, at this moment, he had no desire under heaven to set foot in Washington.

Two weeks later, Daffyd op Owen, in a swivet of anxiety which no perception could dispel, disembarked from

the heli-jet on the Senate landing pad. Mara Helm and
Joel Andres were waiting for him. Daffyd had no eyes for
anyone but the senator who strode forward, grinning
broadly, eagerly grasping the telepath's hand, forgetting
in the excess of his welcome that Daffyd avoided casual
physical contacts.

However, op Owen wanted more than anything to
touch-sense his friend. And was reassured by the
vigorous sensation he felt equally strong through mind and
body. He might disbelieve the evidence of his eyes as he
stared at Andres's clear pupils, the healthy tanned skin
with no trace of the yellow, indicative of liver disorder.
Op Owen could not deny the feeling of health and energy
that coursed to him in that hearty handclasp.

"What happened?" he asked hoarsely.

"Who knows?" Joel replied. "The medics called it a
spontaneous remission. Said my body had started manu-
facturing the right enzymes again. Something to do with a
shift in the RNA messenger proteins or some rot like that.
Anyhow, no more amyloids in the perivascular spaces—
if that makes any sense to you—the old liver and spleen
are back to normal size and I can *feel* that. So, friend, *I* no
longer need that neo-protein research that Zeusman
scrapped."

Mara Helm remained aside, smiling benevolently at the
two men, until they finally remembered her presence.

"Dai, see?" and she laid a finger fleetingly on his sleeve.
"You're here as predicted!"

"Did you bring the graphs and records I asked for?"
Joel inquired.

"Here they are," and Daffyd handed the neat package
over.

"Good," and the senator's expression was maliciously
gleeful. "We're going to hoist Senator Mansfield Zeusman
today on *his* petard. However," and black anger surged
across Andres's face, "I beg your indulgence, Daffyd. Certain—what would you call them, Mara—security measures?"

Mara's lips twitched but there was an answering indignant sparkle in her eyes.

"A shielded cage?" Daffyd asked.

"Yeah," and the sound was more of a growl than an affirmative. "Don't think I didn't protest that insulting . . ."

"In fact," Mara said, "he ranted and screamed at the top of his voice. All Washington heard. I elected to keep you company in the gilt-wired gold-fish bowl," and she gave op Owen a flirtatious wink.

"You'll have an advantage over me," Andres said. "You can switch off the sound of Zeusman's voice."

"Who? Me?" Daffyd asked and the three entered the Senate Building laughing.

Op Owen was not surprised at Mansfield Zeusman's insulting treatment. He expected little else. Although the senator had initiated the investigation of all the Centers, he had never personally entered one. Obviously Zeusman was among those who believed that any telepath could read every mind: he would be unlikely to believe that telepaths performed their services much as a surgeon does an exploratory operation in the hope of uncovering a patient's malignant disease. Zeusman also decried the psychiatric sciences, so his attitude was at least consistently narrow-minded.

"One more thing," Andres said as he held open the door into the shielded room, "you're here at the Committee's request, not Zeusman's, or mine. They may want to question you. Please, Dave, don't tell *all* you know?"

"I'll be a verbal miser, I promise."

"That'll be our saving," Andres replied. He obviously distrusted op Owen's sudden meek compliance.

"Doesn't Joel look wonderful?" whispered Mara as they seated themselves.

"Yes," Daffyd replied and then shut his lips. Even that interchange, broadcast into the chamber beyond, drew every eye to them. Op Owen crossed his legs, clasped his hands and composed himself outwardly.

Zeusman was not as large a man as op Owen thought he'd be. Nor was he a small man in stature which might have explained the aggressive, suspicious personality. He resembled a professor more than a senator, except for the elaborate gesticulations which were decidedly oratorical. And he was expatiating at length now with many gestures, pointedly ignoring Andres who took his place at the conference table.

The other five members of the Committee nodded towards Andres as if they welcomed his arrival. Their smiles faded as they turned back to the speaker. It was apparent to Daffyd that Zeusman's audience was heartily bored with him and had heard the same arguments frequently.

"These Experts claim . . ." and Zeusman paused to permit his listeners to absorb the vitriol he injected into that label, "that even the advertisement of that precognitive word changes events. Now that's a cowardly evasion of the consequences of their pernicious meddling."

"We've been through that argument from stem to stern before, Mansfield," the lanky bald man with a hawk nose said. Op Owen identified him as Lambert Gould McNabb, the senior Senator from New England. "You called this extraordinary session because you claim you have real evidence prejudicial to this Bill."

Zeusman glared at McNabb. McNabb calmly tamped down his pipe, relit it, pinched his nose between thumb and forefinger, blowing against the pressure to relieve his eardrums, sniffed once or twice, put the pipe back in his mouth and turned an expectant face towards Zeusman.

"Well, Mansfield, either hang 'em or cut 'em down."

"I have your attention, Senator McNabb?"

"At the moment."

"My contention has always been that protection for these meddlers is against common sense, ethics, and all the laws of man and God. They usurp the position of the Almighty by deciding who's to live and who's to die."

"To the point, Mansfield," McNabb said.

"Senator McNabb, will you desist from interrupting me?"

"Senator Zeusman, I will—if you will desist from jawing."

Zeusman looked around for support from the other five members of the Committee and found none.

"On the 14th of June, I left my offices in this building for the purpose of visiting several of the universities requesting the renewal of Research Funds. As you know, it is my custom to arrive unannounced. Therefore, it was not until we were airborne that I gave my pilot his directions."

"What time was that?" asked Andres quickly.

"The time is irrelevant."

"No, it isn't. I repeat, at what time did you give your pilot his flight directions?"

"I fail to see what bearing . . ."

"I have a transcript of the pilot's log, from the files of the Senate Airwing," Andres said and passed the copy over to McNabb.

"Ten-twelve, Daylight Saving time, the record says," McNabb said in a drawl, his eyes twinkling as he casually flipped the record across the table to the others.

Zeusman watched, frowning bleakly.

"I have here," Joel went on before Zeusman could grab the floor, "authenticated graph readings of four precognitive Incidents: one from Eastern American Center, the Washington Bureau, Delta Center and Quebec. The period, allowing for time zones, in which these precogs occurred is between 10:12 and 10:16. Excuse the interruption, Zeusman, but I'm trying to keep things chronological."

Zeusman awarded Andres a vicious smile and then a keener look. Op Owen wondered if Zeusman was only now aware of Andres's improved health.

"Ahem. When my heli-jet landed at North East University, I and my party were physically restrained by Dr.

Henry Rizor, the Research Dean and members of his staff, from conducting our investigation of their project on the specious grounds that a precog had been issued, predicting a flaming death for me and my party, due to a faulty heat converter which was supposed to explode. Well, gentlemen, I fathomed this little trap immediately."

"Whoa, whoa, Mansfield," Robert Teague said, tapping the material now in front of him. "The precog reports I have here . . . by God, I'm getting so I don't need an expert to translate them for me anymore . . . indicate that's exactly what was to have happened. At . . . ah, shortly before noon. When did you arrive at North East?"

"Quarter to twelve."

"Then you'd've been in the building around twelve. I'd say you owed these precogs your life."

"My life? Don't be ridiculous!"

"I'm not. You are," Teague replied with considerable exasperation.

"I'm no fool, Bob. I know when I'm being had, in spite of all the forged records going. The whole business was rigged. Heat converters don't blow."

"Right, so how could one be rigged to blow at precisely twelve noon at North East when no one, including yourself, knew when or where you were going that morning until 10:12?"

"A flaw was discovered when the heat converter was dismantled: air bubble in the steel tank," Joel Andres said, passing another affadavit to Teague. "The main chamber has been replaced. It could have blown, through that air-bubble flaw, under just such circumstances of overload as predicted."

"But it didn't!" Zeusman said in a roar.

"No, because it had been turned off to prevent such an occurrence."

"Exactly. The whole thing was a hoax. Ten-twelve, twelve noon, whatever. *And,*" Zeusman rattled the words out so loud and so fast that no one could interrupt him, "in turning off that so-called faulty converter, the experiment then in progress, paid for by government funds, was ruined just before what was certain to be a successful conclusion of a highly delicate, valuable project. I've papers of my own to present"—he dramatically flung stapled sheets to the table—"despositions from the various qualified, highly trained, highly reputable scientists in charge of the neo-protein research. And here is where these . . . these meddling godlets overreach themselves. That neo-protein research, so rudely interrupted on the brink of success would have produced, by *scientific* methods—accurate, repeatable, proven—a substance that would prevent certain all-too-common and terribly painful deaths due to liver failure. Prevent an agonizing death facing a certain member of this august Committee. And, if these precogs are so omniscient, so benign, so altruistic, so wise, why—I ask you, *why,* did they not foresee the effects of their own meddling on their avowed champion?"

Op Owen's altruism and benignity hit an all-time low and he found himself obsessed with an intense desire to turn kinetic and clog Zeusman's windpipe permanently.

"Ah ha," crowed Joel Andres, leaping to his feet, "why should they foresee my demise, my dear colleague? Due to liver failure? How interesting! Of course, you have a paper to prove it, Senator, such as my death certificate?"

"Easy, Joel," said McNabb, squinting at Andres keenly, "Anyone can see you're healthy as a hog, though I must admit you had been looking a bit jaundiced. You look great now, though."

"But I had a report that he was dying of liver failure," Zeusman said.

"Got that authenticated?" Teague asked sarcastically.

"Easy, Bob. We know Mansfield's been doing the job he was elected to do, protect his constituents and this country. That used to be as easy to do," McNabb paused to drag on his pipe, "as finding decent substitute tobacco. But Mansfield *proved* that was bad for most of us."

"We're discussing experts, not tobacco," Zeusman reminded him.

"No, we're discussing progress, on a level some of us find as hard to take as giving up tobacco. However, it was proved that tobacco was unhealthy. These people have proved that their Centers protect health and property, and they go about it scientifically. Everything I've heard today," and McNabb jerked his pipe stem at Zeusman as the latter started to interrupt, "*proves* conclusively to me that you've been putting the wrong eggs in the right basket. That precog was for *your* health and well-being, Mansfield, which these people are pledged to protect: you didn't have to take the warning . . ."

"I was forced . . ."

"Lots of us were forced to stop smoking, too," McNabb said, grinning. "This artificial stuff still doesn't taste right but I *know* it's better for me.

"Most important of all, Mansfield, and it seems to have completely escaped your logical, scientific, one-track mind, is the very fact that these people warned *you!* Whether they knew the consequences to Joel Andres or not if they also stopped the experiment, they had to warn *you* and your party! So stop your maundering on about their ethics and meddling. *I'd've* let you burn!"

Zeusman sank down into a chair, blinking at McNabb's craggy face. Then the New England senator rose, a slight smile on his lips.

"Gentlemen, we've hassled this Bill back and forth for close to two years. We've satisfied ourselves the provisions protecting the parapsychic professions, as outlined in Articles IV and V, do not threaten the safety of the citizens of this country, do not jeopardize personal liberty, et cetera and all that, and, hell, let's place it on the agenda and start protecting these poor idealistic bastards from . . . from them as don't wish to be protected."

McNabb's grin was pure malice but he didn't glance in Zeusman's direction nor was the midwesterner aware of anything but this unexpected defeat.

Op Owen reached the Center after full dark of the late spring evening. The pleasant sense of victory still enveloped him in contentment. He found himself, however, turning toward the apartments rather than his own quarters. The news that the Andres Bill had left Committee and would be presented to the Senate next session had already been relayed to the Center. He heard echoes of the celebrating which appeared to be going on all over the grounds.

A little premature, he thought to himself, for the Bill must pass Senate and Congress. There would be sharp debate but they predicted it would pass. The President was already in favor of protection for the Talented since he benefited from their guardianship.

Op Owen entered the building where the Horvaths lived. He hesitated at the elevator, then made for the steps, pleased to arrive without breathlessness at their apartment door.

He had a split second of concern that he might be interrupting the young couple but it was quickly dispelled when Lajos, still dressed, flung the door wide.

"Mr. op Owen!" The precog's face was a study in incredulous amazement. "Good evening, sir!"

"I'm sorry. Were you expecting someone?"

"No, no one. Exactly. Please, come in. It's just . . . well, everyone's been apartment hopping since the news came . . ."

"The Director is immune to jubilation?"

Lajos was spared the necessity of answering because Ruth entered from the kitchen, her face lighting up as she rushed forward to greet their guest. Op Owen was relieved at her obvious welcome: she could have developed a subconscious antipathy for him after their recent session.

"I don't think anyone expected you back tonight, sir," Lajos was saying, pressing a drink on op Owen.

"We're all so proud of you, sir," Ruth added shyly.

"I did nothing," op Owen replied. "I sat in a shielded room and listened. It was Lajos's precog . . ."

"There were three other reports, sir," Lajos said, "but is it really confirmed that Senator Andres has had a remission of that liver ailment?"

"Yes, absolutely, demonstrably true. I know we've all felt burdened with a certain . . . regret, on that aspect of the North East Incident. It is the inevitable concomitant of the precognitive gift."

"And Dr. Rizor's grant will be restored?"

Op Owen was taken by surprise. "I'm embarrassed to say I didn't think to inquire." He felt himself coloring.

"We can't think of everything, can we?" Ruth asked, her lips twitching with a mischievous smile.

Op Owen burst out laughing and, after a startled pause, Lajos joined him.

"I'll bet it will be restored," Ruth went on, "and that's no precog: just plain justice."

"How's Dorotea?" op Owen asked.

"She's asleep," and there was nothing but pride and pleasure in Ruth's face as she glanced towards the closed nursery door. "It's fascinating to *listen* to her figuring out how to get out from under the table."

Lajos echoed her pleasure. Op Owen rose, suddenly conscious of the rippling undercurrent between the two young people. His presence constituted a crowd.

"I wanted you to know about Joel Andres, Lajos."

"Thank you sir, I do appreciate it."

"It was good of you to tell us. You must be so tired," Ruth said, linking arms with her husband and standing very close to him.

"Save your maternal instincts for your children, Ruth," he said kindly and left.

Once again in the soft night air, op Owen felt extremely pleased with life. Obeying an impulse, he glanced over his shoulder and noticed that the lights in the Horvath apartment were already out. He had interrupted them after all. Sometimes, shield as he could, the stronger emotions, sex being one of them, seeped through.

He took his time walking back through the grounds, permitting himself the rare luxury of savoring the happy aura that permeated the Center. He stored up the fragrance of the joyful night, the exuberance that penetrated the dark, the hopefulness that softened the chill of the breeze, against those desperate hours that are the commoner lot of man. These times of harmony, concert, attunement came all too seldom for the Talented. They were rare, glorious, treasured.

Habit made him stop in at the huge control room. Surprise prompted him to enter——for Lester Welch, a dressing robe thrown over his nightclothes and a drink in one hand, was bending over the remote graph panels. His attitude, as well as that of the duty officer, was of intense concentration.

"Never seen anything like that before in a coital graph," Welch was muttering under his breath.

"Turned graphic voyeur, Lester?" Daffyd asked with tolerant amusement.

"Voyeur, hell. Take a look at these graphs. Ruth Horvath's doing it again. And at a time like this? Why?"

Welch was scarcely a prurient man. Stifling his own dislike of such an unwarranted invasion of privacy, op Owen glanced at the two graphs, needles reacting wildly in response to the sexual stimuli mutually enjoyed. Lajos's graph showed the normal agitated pattern: Ruth's matched his except for the frenetic action of the needle, trying valiantly to record the cerebrally excited and conflicting signals its sensitive transistors picked up. The needle gouged deep into the fragile paper, flinging its tip back and forth. Yet the pattern of deviation emerged throughout the final high——a tight, intense, obviously kinetic pattern.

Abruptly the frantic activity ceased, the lines wandered slowly back to normal-fatigue patterns.

"That was most incredible. The most prodigious performance I have ever witnessed."

Op Owen shot Welch a stern glance, only to realize that the man meant the electronic record. He was momentarily embarrassed at his own thoughts.

"What does she do?" Welch continued speaking and the technician glanced up quickly, startled and flushing. "The kinetic energy is expended for what reason? Not that she'd be able to tell us anyhow."

"For what reason?" op Owen asked quietly, answering the safest question. "For the exercise of a very womanly talent." He waited, then sighed at their obtuseness. "What is the fundamental purpose of intercourse between members of the opposite sex?"

"Huh?" It was Welch's turn to be shocked.

"The propagation of their species," op Owen answered his own inquiry.

"You mean . . . you can't mean . . ." Welch sank, stunned, into a chair as he began to comprehend.

"It hadn't occurred to me before now," op Owen went on conversationally, "that it is rather odd that a brown-eyed, black-haired father and a grey-eyed, brown haired mother could produce a blue-eyed blonde. Not impossible. Just quite improbable. Now Lajos is precog, and we have to grant that Ruth is kinetic. So how do these genes produce a strong, strong telepath?"

"What did she do?" Welch asked softly. His eyes knew the answer but he had to hear op Owen voice it.

"She rearranged the protein components of the chromosome pairs which serve as gene locks and took the blue-eyed genes and the blonde-haired ones out of cell storage. And what ever else she wanted to create Dorotea. That would be my educated guess. Just the way she unlocked the RNA messengers for . . ." Op Owen hesitated: no, not even Lester Welch needed to know *that* bit of Ruth's tinkering——"whatever it is she has in mind for this child." Welch had not apparently noticed his hesitation. "It'll be interesting to see the end product."

Welch was speechless and the technician pretended great industry at another panel. Op Owen smiled gently.

"This is classified, gentlemen. I'll want those records removed as soon as you can break into the drums," he told the technician, who managed to respond coherently.

"I'm glad of that," Welch said with open relief. "I'm glad that you're not blabbing all this to the world. Are you going to tell Lajos?"

"No," Daffyd replied with deliberation. "He obviously intends to cooperate. And they'll be happier parents without that knowledge."

Welch snorted, himself again.

"You sound like you're getting common sense, Dave. Thank God for that." He frowned as the drum wound the last of that Incident out of sight. "She can actually unlock the genes!" He whistled softly.

" 'One science only will one genius fit.
    So vast is art, so narrow human wit!' "

"How's that again, Dave?"

"A snitch of Popery!" op Owen remarked as he left.

3

Apple

Apple

The theft was the lead morning 'cast and ruined Daffyd op Owen's appetite. As he listened to the description of the priceless sable coat, the sapphire necklace, the couture model gown and the jewel-strap slippers, he felt as if he were congealing to his chair as his breakfast cooled and hardened on the plate. He waited, numbed, for the commentator to make the obvious conclusion: a conclusion which would destroy all that the East American Parapsychic Center had achieved so slowly, so delicately. For the only way in which such valuable items could have been removed from a store dummy in a scanned, warded, very public display window in the five-minute period between the fixed TV frames was by kinetic energy.

"The police have several leads and expect to have a solution by evening. Commissioner Frank Gillings is taking charge of the investigation.

" 'I keep my contractual obligations to the City,' Gillings is reported to have told the press early this morning as he personally supervised the examination of the display window at Coles, Michaels and Charny Department Store. 'I have reduced street and consensual crimes and contained riot activity. Jerhattan is a safe place for the law-abiding. Unsafe for law-breakers.' "

The back-shot of Gillings's stern face was sufficient to break op Owen's stasis. He rose and strode toward the comuit just as it beeped.

"Daffyd, you heard that 'cast?" The long, unusually grim face of Lester Welch appeared on the screen. "Goddammit, they promised no premature announcement. Mediamen!" His expression boded ill for the first unwary reporter to approach him. Over Les's shoulder, op Owen could see the equally savage face of Charlie Moorfield, duty officer of the control room of the Center.

"How long have *you* known about the theft?" Op Owen couldn't quite keep the reprimand from his voice. Les had a devoted habit of trying to spare his superior, particularly these days when he knew op Owen had been spreading himself very thin in the intensive public educational campaign.

"Ted Lewis snuck in a cautious advice as soon as Headquarters scanned the disappearance. He also can't 'find' a thing. And, Dave, there wasn't a wrinkle or a peak between 7:03 and 7:08 on any graph that shouldn't be there, with every single Talent accounted for!"

"That's right, Boss," Charlie added. "Not a single Incident to account for the kinetic 'lift' needed for the heist."

"Gillings is on his way here," said Les, screwing his face up with indignation.

"Why?" Daffyd op Owen exploded. "Didn't Ted clear us?"

"Christ, yes, but Gillings has been at Cole's and his initial investigation proves conclusively to him that one of our people is a larcenist. One of our women, to be precise, with a secret yen for sable, silk and sapphires."

Daffyd forced himself to nullify the boiling anger he felt. He could not afford to cloud reason with emotion. Not with so much at stake. Not with the Bill which would provide legal protection for Talents only two weeks away from passing.

"You'll never believe me, will you, Dave," Les said, "that the Talented will always be suspect?"

"Gillings has never caviled at the use of Talents, Lester."

"He'd be a goddamned fool if he did." Lester's eyes sparkled angrily. He jabbed at his chest. "*We've* kept street and consensual crime low. Talent did his job for him. And now he's out to nail us. With publicity like this, we'll never get that Bill through. Christ, what luck! Two bloody weeks away from protection."

"If there's no Incident on the graphs, Les, even Gillings must admit to our innocence."

Welch rolled his eyes heavenwards. "How can you be so naive, Dave? No matter what our remotes prove, that heist was done by a Talent."

"Not one of ours." Daffyd op Owen could be didactic, too.

"Great. Prove it to Gillings. He's on his way here now and he's out to get us. We've all but ruined his spotless record of enforcement and protection. That hits his credit, monetary and personal." Lester paused for a quick breath. "I told you that public education program would cause more trouble than it's worth. Let me cancel the morning 'cast."

"No." Daffyd closed his eyes wearily. He didn't need to resume that battle with Les now. In spite of this disastrous development, he was convinced of the necessity for the campaign. The general public must learn that they had nothing to fear from those gifted with a parapsychic Talent. The series of public information programs, so carefully planned, served several vital purposes: to show how the many facets of Talent served the community's best interests; to identify those peculiar traits that indicated the possession of a Talent; and most important, to gain public support for the Bill in the Senate which would give Talents professional immunity in the exercise of their various duties.

"I haven't a vestige of Talent, Dave," Les went on urgently, "but I don't need it to guess some dissident in the common mass of have-nots listened to every word of those 'casts and put what you should never have aired to good use . . . for him. And don't comfort me with how many happy clods have obediently tripped up to the Clinic to have their minor Talents identified. One renegade apple's all you need to sour the barrel!"

"Switch the 'cast to the standard recruiting tape. To pull the whole series would be worse. I'm coming right over."

Daffyd op Owen looked down at the blank screen for a long moment, gathering strength. It was no precog that this would be a very difficult day. Strange, he mused, that no precog had foreseen this. No. *That* very omission indicated a wild Talent, acting on the spur of impulse. What was it Les had said? "The common mass of have-nots?" Even with the basic dignities of food, shelter, clothing and education guaranteed, the appetite of the have-not was continually whetted by the abundance that was not his. In this case, hers. Daffyd op Owen groaned. If only such a Talent had been moved to come to the Center where she could be trained and used. Where had their so carefully worded programming slipped up? She could have had the furs, the jewels, the dresses on overt purchase . . . and enjoyed them openly. The Center was well enough endowed to satisfy any material yearning of its members. Surely Gillings would admit that.

Op Owen took a deep breath and exhaled regret and supposition. He must keep his mind clear, his sensitivities honed for any nuance that would point a direction toward success.

As he left his shielded quarters at the back of the Center's extensive grounds, he was instantly aware of tension in the atmosphere. Most Talented persons preferred to live in the Center, in the specially shielded buildings that reduced the 'noise' of constant psychic agitation. The Center preferred to have them here, as much to protect as to help their members. Talent was a double-edged sword; it could incise evil but it neatly separated its wielder from his fellow man. That was why these broadcasts were so vital. To prove to the general public that the psychically gifted were by no means supermen. Research had indicated there were more people with the ability than would admit it. There were, however, definite limitations to most Talents.

The Parapsychic had been raised, in Daffyd's lifetime, to the level of a science with the development of the Goos-egg, ultra-sensitive electroencephalographs which could record, and identify the type of "Talent" by the minute electrical impulses generated in the cortex by the application of psychic powers. Daffyd op Owen sometimes thought the word "power" was the villain in perpetuating the public misconceptions. Power means "possession of control" but such synonyms as "domination," "sway," "command" leapt readily to the average mind and distorted the actual definition.

Daffyd op Owen was roused from his thoughts by the heavy beat of a copter. He turned onto the path leading directly to the main administration building and had a clear view of the Commissioner's marked copter landing on the flight roof, to the left of the control tower with its forest of antennal decorations.

Immediately he perceived a reaction of surprise, indignation and anxiety. Surely every Talent who'd heard the news on the morning 'cast and realized its significance could not be surprised by Gillings's arrival. Op Owen quickened his pace.

"Orley's loose!" The thought was as loud as a shout.

People paused, turned unerringly towards the long low building of the Clinic where applicants were tested for sensitivity and trained to understand and use what Talent they possessed: and where the Center conducted its basic research in psionics.

A tall, heavy figure flung itself from the Clinic's broad entrance, charged down the lawn, in a direct line to the tower. The man leaped the ornamental garden, plunged through the hedges, swung over the hood of a parked lawn-truck, straight-armed the overhanging branches of trees, and brushed aside several men who tried to stop him.

"Project reassurance! Project reassurance!" the bull-horn from the tower advised. "Project happiness!"

"Get those cops in my office!" Daffyd projected on his

own as he began to run towards the building. He hoped that Charlie Moorfield or Lester had already done so. Orley didn't look as if anything short of a tranquilizer bullet would stop him. Who had been dim-witted enough to let the telempath out of his shielded room at a time like this? The moron was the most sensitive barometer to emotion Daffyd had ever encountered and he was physically dangerous if aroused. By the speed of that berserker-charge, he had soaked up enough fear/anxiety/anger to dismember the objects he was homing in on.

The only sounds now in the grounds were those of op Owen's shoes hitting the permaplast of the walk and the thud-thud of Orley's progress on the thick lawn. One advantage of being Talented is efficient communication and total comprehension of terse orders. But the wave of serenity/reassurance was not penetrating Orley's blind fury: the openness dissipated its effect.

Three men walked purposefully out of the administration building and down the broad apron of steps. Each carried slim-barreled hand weapons. The man on the left raised and aimed his at the audibly-panting, fast approaching moron. The shot took Orley in the right arm but did not cause him to falter. Instantly the second man aimed and fired. Orley lost stride for two paces as the shot penetrated his thigh but incredibly he recovered. The third man—op Owen recognized Charlie Moorfield—waited calmly as Orley rapidly closed the intervening distance. In a few more steps Orley would crash into him. Charlie was swinging out of the way, his gun slightly raised for a chest shot, when the moron staggered and, with a horrible groan, fell to his knees. He tried to rise, one clenched fist straining towards the building.

Instantly Charlie moved to prevent Orley from gouging his face on the coarse-textured permaplast.

"He took two double-strength doses, Dave," Moorfield exclaimed with some awe as he cradled the moron's head in his arms.

"He would. How'n'hell did he get such an exposure?"

Charlie made a grimace. "Sally was feeding him on the terrace. She hadn't heard the news 'cast. Said she was concentrating on keeping him clean and didn't 'read' his growing restlessness as more than response to her until he burst wide open."

"Too much to hope that our unexpected guests didn't see this?"

Charlie gave a sour grin. "They caused it, Boss. Stood there on the roof, giving Les a hard time, broadcasting basic hate and distrust. You should've seen the dial on the psychic atmosphere gauge. No wonder Orley responded." Charlie's face softened as he glanced down at the unconscious man. "Poor damned soul. Where is that med-team? I 'called' them when he got outside."

Daffyd glanced up at the broad third floor windows that marked his office. Six men stared back. He put an instant damper on his thoughts and emotions, and mounted the steps.

The visitors were still at the window, watching the med-team as they lifted the huge limp body onto the stretcher.

"Orley acts as a human barometer, gentlemen, reacting instantly to the emotional aura around him," Les was saying in his driest, down-east tone. To op Owen's wide-open mind, he emanated a raging anger that almost masked the aura projected by the visitors. "He has an intelligence factor of less than 50 on the New Scale which makes him uneducable. He is, however, invaluable in helping identify the dominating emotion of seriously disturbed mental and hallucinogenic patients which could overcome a rational telepath."

Police Commissioner Frank Gillings was the prime source of the fury which had set Harold Orley off. Op Owen felt sorry for Orley, having to bear such anger, and sorrier for himself and his optimistic hopes. He was momentarily at a loss to explain such a violent reaction from

Gillings, even granting the validity of Lester Welch's assumption that Gillings was losing face, financial and personal, on account of this affair.

He tried a "push" at Gillings's mind to discover the covert reasons and found the man had a tight natural shield, not uncommon for a person in high position, privy to sensitive facts. The burly Commissioner gave every outward appearance of being completely at ease, as if this were no more than a routine visit, and not one hint of his surface thoughts leaked. Deep-set eyes, barely visible under heavy brows, above fleshy cheeks in a swarthy face that missed nothing, flicked from Daffyd to Lester and back.

Op Owen nodded to Ted Lewis, the top police "finder" who had accompanied the official group. He stood a little to one side of the others. Of all the visitors, his mind was wide open. Foremost was the thought that he hoped Daffyd would read him, so that he could pass the warning that Gillings considered Orley's exhibition another indication that Talents could not control or discipline their own members.

"Good morning, Commissioner. I regret such circumstances bring you on your first visit to the Center. This morning's newscast has made us all extremely anxious to clear our profession."

Gillings's perfunctory smile did not acknowledge the tacit explanation of Orley's behavior.

"I'll come to the point, then, Owen. We have conclusively ascertained that there was no break in store security measures when the theft occurred. The 'lectric wards and spy-scanner were not tampered with nor was there any evidence of breaking or entering. There is only one method in which sable, necklace, dress and shoes could have been taken from that window in the five minutes between TV scans.

"We regret exceedingly that the evidence points to a person with psychic talents. We must insist that the larcenist be surrendered to us immediately and the merchandise returned to Mr. Grey, the representative from Cole's." He indicated the portly man in a conservative but expensive grey fitted.

Op Owen nodded and looked expectantly towards Ted Lewis.

"Lewis can't 'find' a trace anywhere so it's obvious the items are being shielded." A suggestion of impatience crept into Gillings's bass voice. "These grounds are shielded."

"The stolen goods are not here, Commissioner. If they were, they would have been found by a member the instant the broadcast was heard."

Gillings's eyes snapped and his lips thinned with obstinacy.

"I've told you I can read on these grounds, Commissioner," Ted Lewis said with understandable indignation. "The stolen . . ."

A wave of the Commissioner's hand cut off the rest of Lewis's statement. Op Owen fought anger at the insult.

"You're a damned fool, Gillings," said Welch, not bothering to control his, "if you think we'd shelter a larcenist at this time."

"Ah yes, that Bill pending Senate approval," Gillings said with an unpleasant smile.

Daffyd found it hard to nullify resentment at the smug satisfaction and new antagonism which Gillings was generating.

"Yes, that Bill, Commissioner," op Owen repeated, "which will protect any Talent *registered* with a parapsychic center." Op Owen did not miss the sparkle of Gillings's deep-set eyes at the deliberate emphasis. "If you'll step this way, gentlemen, to our remote-graph control system, I believe that we can prove, to your absolute satisfaction, that no registered Talent is responsible. You haven't been here before, Commissioner, so you are not familiar with our method of recording incidents in which psychic powers are used.

"Power, by the way, means 'possession of control', personal as well as psychic, which is what this Center teaches each and every member. Here we are. Charles Moorfield is the duty officer and was in charge at the time of the robbery. If you will observe the graphs, you'll notice that that period—between 7:03 and 7:08 was the time give by the 'cast—has not yet wound out of sight on the storage drums."

Gillings was not looking at the graphs. He was staring at Charlie.

"Next time, aim at the chest first, mister."

"Sorry I stopped him at all . . . mister," replied Charlie, with such deliberate malice that Gillings colored and stepped towards him.

Op Owen quickly intervened. "You dislike, distrust and hate us, Commissioner," he said, keeping his own voice neutral with effort. "You and your staff has prejudged us guilty, though you are at this moment surrounded by incontrovertible evidence of our collective innocence. You arrived here, emanating disruptive emotions—no, I'm *not* reading your minds, gentlemen." Daffyd had all Gillings's attention with that phrase. "That isn't necessary. You're triggering responses in the most controlled of us—not to mention that poor witless telempath we had to tranquilize. And, unless you put a lid on your unwarranted hatred and fears, I will have no compunction about pumping you all full of tranks, too!"

"That's coming on mighty strong for a man in your position, Owen," Gillings said in a tight hard voice, his body visibly tense now.

"You're the one that's coming on strong, Gillings. Look at that dial behind you."

Gillings did not want to turn, particularly not at op Owen's command, but there is a quality of righteous anger that compels obedience.

"That registers—as Harold Orley does—the psychic intensity of the atmosphere. The mind gives off electrical impulses, Gillings, surely you have to admit that. Law enforcement agencies used that premise for lie detection. Our instrumentation makes those early registers as archaic as space ships make oxcarts. We have ultra-delicate equipment which can measure the minutest electrical impulses of varying frequencies and duration. And this PA dial registers a dangerous high right now. Surely your eyes must accept scientific evidence.

"Those rows of panels there record the psychic activity of each and every member registered with this Center. See, most of them register agitation right now. These red divisions indicate a sixty-minute time span. Each of those drums exposes the graph as of the time of that theft. Notice the difference. Not one graph shows the kinetic activity required of a 'lifter' to achieve such a theft. But every one shows a reaction to your presence.

"There is no way in which a registered Talent can avoid these graphs. Charlie, were any kinetics out of touch at the time of the theft?"

Charlie, his eyes locked on Gillings, shook his head slowly.

"There never has been so much as a civil misdemeanor by any of our people. No breach of confidence, nor integrity. No crime could be shielded from fellow Talents.

"And can you rationally believe that we would jeopardize years and years of struggle to become accepted as reliable citizens of indisputable integrity for the sake of a fur coat and a string of baubles? When there are funds available to any Talent who might want to own such fripperies?" Op Owen's scorn made the Cole man wince.

"Now get out of here, Gillings. Discipline your emotions and revise your snap conclusion. Then call through normal channels and request our cooperation. Because, believe me, we are far more determined . . . and better equipped . . . to discover the real criminal than you could ever be, no matter what *your* personal stake in assigning guilt might conceivably be."

Op Owen watched for a reaction to that remark but Gillings, his lips thin and white with anger, did not betray himself. He gestured jerkily towards the one man in police blues.

"Do not serve that warrant now, Gillings!" op Owen said in a very soft voice. He watched the frantic activity of the needle on the PA dial.

"Go. Now. Call. Because if you cannot contain your feelings, Commissioner, you had better maintain your distance."

It was then that Gillings became aware of the palpable presence of those assembled in the corridor. A wide aisle had been left free, an aisle that led only to the open elevator. No one spoke or moved or coughed. The force exerted was not audible nor physical. It was, however, undeniably unanimous. It prevailed in forty-four seconds.

"My firm will wish to know what steps are being taken," the Cole's man said in a squeaky voice as he began to walk, with erratic but ever quickening steps, towards the elevator.

Gillings's three subordinates were not so independent, but there was no doubt of their relief as Gillings turned and walked with precise, unhurried strides to the waiting car.

No one moved until the thwapping rumble of the copter was no longer audible. Then they turned for assignments from their director.

City Manager Julian Pennstrak, with a metropolis of some four million to supervise, had a habit of checking up personally on any disruption to the smooth operation of his city. He arrived as the last of the organized search parties left the Center.

"I'd give my left kidney and a million credits to have enough Talent to judge a man accurately, Dave," he said as he crossed the room. He knew better than to shake hands unless a Talented offered but it was obvious to Daffyd, who liked Pennstrak, that the man wanted somehow to convey his personal distress over this incident. He stood for a moment by the chair, his handsome face without a trace of his famous genial smile. "I'd've sworn Frank Gillings was pro-Talent," he said, combing his fingers through his thick, wavy black hair, another indication of his anxiety. "He certainly has used your people to their fullest capabilities since he became LEO Commissioner."

Lester Welch snorted, looking up from the map he was annotating with search patterns. "A man'll use any tool that works . . . until it scratches him, that is."

"But you could prove that no registered Talent was responsible for that theft."

" 'A man convinced against his will, is of his own opinion still,' " Lester chanted.

"Les!" Op Owen didn't need sour cynicism from any quarter, even one dedicated to Talent. "No *registered* Talent was responsible."

Pennstrak brightened. "You did persuade Gillings that it's the work of an undiscovered Talent?"

Welch made a rude noise. "He'll be persuaded when we produce both missing person and missing merchandise. Nothing else is going to satisfy either Gillings or Cole's."

"True," Pennstrak agreed, frowning thoughtfully. "Nor the vacillating members of my own Council. Oh, I know, it's a flash reaction but the timing is so goddamned lousy, Dave. Your campaign bore down heavy on the integrity and good citizenship of the Talented."

"It's a deliberate smear job . . ." Welch began gloomily.

"I thought of that," Pennstrak interrupted him, "and had my own expert go over the scanner films. You know the high security risk set-up: rotating exposures on the stationary TV eyes. One frame the model was clothed; next, exposed in all its plastic glory. It was a 'lift' all right. No possibility of tampering with that film." Pennstrak leaned forward to Dave, though there was scarcely any need to guard his statements in this company. "Furthermore, Pat came along. She 'read' everyone at the store, and Gillings's squad. Not Gillings, though. She said he has a natural shield. The others were all clean . . . at least of conspiracy." Pennstrak's snide grin faded quickly. "I made her go rest. That's why there's no one with me."

Op Owen accepted the information quietly. He had half-hoped . . . it was an uncharacteristic speculation for him. However, it did save time and Talent to have had both store and police checked.

It had become general practice to have a strong tele-pathic receiver in the entourage of any prominent or con-troversial public figure. That Talent was rarely identified publicly. He or she usually performed some obvious ser-vice so that their constant presence was easily explicable. Pat Tawfik was overtly Pennstrak's chief speech writer.

"I have, however," Pennstrak continued, "used my offi-cial prerogative to supervise the hunt. There're enough sympathetic people on the public media channels to play down the Talent angle—at my request—but you know what this kind of adverse publicity is going to do to you, this Center and the Talented in general. One renegade can discredit a hundred honest injuns. So, what can I do to help?"

"I wish I knew. We've got every available perceptive out on the off-chance that this—ah—renegade happens to be broadcasting joy and elation over her heist."

"Her?"

"The concensus is that while a man might lift furs and jewels, possibly the dress, only a woman would take the shoes, too. Top finders are coming in from other Cen-ters . . ."

"A 'find' is reported, Boss," said Charlie over the inter-com. "Block Q."

As Pennstrak and op Owen reached the map, Welch announced with a groan. "Gawd, that's a multi-layer apart-ment zone."

"A have-not," added op Owen.

"Gil Gracie made the find, Boss," Charlie continued. "And the fur is not all he's found but he's got a problem."

"You just bet he has," Les said under his breath as he grimaced down at the map coordinates.

"Charlie, send every finder and perceptive to Block Q. If they can come up with a fix . . ."

"Boss, we got a fix, but there's one helluva lot of similarities."

"What's the problem?" asked Pennstrak.

"We'll simply have to take our time and eliminate, Charlie. Send anyone who can help." Then op Owen turned to Pennstrak. "In reporting a 'find,' the perceptive is aware of certain particular spatial relationships between the object sought and its immediate surroundings. It isn't as if he has seen the object as a camera sees it. For example, have you ever entered a room, turned down a street, or looked up quickly and had the feeling that you had seen just (and Daffyd made a bracket of his hands) that portion of the scene before, with exactly the same lighting, exactly the same components? But only that portion of the scene, so that the rest was an indistinguishable blur?"

Pennstrak nodded.

" 'Finding' is like that. Sometimes the Talent sees it in lucid detail, sometimes it's obscured or, as in this case, there are literally hundreds of possibilities . . . apartments with the same light exposure, same scene out the window, the same floor plan and furnishings. Quite possible in this instance since these are furnished, standard subsistence dwellings. Nothing to help us single out, say Apartment 44E, Building 18, Buhler Street."

"There happens to be a Building 18 on Buhler Street, Boss," Les Welch said slowly, "and there are 48 levels, 10 units per floor."

Pennstrak regarded op Owen with awe.

"Nonsense, this office is thoroughly shielded and I'm *not* a precog!"

"Before you guys took the guesswork out of it, there were such things as hunches," Pennstrak suggested.

For op Owen's peace of mind and Lester's pose of

misogyny, it was neither Building 18 nor Buhler Street nor Apartment 44. It was Apartment 1E, deep in the center of Q Block. No one had entered nor left it—by normal means—since Gil Gracie and two other finders had made a precise fix. Gil handed op Owen the master key obtained from the dithering super.

"My Gawd," Pennstrak said in a voice muted with shocked surprise, as they swung open the door. "Like an oriental bazaar."

"Indiscriminate pilfering on a wholesale basis." Op Owen corrected him, glancing around at the rich brilliant velvet drapes framing the dingy window to the wildly clashing pillows thrown on the elegant Empire loveseat. A marble-topped table was a jumble of pretty vases, silver boxes and goblets. Priceless china held decaying remains of food. Underneath the table were jaggedly opened, empty cans bearing the label of an extremely expensive caterer. Two empty champagne bottles pointed green, blind eyes in their direction. A portable color 'caster was piled with discarded clothing; a black-lace sheer body stocking draped in an obscene posture across the inactive screen. "A magpie's nest rather," he sighed, "and I'd hazard that Maggie is very young and has been poor all her life until . . ." He met Pennstrak's sympathetic gaze. "Until our educational program gave her the hints she needed to unlock her special Talent."

"Gillings is going to have to work with you on this, Dave," Pennstrak said reluctantly as he reached for the intercom at his belt. "But first he's going to have to apologize."

Op Owen shook his head vigorously. "I want his cooperation, Julian, grudged or willing. *When* he really believes in Talent, then he will apologize voluntarily . . . and obliquely."

To op Owen's consternation, Gillings arrived noisily in the cowlike lab copter, sirens going, lights flashing.

"Don't bother now," op Owen said to Pennstrak for he could see the City Manager forming a furious reprimand.

"She might have been warned by the finders' activity any-how."

"Well, she's certainly been warned off now." Pennstrak stalked off, to confer with one of his aides just as Gillings strode into the corridor with his technicians.

According op Owen and Gracie the merest nod, Gillings began issuing crisp orders. He knew his business, op Owen thought, and he evidently trusted *these* technicians for he didn't bother to crowd into the tiny apartment to oversee them.

"As soon as your men have prints and a physical pro-file, Commissioner, we'd like to run the data through our computer. There's the chance that the girl did take ad-vantage of the open Talent test the Center has been adver-tising."

"You mean you don't *know* who it is *yet?*"

"I could 'find' the coat only because I *knew* what it looked like," Gil Gracie said, bristling at Gillings's manner.

"Then where is it?" and Gillings gestured preemptorily to the sable-less apartment.

"These are the shoes, Commissioner," said one of his team, presenting the fragile strap and jeweled footwear, now neatly sealed in clear plastic. "Traces of dirt, dust, fleck of nail enamel and from the 'scope imprint, I'd say they were too big for her."

Gillings stared at the shoes disinterestedly. "No sign of the dress?"

"Still looking."

"Odd that you people can't locate a girl with bare feet in a sable coat and a bright blue silk gown?"

"No odder than it is for your hundreds of patrolmen throughout the city, Commissioner, to overlook a girl so bizarrely dressed," said op Owen with firm good humor. "When you 'saw' the coat, Gil, where was it?"

"Thrown across the loveseat, one arm hanging down to the floor. I distinguished the edge of the sill and the tree outside, the first folds of the curtain and the wall heating unit. I called in, you sent over enough finders so that we were able to eliminate the similarities. It took us nearly an hour . . ."

"Were you keeping an 'eye' on the coat all the time?" Gillings demanded in a voice so devoid of expression that his contempt was all the more obvious.

Gil flushed, bit his lip and only partially inhibited by op Owen's subtle warning, snapped back, "Try keeping your physical eye on an object for an hour!"

"Get some rest, Gil," op Owen said gently. He waited until the finder had turned the corner. "If you are as determined to find this criminal as you say you are, Commissioner Gillings, then do not destroy the efficiency of my staff by such gratuitous criticism. In less than four hours, on the basis of photographs of the stolen objects, we located this apartment . . ."

"But not the criminal, who is still in possession of a sable coat which you found once but have now unaccountably lost."

"That's enough, Gillings," said Pennstrak who had rejoined them. "Thanks to your arrival, the girl must know she's being sought and is shielding."

Pennstrak gestured toward the dingy windows of the flat, through which the vanes of the big copter were visible. A group of children, abandoning the known objects of the development play-yard, had gathered at a respectful, but curiosity-satisfying distance.

"Considering the variety of her accomplishments," op Owen said, not above using Pennstrak's irritation with his Commissioner to advantage, "I'm sure she knew of the search before the Commissioner's arrival, Julian. Have any of these items been reported, Commissioner?"

"That console was. Two days ago. It was on 'find,' too."

"She has been growing steadily bolder, then," op Owen went on, depressed by Gillings's attitude. And depressed that such a Talent had emerged twisted, perverted, selfish. Why? Why? "If your department ever gets the chronology of the various thefts, we'd appreciate the copy."

"Why?" Gillings turned to stare at op Owen, surprised and irritated.

"Talent takes time to develop—in ordinary persons. It does not, like the ancient goddess Athena, spring full-grown from the forehead. This girl could not, for instance, have lifted that portable set the first time she used her Talent. The more data we have on . . . the lecture is ill-timed."

Gillings's unspoken "you said it" did reach op Owen whose turn it was to stare in surprise.

"Well, your 'finders' are not novices," the Commissioner said aloud. "If they traced the coat once, why not again?"

"Every perceptive we have is searching," op Owen said. "But, if she was able to leave this apartment after Gil found the coat, taking it with her, because it obviously is not here, she also is capable of shielding herself and that coat. And, until she slips that guard, I doubt we'll find it or her."

The report on the laboratory findings was exhaustive. There was a full set of prints, foot and finger. None matched those on file in the city records, or Federal or Immigration. She had not been tested at the Center. Long coarse black hair had been found. Analysis of skin flakes suggested an olive complexion. Thermo-photography placed her last appearance in the room at approximately the time the four 'finders' fixed on her apartment, thus substantiating op Owen's guess. The thermal prints also revealed that she was of slender build, approximately 5'4", weighing 105 pounds. Stains on a paring knife proved her to possess blood type O. No one else had occupied the apartment within the eight day range of the thermography used.

From such records, the police extrapolator made a rough sketch of "Maggie O" which she was called for want of a better name. The sketch was taken around the neighborhood with no success. People living in Block Q didn't bother people who didn't bother them.

It was Daffyd op Owen who remembered the children crowding the police copter. From them he elicited the information that she was new in the building. (The records indicated that the apartment should be vacant.) She was always singing, dancing to the wall 'caster, and changing her clothes. Occasionally she'd play with them and bring out rich food to eat, promising they could have such good things if they'd think hard about them. While the children talked, Daffyd "saw" Maggie's face reflected in their minds. The police extrapolator had been far short of the reality. She was not much older than the children she had played with. She had not been pretty by ordinary standards but she had been so "different" that her image had registered sharply. The narrow face, the brilliant eyes, slightly slanted above sharp cheekbones, the thin, small mouth and the pointed chin were unusual even in an area of ethnic variety.

This likeness and a physical description were circulated quickly to be used at all exits to the city and all transportation facilities. It was likely she'd try to slip out during the day-end exodus.

The south and west airstrips had been under a perceptive surveillance since the search had been inaugurated. Now every facility was guarded.

Gil Grace "found" the coat again.

"She must have it in a suitcase," he reported on the police-provided handunit from his position in the main railroad concourse. "It's folded and surrounded by dark. It's moving up and down. But there're so many people. So many suitcases. I'll circulate. Maybe the find'll fix itself."

Gillings gave orders to his teams on the master unit which had been set up in the Center's control room to coordinate the operations.

"You better test Gil for precog," Charlie muttered to op

Owen after they'd contacted all the sensitives. "He *asked* for the station."

"You should've told me sooner, Charlie. I'd've teamed him with a sensitive."

"Look at that," Charlie exclaimed, pointing to a wildly moving needle on one of the remotes.

Les was beside it even as the audio for the Incident went on.

"Not that track! Oh! Watch out! Baggage. On the handcart! Watch out. Move, man. Move! To the right. The right! Ahhhh." The woman's voice choked off in an agonized cry.

Daffyd pushed Charlie out of the way, to get to the speaker.

"Gil, this is op Owen. Do not pursue. Do not pursue that girl! She's aware of you. Gil, come in. Answer me, Gil. . . . Charlie, keep trying to raise him. Gillings, contact your men in the station. Make them stop Gil Gracie."

"Stop him? Why?"

"The precog. The baggage on the handcart," shouted Daffyd, signaling frantically to Lester to explain in detail. He raced for the emergency stairs, up the two flights, and slammed out onto the roof. Gasping physically for breath, he clung to the high retaining wall and projected his mind to Gil's.

He knew the man so well, had trained Gil when an employee brought in the kid who had a knack for locating things. Op Owen could see him ducking and dodging through the trainward crowds, touching suitcases, ignoring irate or astonished carriers; every nerve, every ounce of him receptive to the "feel" of a dense, dark sable fur. And so singleminded that Daffyd could not "reach" him.

But op Owen knew the instant the loaded baggage cart swerved and crushed the blindly intent Talent against an I-beam. He bowed his head, too fully cognizant that a double tragedy had occurred. Gil was lost . . . and so now was the girl.

There was no peace from his thoughts even when he returned to the shielded control room. Lester and Charlie pretended to be very busy. Gillings was. He directed the search of the railway station, arguing with the station-master that the trains were to be held and that was that. The drone of his voice began to penetrate op Owen's remorse.

"All right, then, if the Talents have cleared it and there's no female of the same height and weight, release that train. Someone tried the johns, didn't they? No, Sam, you can detain anyone remotely suspicious. That girl is clever, strong, and dangerous. There's no telling what else she could do. But she damn well can't change her height, weight and blood type!"

"Daffyd. Daffyd." Lester had to touch him to get his attention. He motioned op Owen towards Charlie who was holding out the handunit.

"It's Cole's, sir."

Daffyd listened to the effusively grateful store manager. He made the proper responses but it wasn't until he had relinquished the handunit to Charlie that the man's excited monologue made sense.

"The coat, the dress and the necklace have reappeared on the store dummy," op Owen said. He cleared his throat and repeated it loud enough to be heard.

"Returned?" Gillings echoed. "Just like that? Why, the little bitch! Sam, check the ladies rooms in that station. Wait, isn't there a discount dress store in that station? Have them check for missing apparel. I want an itemized list of what's gone, and an exact duplicate from their stock shown to the sensitives. We've got her scared and running now."

"Scared and running now." Gillings's smug assessment rang ominously in Daffyd's mind. He had a sudden flash. Superimposed over a projection of Maggie's thin face was the image of the lifeless store dummy, elegantly re-clad in the purloined blue gown and dark fur. "Here, take them back. I don't want them anymore. I didn't mean to kill him. I didn't mean to. See, I gave back what you wanted. Now leave me alone!"

Daffyd shook his head. Wishful thinking. Just as futile as the girl's belated gesture of penance. Too much too soon. Too little too late.

"We don't want her scared," he said outloud. "She was scared when she toppled that baggage cart."

"She *killed* a man when she toppled that baggage cart, op Owen!" Gillings was all but shouting.

"And if we're not very careful, she'll kill others."

"If you think I'm going to velvet glove a homicidal maniac . . ."

A shrill tone issuing from the remote unit forced Gillings to answer. He was about to reprimand the caller but the message got stunned attention.

"We can forget the paternal bit, Owen. She knocked down every one of your people and mine at the Oriole Street entrance. Your men are unconscious. Mine and about twenty or more innocent commuters are afflicted with blinding headaches. Got any practical ideas, Owen, on catching this monster you created?"

"Oriole? Was she heading east or west?" He had to stop that line of talk.

"Does it matter?"

"If we're to catch her it does. And we must catch her. She's operating at a psychic high. There's no telling what she's capable of now. Such Talent has only been a theoretic possibility . . ."

Gillings lost all control on himself. The fear and hatred burst out in such a wave that Charlie Moorfield, caught unawares, erupted out of his chair towards Gillings in an instinctive defense reaction.

"Gillings!" "Charlie!" Les and Daffyd shouted together, each grabbing the wild combatants. But Charlie, his face white with shock at his own reaction, had himself in hand. Sinking weakly back into his chair, he gasped out an apology.

"You mean, you *want* to have more monsters like her

and him?" Gillings demanded. Between his voice and the violent emotions, Daffyd's head rang with pain and confusion.

"Don't be a fool," Lester said, grabbing the Commissioner by the arm. "You can't spew emotions like that around a telepath and not get a reaction. Look at Daffyd! Look at Charlie! Christ man, you're as bad as the scared, mixed-up kid . . ." and then Les dropped Gillings's arm and stared at him in amazement. "Christ, you're a telepath yourself!"

"Quiet, everybody," Daffyd said with such urgency he had their instant attention. "I've the solution. And there's no time to waste. Charlie, I want Harold Orley airbound in the Clinic's copter heading south to the Central Station in nothing flat. We'll correct course en route. Gillings, I want two of the strongest, most stable patrolmen on your roster. I want them armed with fast-acting, double-strength trank guns and airborne to rendezvous near Central Station."

"Harold?" Les echoed in blank astonishment. Then relief colored his face as he understood Daffyd's intentions. "Of course. Nothing can stop Harold. And no one can read him coming."

"Nothing. And no one," op Owen agreed, bleakly.

Gillings turned from issuing his orders to see an ambulance copter heading west across the sky.

"We're following?"

Daffyd nodded and gestured for Gillings to precede him to the roof. He didn't look back but he knew what Les and Charlie did not say.

She had been seen running east on Oriole. And she was easy to follow. She left people doubled up with nausea and crying with head pains. That is, until she crossed Boulevard.

"We'll head south, south east on an intercept," Gillings told his pilot and had him relay the correction to the ambulance. "She's heading to the sea?" he asked rhetorically as he rummaged for the correct airmap of the city. "Here. We can set down at Seaman's Park. She can't have made it that far . . . unless she can fly suddenly." Gillings looked up at op Owen.

"She probably could teleport herself," Daffyd answered, watching the Commissioner's eyes narrow in adverse reaction to the admission. "But she hasn't thought of it yet. As long as she can be kept running, too scared to think . . ." That necessity plagued Daffyd op Owen. They were going to have to run her out of her mind.

Gillings ordered all police hovercraft to close in on the area where she was last seen, blocks of residences and small businesses of all types.

By the time the three copters had made their rendezvous at the small Park, there were no more visible signs of Maggie O's retreat.

As Gillings made to leave the copter, Daffyd op Owen stopped him.

"If you're not completely under control, Gillings, Harold will be after you."

Gillings looked at the director for a long moment, his jaw set stubbornly. Then, slowly, he settled into the seat and handed op Owen a remote comunit.

"Thanks, Gillings," he said, and left the copter. He signaled to the ambulance to release Harold Orley and then strode across the grass to the waiting officers.

The two biggest men were as burly as he could wish. Being trained law enforcers, they ought to be able to handle Orley. Op Owen "pushed" gently against their minds and was satisfied with his findings. They possessed the natural shielding of the untemperamental which made them less susceptible to emotional storms. Neither Webster or Heis were stupid, however, and had been briefed on developments.

"Orley has no useful intelligence. He is a human barometer, measuring the intensity and type of emotions which surround him and reacting instinctively. He does not broadcast. He only receives. Therefore he cannot be harmed or identified by . . . by Maggie O. He is the only Talent she cannot 'hear' approaching."

"But, if he reaches her, he'd . . ." Webster began, measuring Harold with the discerning eye of a boxing enthusiast. Then he shrugged and turned politely to op Owen.

"You've the double strength tranks? Good. I hope you'll be able to use them in time. But it is imperative that she be apprehended before she does more harm. She has already killed one man. . . ."

"We understand, sir," Heis said when op Owen did not continue.

"If you can, shoot her. Once she stops broadcasting, he'll soon return to a manageable state." But, Daffyd amended to himself, remembering Harold sprawled on the ground in front of the building, not soon enough. "She was last seen on the east side of the Boulevard, about eight blocks from here. She'd be tired, looking for someplace to hide and rest. But she is also probably radiating sufficient emotion for Harold to pick up. He'll react by heading in a straight line for the source. Keep him from trying to plow through solid walls. Keep your voices calm when you speak to him. Use simple commands. I see you've got handunits. I'll be airborne; the copter's shielded but I'll help when I can."

Flanking Harold, Webster and Heis moved west along Oriole at a brisk, even walk: the two officers in step, Harold's head bobbing above theirs, out of step—a cruel irony.

Daffyd op Owen turned back to the copter. He nodded to Gillings as he seated himself. He tried not to think at all.

As the copters lifted from the Park and drifted slowly west amid other air traffic, op Owen looked sadly down at the people on the streets. At kids playing on the sidewalks. At a flow of men and women with briefcases or shopping bags, hurrying home. At snub-nosed city cars and squatty trucks angling into parking slots. At the bloated cross-city helibuses jerking and settling to disgorge their passengers at the street islands.

"He's twitching," reported Heis in a dispassionate voice.

Daffyd flicked on the handset. "That's normal. He's beginning to register."

"He's moving faster now. Keeps wanting to go straight through the buildings." Reading Heis's undertone, op Owen knew that the men hadn't believed his caution about Orley plowing through solids. "He's letting us guide him, but he keeps pushing us to the right. You take his other arm, Web. Yeah, that's better."

Gillings had moved to the visual equipment along one side of the copter. He focused deftly in on the trio, magnified it and threw the image on the pilot's screen, too. The copter adjusted direction.

"Easy, Orley. No, don't try to stop him, Web. Stop the traffic!"

Orley's line of march crossed the busier wide north-south street. Webster ran out to control the vehicles. People turned curiously. Stopped and stared after the trio.

"Don't," op Owen said as he saw Gillings move a hand towards the bullhorn. "There's nothing wrong with her hearing."

Orley began to move faster now that he had reached the farther side. He wanted to go right through intervening buildings.

"Guide him left to the sidewalk, Heis," op Owen said. "I think he's still amenable. He isn't running yet."

"He's breathing hard, Mr. Owen," Heis sounded dubious. "And his face is changing."

Op Owen nodded to himself, all too familiar with the startling phenomenon of watching the blankness of Orley's face take on the classic mask of whatever emotions he was receiving. It would be a particularly unnerving transition under these conditions.

"What does he show?"

"I'd say . . . hatred," Heis's voice dropped on the last word. Then he added in his usual tone, "He's smiling, too, and it isn't nice."

They had eased Orley to the sidewalk heading west. He kept pushing Webster to the right and his pace increased until it was close to a run. Webster and Heis began to gesture people out of their way but it would soon be obvious to the neighborhood that something was amiss. Would it be better to land more police to reassure people and keep their emanations down? Or would they broadcast too much suppressed excitement at police interference? She'd catch that. Should he warn Heis and Webster to keep their thoughts on Harold Orley? Or would that be like warning them against all thoughts of the camel's left knee?

Orley broke into a run. Webster and Heis were hard put to keep him to the sidewalk.

"What's in the next block?" op Owen asked Gillings.

The Commissioner consulted the map, holding it just above the scanner so he could keep one eye on the trio below.

"Residences and an area parking facility for interstate trucking." Gillings turned to op Owen now, his heavy eyebrows raised in question.

"No, she's still there because Orley is homing in on her projection."

"Look at his face! My God!" Heis exclaimed over the handunit. On the screen, his figure had stopped. He was pointing at Orley. But Webster's face was clearly visible to the surveillers and what he saw unnerved him.

Orley broke from his guides. He was running, slowly at first but gathering speed steadily, mindlessly brushing aside anything that stood in his way. Heis and Webster went after him but both men were shaking their heads as if something were bothering them. Orley tried to plunge through a brick store wall. He bounced off it, saw the unimpeded view of his objective and charged forward. Web-

ster had darted ahead of him, blowing his whistle to stop
the oncoming traffic. Heis alternately yelled into the handunit and at startled bystanders. Now some of them were
afflicted and were grabbing their heads.

"Put us on the roof," op Owen told the pilot. "Gillings,
get men to cover every entrance and exit to that parking
lot. Get the copters to hover by the open levels. The men'll
be spared some of the lash."

It wouldn't do much good, op Owen realized, even as
he felt the first shock of the girl's awareness of imminent
danger.

"Close your mind," he yelled at the pilot and Gillings.
"Don't think."

"My head, my head." It was Heis groaning.

"Concentrate on Orley," op Owen said, his hands
going to his temples in reaction to the knotting pressure.
Heis's figure on the scanner staggered after Orley who
had now entered the parking facility.

Op Owen caught the mental pressure and dispersed it,
projecting back reassurance/help/protection/compassion.
He could forgive her Gil Gracie's death. So would any
Talent. If she would instantly surrender, somehow the
Center would protect her from the legal aspects of her act.
Only surrender now.

Someone screamed. Another man echoed that piercing
cry. The copter bucked and jolted them. The pilot was
groaning and gasping. Gillings plunged forward, grabbing
the controls.

Op Owen, fighting an incredible battle, was blind to
physical realities. If he could just occupy all the attention
of that over-charged mind . . . hold it long enough . . .
pain/fear/black/red/moiled-orange/purples . . . breathing . . . shock. Utter disbelief/fear/loss of confidence.
Frantic physical effort.

Concrete scraped op Owen's cheek. His fingers bled
as he clawed at a locked steel exit door on the roof. He
could not enter. *He had to reach her* FIRST!

Somehow his feet found the stairs as he propelled himself down the fire escape, deliberately numbing his mind to the intensive pounding received. A pounding that became audible.

Then he saw her, fingers clawing for leverage on the stairpost, foot poised for the step from the landing. A too-thin adolescent figure, frozen for a second with indecision and shock; strands of black hair like vicious scars across a thin face, distorted and ugly from the tremendous physical and mental efforts of the frantic will. Her huge eyes, black with insane fury and terror, bloodshot with despair and the salty sweat of her desperate striving for escape, looked into his.

She knew him for what he was; and her hatred crackled in his mind. Those words—after Gil Gracie's death—had been hers, not his distressed imagining. She had known him then as her real antagonist. Only now was *he* forced to recognize her for what she was, all she was—and regrettably, all she would not be.

He fought the inexorable decision of that split-second confrontation, wanting more than anything else in his life that it did not have to be so.

She was the wiser! She whirled!

She was suddenly beyond the heavy fire door without opening it. Harold Orley, charging up the stairs behind her, had no such Talent. He crashed with sickening force into the metal door. Daffyd had no alternative. She had teleported. He steadied the telempath, depressed the lock bar and threw the door wide.

Orley was after the slender figure fleeing across the dimly lit, low-ceiling concrete floor. She was heading towards the down ramp now.

"Stop, stop," op Owen heard his voice begging her.

Heis came staggering from the stairway.

"Shoot him. For Christ's sake, shoot Orley, Heis," op Owen yelled.

Heis couldn't seem to coordinate. Op Owen tried to

push aside his fumbling hands and grab the trank gun himself. Heis's trained reflexes made him cling all the tighter to his weapon. Just then, op Owen heard the girl's despairing shriek.

Two men had appeared at the top of the ramp. They both fired, the dull reports of trank pistols accentuated by her choked gasp.

"Not her. Shoot Orley. Shoot the man," op Owen cried but it was too late.

Even as the girl crumpled to the floor, Orley grabbed her. Grabbed and tore and beat at the source of the emotions which so disturbed him. Beat and tore and stamped her physically as she had assaulted him mentally.

Orley's body jerked as tranks hit him from all sides, but it took far too long for them to override the adrenal reactions of the overcharged telempath.

There was pain and pity as well as horror in Gillings's eyes when he came running onto the level. The police stood at a distance from the blood-spattered bodies.

"Gawd, couldn't someone have stopped him from getting her?" the copter pilot murmured, turning away from the shapeless bloodied thing half-covered by Orley's unconscious body.

"The door would have stopped Orley but he," and Heis grimly pointed at op Owen, "opened it for him."

"She teleported through the door," op Owen said weakly. He had to lean against the wall. He was beginning to shudder uncontrollably from reaction. "She had to be stopped. Now. Here. Before she realized what she'd done. What she could do." His knees buckled. "She teleported through the door!"

Unexpectedly it was Gillings who came to his aid, a Gillings whose mind was no longer shielded but broadcasting compassion and awe, and understanding.

"So did you."

The phrase barely registered in op Owen's mind when he passed out.

"That's all that remains of the late Solange Boshe," Gillings said, tossing the file reel to the desk. "As much of her life as we've been able to piece together. Gypsies don't stay long anywhere."

"There're some left?" Lester Welch asked, frowning at the three-inch condensation of fifteen years of a human life.

"Oh there are, I assure you," Gillings replied, his tone souring slightly for the first time since he had entered the office. "The tape also has a lengthy interview with Bill Jones, the cousin the social worker located after Solange had recovered from the bronchial pneumonia. He had no idea," Gilllings hastily assured them, "that there is any reason other than a routine check on the whereabouts of a runaway county ward. He had a hunch," and Gillings grimaced, "that the family had gone on to Toronto. They had. He also thought that they had probably given the girl up for dead when she collapsed on the street. The Toronto report substantiates that. So I don't imagine it will surprise you, op Owen, that her tribe, according to Jones, are the only ones still making a living at fortune-telling, palm-reading, tea-leaves and that bit."

"Now, just a minute, Gillings," Lester began, bristling. He subsided when he saw that his boss and the Police Commissioner were grinning at each other.

"So . . . just as you suspected, op Owen, she was a freak Talent. We know from the ward nurses that she watched your propaganda broadcasts during her hospitalization. We can assume that she was aware of the search either when Gil Gracie 'found' the coat, or when the definite fix was made. It's not hard to guess her motivation in making the heist in the first place, nor her instinctive desire to hide." Gillings gave his head an abrupt violent jerk and stood up. He started to hold out his hand, remembered and raised it in a farewell gesture. "You are continuing those broadcasts, aren't you?"

Lester Welch glared so balefully at the Commissioner that op Owen had to chuckle.

"With certain deletions, yes."

"Good. Talent must be identified and trained. Trained young and well if they are to use their Talent properly." Gillings stared op Owen in the eye. "The Boshe girl was bad, op Owen, bad clear through. Listen to what Jones said about her and you won't regret Tuesday too much. Sometimes the young are inflexible, too."

"I agree, Commissioner," Daffyd said, escorting the man to the door as calmly as if he hadn't heard what Gillings was thinking so clearly. "And we appreciate your help in the cover yarns that explained Tuesday's odd occurrences."

"A case of mutual understanding," Gillings said, his eyes glinting. "Oh, no need to see me out. *I* can open this door."

That door was no sooner firmly shut behind him than Lester Welch turned on his superior.

"And just who was scratching whose back then?" he demanded. "Don't you dare come over innocent, either, Daffyd op Owen. Two days ago that man was your enemy, bristling with enough hate and distrust to antagonize me."

"Remember what you said about Gillings Tuesday?"

"There's been an awful lot of idle comment around here lately."

"Frank Gillings *is* telepathic." Then he added as Lester was choking on the news: "And he doesn't want to be. So he's suppressed it. Naturally he'd be antagonistic."

"Hah!"

"He's not too old, but he's not flexible enough to adapt to Talent, having denied it so long."

"I'll buy that. But what was that parting shot—'*I* can open this door'?" Lester mimicked the Commissioner's deep voice.

"I'm too old to learn new tricks, too, Les. I teleported through the roof door of that parking facility. He saw me do it. And *she* saw the memory of it in my mind. If she'd lived, she'd've picked my mind clean. And—I didn't *want* her to die."

Op Owen turned abruptly to the window, trying to let the tranquillity of the scene restore his equilibrium. It did—until he saw Harold Orley plodding along the path with his guide. Instantly a white, wide-eyed, hair-streaked face was superimposed over the view.

The intercom beeped and he depressed the key for his sanity's sake.

"We've got a live one, Boss," and Sally Iselin's gay voice restored him. "A strong precog with kinetic possibilities. And guess what?" Sally's excitement made her voice breathless. "He said the cop on his beat told him to come in. He doesn't want any more trouble with the cops so he . . ."

"Would his name be Bill Jones?"

"However did you know?"

"And that's no precog, Sally," op Owen said with a ghost of a laugh, aware he was beginning to look forward again. "A sure thing's no precog, is it, Les?"

4

A Bridle
for Pegasus

A Bridle for Pegasus

Julian Pennstrak, Jerhattan City Manager, Daffyd op Owen, Director of the East American Parapsychic Center, and Frank Gillings, Commissioner of Law Enforcement and Order, had gathered in the latter's office: an appropriate setting as the four sides of the tower office were tough plexiglass so the occupants had a full panoramic view of the city they managed or foresaw and protected.

"The Maggie O affair was not without some reward," Daffyd op Owen reminded the other two. "Her . . . relation . . . in whatever degree of cousinship Bill Jones stood . . . is proving to be a sound precog."

Gillings grunted and rubbed the side of his fleshy nose, registering skepticism.

"Half a city semi-paralyzed with blinding headaches, two dead, and a lot of public lying and you say there was some reward!"

"You do tend to adopt a negative attitude, don't you, Frank?" the City Manager remarked, half amused. He was watching op Owen from the corner of his eye. He knew that the Director of the Parapsychic Center had been deeply shaken by the deaths of Gil Gracie and Solange Boshe, a.k.a. Maggie O. And the curious sparring between Gillings and op Owen dated from that incident: the one grudging admiration and the other exhibiting wistful regret. Well, Pennstrak possessed a certain empathy himself which told him not to delve too deeply into the denouement of that incident. Suffice it to say, the

159

truth about Maggie's sudden rise and demise had been successfully obscured from public notice and, if Daffyd were satisfied that some profit existed on the black side of the ledger, the City Manager would be content. "Nonetheless," Julian Pennstrak continued, "the Professional Immunity Law is now, as of yesterday, programmed into Federal Books and State Law Machinery. What's your problem now, Frank?"

"It's this: if renegades like Solange Boshe can exist, how do we smell 'em out before they cause trouble? Now," and he held up his hand as Daffyd op Owen opened his mouth to speak, "I know you've got a subliminal TRI-D program going, Dave, but just how successful is it in routing out the odd-balls?"

Op Owen winced at Gillings's phraseology.

"Unfortunately only time will tell. We do have Bill Jones, Maggie O's cousin, and he'll be a first rate precog. Sally Iselin at the Testing Clinic has upwards of fifty applicants a day." He sighed. "Most are wishful thinkers, I'm afraid, but occasionally a live one does come in. You can't make people get Talent-tested."

"What we need," the LEO Commissioner said in a deadly voice, "is enforced testing."

"Of nine million people?" asked Pennstrak, good-humoredly aghast.

Gillings grunted. "The mavericks cost us more."

Pennstrak agreed to that.

"Better still, early testing would be a tremendous help," Daffyd op Owen said. "Our sensitives in the maternity wards do catch the occasional strong one at birth. But we lack adequate facilities and more important, the personnel. It takes a special kind of Talent, in itself, to spot embryo Talents. Sally Iselin is acutely sensitive in this area and I thank Providence for her presence in the Clinic. She's never been wrong in her assessments. But she's the only one Eastern has and she's overworked as it is." Daffyd smiled and decided against what he'd been about to confide. The dour face of Lester Welch leered at him: For Christ's sake, Dave, don't tell everybody everything you know. They don't always want to hear it. For instance, Daffyd doubted that Frank Gillings would take kindly to the notion that Sally Iselin's chief assistant at the moment was the two-year-old Dorotea Horvath, the extraordinarily Talented daughter of two of his people. Dorotea came every morning and afternoon to the Clinic, to "play" in the room full of applicants. She'd instinctively approach anyone with the least vestige of Talent so that Sally could give the deeper testing. The others could be dismissed after the routine examinations, none the wiser for the pre-selection. Dorotea was blissfully unaware of what she could do—she simply did it.

"Talent is sometimes latent," Daffyd told Gillings, "as it was in Solange Boshe, springing into maturity under pressure. But different minds react to different stimuli and the powerful Talent, such as Solange's, to another set entirely. Talent can also be consciously or subconsciously suppressed since any Talent singles one out for the unwelcome attentions of the less gifted. We do try to alleviate that envy with our public information broadcasts on what Talent does to relieve . . ."

Gillings cut him off with a brusque wave of his hand. As much, Daffyd op Owen thought wryly, because Gillings was a latent who had no wish to be trained or reminded of this defection.

"Sorry for the lecture," op Owen said with an apologetic grin, "but you must realize that we are limited in what we can do even with all the Talent at our disposal. Nor can we foresee the stray maturing of Talent. Your LEO operatives, Frank, have all the information we've collated on how to spot the latent or unconscious Talent. What more can we do?"

"Get your Senator friend to write a rider on that Immunity Law," said Gillings in a growl, "that it's illegal to be Talented and conceal it."

Daffyd returned Gillings's half guilty glare with a wide-eyed look of surprise. Gillings's perception was not dull:

he knew what was behind op Owen's grin and he scowled fiercely at him.

"I'll suggest it to Joel Andres when next we meet," op Owen said politely. "It's a point well taken."

"How in hell could you implement such a statute under the conditions you've just cited, Daffyd?" demanded Pennstrak with understandable disgust. "No facilities, not enough Talent. Besides, latents wouldn't know and therefore wouldn't register, and a Talent who knew of his ability could claim he didn't."

"Well, it'd be a help to me," Gillings said, still in a growling mood. Yet he glanced at op Owen with less choler. Obviously the telepath hadn't mentioned Gillings's latent abilities to the City Manager. The man knew when to keep his mouth shut. "I could shut up suspects and keep them from running amok like that gypsy girl."

Op Owen's smile faded.

"You can't suppress or contain Talent, Frank. That'd put exactly the sort of pressure on them we'd want at all costs to avoid. There's so much we don't know about the parapsychic, so much."

"Like what for instance?" asked the LEO Commissioner, steeling himself for unwelcome information.

Op Owen spread his hands wide. "I can't tell you. I'm not a precog." To which he added a devout and silent "Amen!"

Gillings unloosed another grunt. "Now, on that score, have your Talents come up with anything on this ethnic employment allocation nonsense? You guys are, I sincerely trust, pan-ethnic?"

"Demonstrably."

Gillings gave him a long look as if he suspected op Owen of facetiousness. Julian Pennstrak cleared his throat hastily.

"That's one less headache at any rate," the LEO man went on, "but your precogs haven't had any Incidents beyond this nebulous warning?" He tapped the Incident readings which had been sent to his office the previous day.

Daffyd shook his head. "The precognitive faculty is the most erratic but generally speaking, the larger the number of people involved, the greater the possibility of detailed Incidents. Or, conversely, the severer the change to a prominent person or a linked or emotional association, the more likelihood of a definitive Incident.

"The old tea-leaf and card readers attempted to tell the future, anyone's future: and while I suppose they could generalize for the average soul well enough, the best of them were only accurate when predicting the future of lives which affected a large section of general mankind. Some precogs operate only on a direct confrontation with a personality, which is why we keep key personnel folders with those sensitives. But you can't actually provoke a precog.

"In the instance of Maggie O: she was a fluke to begin with, an isolated case, unintegrated in any group or with any affiliation that would cause one of our precogs to 'read' for her. That is, until circumstances put her in a position to cross Gil Gracie's lifeline. Then we had a reading on *him,* but only because the precog was tuned to Gil.

"There are, as I keep saying ad nauseam I know, a lot of parapsychic manifestations about which we know nothing. Every time I believe I understand one combination or facet, exceptions to that comprehension appear to confound me.

"Henry Darrow said that having any Talent is like riding a winged horse, you get a magnificent view but you can't always dismount when you want to."

Gillings had waited patiently through op Owen's peroration; now he rattled the urgently tagged tapes on his desk. Pennstrak regarded the Director with new insight.

"I'd always thought that Pegasus was the symbol of poetry . . . flights of verbal fantasy. But I must say, I like your notion, Dave. A winged horse is an appropriate mount for you people. Not that I'd have the courage to hop on its back."

"If you two would deign to consider the mundane problems of the earthbound," Gillings said in an acid tone of voice, "just how in hell are we going to find jobs for all these eager mud-grubbers?"

On a morning some two months later when Daffyd op Owen reached his office, there was a message on his desk to call Sally Iselin as soon as he had a moment. To a semantically-sensitive personality, the phrasing was provocative, added to the fact that Sally Iselin was in charge of recruit-testing. Daffyd punched her call numbers as soon as he read the note, disregarding other red and white flagged tapes and messages. If only one psi-latent was uncovered in a month of public information broadcasts, the program would be worth its cost.

"Daffyd here, Sally. You rang me?"

"Oh, Daffyd!" She sounded surprised and a tinge embarrassed. "I'm not really certain if I should bother you . . ."

"My great-grandmother used to say, 'If it's doubtful, it's dirty.' "

"I'm not talking about a shirt, Daffyd," and Sally's usual levity was missing. "I'm talking about people."

"Which people?" It was like pulling screws from wood: intriguingly un-Sallyish.

"Well, Daffyd, I'd hate to prejudice you. But . . . well, would you take me out tonight? There's a place I want you to feel. I *can't* figure out what it is myself and I know something happened."

"Curiouser and curiouser. You've hooked me . . ."

"Oh, damn. I don't want to *hook* you. I've gone and done what I shouldn't ta oughta."

Daffyd laughed. "Sally, all you've done is arouse my very considerable, insatiable curiosity."

"All right, elephant's child. Pick me up at nine; you'll need the copter and *money*." Her voice darkened with baleful implications of wild spending and debauchery, but there was a rippling undercurrent of laughter which told Daffyd that Sally was herself again.

"With as many bundles as Lester will allow me. At 9!"

He depressed the comset button just as the door opened to admit Lester Welch.

"What's on Iselin's alleged mind?"

"I can't 'path over a phone," Daffyd replied, deliberately misinterpreting Lester.

The man swore and glared sourly at his boss. "All right, so you won't talk either. Maybe I've no Talent but I don't need it to know something's got Sally excited. She's so careful to sound calm."

Daffyd shrugged his shoulders and reached for the in-tapes. "Soon as I know, you will. Anything else bothering you this fine morning? And Sally says I need bundles tonight."

Lester eyed him in surprise for a moment and then snorted. He pointed to the finance-coded blue tape among the urgent flags Daffyd was fingering.

"Some local yokel from East Waterless Ford up-state wants to tax the Center's residential accommodations, same as any other apartment block. Claims the revenue on such 'high income residents' would reduce the state's deficit by 9%."

Daffyd whistled appreciatively. "He's probably right but for the fact that this is a registered restricted commune and those high-income residents turn every credit of their salaries over to the Center."

"Listen, Dave, he's building a pretty good case."

Op Owen sighed. There was always something or someone or some committee picking away at the Center, trying to disrupt, destroy or discredit it despite all the careful publicity.

"They did the same thing in New Jersey, you know,

when the Princeton University Complex put up those academician villages to counteract the high price of real estate and taxes," Lester reminded him sourly.

"I'll listen, I'll listen. Now, go away, Les." Daffyd inserted Welch's tape in the console.

Lester growled something under his breath as he left. And Daffyd op Owen listened. He didn't like what he heard but the State Senator had certainly done some of his homework. Revenues from the Center's residential buildings would indeed be a tidy pile in the State's chronically anemic Treasury. Only the Center was in Jerhattan proper by a mile and a half, and therefore its revenues were the City's, if anyone's.

"Get me Julian Pennstrak, please," Daffyd asked his secretary.

The City Manager might be of some assistance here. Certainly he'd be interested in what this up-state character, Aaron Greenfield (am I always to be "fielded," Daffyd wondered wryly, remembering his battle with the US Senator Mansfield Zeusman) is proposing. If Julian didn't already know. Not much slipped past Pennstrak's affable eagle-eye. Pennstrak wasn't available but his secretary tactfully put Daffyd through to Pat Tawfik, Pennstrak's speech writer who was, in actual fact, his Talent guard.

"Yes, Dave, Julian's been keeping an eye on Greenfield's proposal," Pat told him. "In fact, Julian had him in here for a long cozy chat when we first got wind of the scheme. Greenfield's like Zeusman: suspicious and scared of us supermen."

"Julian told him that the residential buildings are communal . . . ?"

"Yes and Julian showed him the figures the Center files every year, plus the auditors' reports. Cut no ice! In fact, if anything," and Pat grimaced, "it only confirmed Greenfield's notion that the Center is a rich source of additional income."

"The Center is also in Jerhattan proper."

"Julian made that point but Greenfield's one of those allocation goons: all for one and one for all . . . all monies being in one kitty—his. He's State Budget Chairman, you see."

Daffyd nodded.

"I didn't want to worry you unnecessarily, Daffyd," Pat went on apologetically.

Daffyd suppressed a tart rejoinder and sighed instead.

"Pat, it's easier to pull a weed if it's small."

"A weed? That's a good one. Greenfield's a weed all right." Pat sounded unusually acerbic. "I'll tell Julian you called and that you're worried."

"No. I'm not worried, Pat. Not yet."

"I would be if I were you," she said, all gloom.

"Is there a precog?"

"No specific ones. But frankly, Dave, I'm far more worried about the city's climate than anything old Aaron Leftfield perpetrates. And so is Julian. He's street-walking today." She gave a reassuring wave of her hand. "Oh, I sent one of the LEO sensitives with him. I can't move so fast these days." She glanced down at her gravid abdomen. "You've seen my report?"

"You sent one in?" Daffyd began riffling through the tapes.

"It should be on your desk. It'd better be on your desk."

Daffyd found the purple-backed City Admin tape and waved it at her.

"It is. Lester Welch had first crack at me."

"And he didn't mention our tape?" She made an exasperated noise. "Look, Dave, listen to it now because, believe me, it's more important than Greenfield even if Lester doesn't think so."

"Is that a precog, Pat?"

"You tell me it's my condition," she said, suddenly angry, "the way Julian does or a vitamin deficiency like my OB and I'll resign." The anger as suddenly drained from her face. "God, don't I just wish I could!"

"Pat, d'you want a few weeks relief?"

Daffyd op Owen caught the shifting emotions on her face: sullen resentment giving way to hope, instantly replaced by resignation. "Don't, Dave."

"I wouldn't and you know it. I can send out a mayday . . ."

"And overwork some other poor Talent?" Pat's chin lifted. "I'll be all right, Dave. Honest! It's just that . . . well, hell, listen to the report. And remember, it's a pan-ethnic problem this year."

"This year?" Another loaded phrase. Daffyd op Owen inserted the City Admin tape and his concern over the Greenfield proposal faded to insignificance as he recognized the more imminent danger of a disturbed City. He began to wonder who else had thought to save their dear Director trouble by not reporting the grim facts he now heard. Because if the Correlation Staff had slipped up on reading precogs, he'd downgrade the lot.

Brief, violent inter-ethnic quarrels over contract employment during the winter had been mediated but, within the City's ethnic sectors, the truce had been uneasy: each segment certain that another had received what plums existed. (Most of the spot employment during the winter had been make-work, paid for by funds pared from other pressing needs to give the proud their sop.) Most of the agitation could be traced to a young Pan-Slavic leader, Vsevolod Roznine. The report noted that Roznine was more feared than popular with his constituents and, although several attempts had been made to cool or placate the agitator, he had neatly avoided the traps. The report closed with the note that Roznine might have latent Talent. However, the only mental contact made had been so distasteful to the Talent that he had broken it off before he could implant any suggestion to go to the Center for testing.

"The man's public mind is a sewer," was the final comment.

Daffyd op Owen made a steeple of his fingers and,

twirling his swivel chair, gazed out his window to the orderly grounds below. He felt unaccountably depressed yet he could be justifiably proud of what Talent in general and Eastern American Center in particular had been able to accomplish in the past decades. Op Owen could appreciate, and it was no precog, how much more had to be done on numerous levels: public, private, civic, clinical, military, spatial, and most important, inner. No matter what the dominant Talent, precog, telepath, teleport, kinetic, empathic, the Talented were still very human people, above and beyond their special gifts which so often complicated adjustment therapy.

They had professional immunity at long last, for all registered Talents. Another giant step forward. They had had acceptance on a commercial level for many years where Talent could steadily show profit to management. Since the first body-Talents had been able to point out assassins in crowds (even before precogs were accepted and acted on by key personnel), they'd been accepted by intelligent people. But the suspicious were the majority and they still had to be convinced that the Talented were not dangerously different.

He'd ruminated on this many times and it wasn't solving the other pressing problems before him. A city torn by the very ethnic strife that had once been hailed as a bonding compromise to the late twentieth century's lack of basic life-style values: summer was a-coming and, despite advances in weather controls, a hot dry spell which could cut the power available for city air-conditioning would only produce riot-breeding conditions.

So far, no major precogs of disasters had been recorded and for such a large unit as Jerhattan, a trouble precog was statistically more probable than one dealing with a small number of people or a single citizen. Scant reassurance, however.

And thank god, Talent was pan-ethnic, thought Daffyd. He didn't have to worry about that ugly head rising against the Center.

He did tape an All-Talent alert on the city's climate. The great minds would now have a single thought. Perhaps they'd also have an answer.

When he picked Sally Iselin up at nine at the Clinic door, she gave him a quick appraising look. Then her anxious-puppy expression changed to a radiant smile.

"I knew it. I knew it." And she all but war-danced a circle as she inspected his costume.

"What?" he asked, turning to keep her face in view.

"You dressed just right. How'd you know? I'm sure I didn't clue you. Are you positive you're not a precog, too, Daffyd?"

"I'd rather not be."

Her vivacity faded instantly. She put a hand out, aborting the sympathetic gesture before she actually made a contact. He touched her fingers lightly in reassurance.

"Not to worry. I just had a tedious day. Felt like wearing glad threads."

Sally's eyes crinkled and her mouth tilted up as she cocked her head to one side. "You are indeed joyous," she said saucily as her glance took in his royal blue black-trimmed coverall.

"Look who's talking," and Daffyd grinned down at Sally in lime green and black swing tunic and matching high boots. Sally's puppy charm was a tonic and he wondered, as he often did in her company, why he didn't make more opportunities to enjoy it.

As he put a helping hand under her elbow to assist her up to the passenger side of the two-spot copter, she gave him a startled sideways glance. He caught the echo of mental astonishment before she started to chatter about the day's hopeful applicants.

"They come, Daffyd, swearing oaths that they'd had this or that perception. Dorotea dosen't tap a one. We go through the routine but even with maximum perceptol, they come over dead dumb and stone blind."

Sally was a compulsive talker but Daffyd became aware that her present garrulity was a shield. He wondered what Sally would need to obscure. Propriety prohibited his making a quick probe but undoubtedly there'd be clues later on. Sally was entirely too open to be devious for very long.

She directed him to Sector K, northwest of the Center, where the worn hills struggled up from old swamplands: not a salubrious area despite reclamation and renovation efforts. There were still ruins of early twentieth-century factories and it was by one such structure, a sprawling half-glass and brick affair, that Sally directed him to land.

"The place seems popular enough," Daffyd said as he had to circle several times to find a site for the copter.

Sally winced, eyeing the ranks of city-crawlers and the presence of both private and public transport copters. "Doesn't take long, does it, for the masses to latch onto a new thrill!"

"Oh? This is new?" He'd caught the worry tone of her thoughts. "Crowd bad for the project?"

"I don't know." She was more than worried. "I just don't know. It's just that . . ." She broke off, firmly pressing her lips together.

They stood in a short queue for billets, paying a credit apiece to get in.

"Milking the golden cow," Sally said with uncharacteristic bitternness as they passed the billets in at massive sliding doors which separated the outer hall from the vast factory space beyond.

"Guarding it, too," Daffyd said, noting the strong-arm types in meshed duty-alls.

"That might make more sense than you'd guess," Sally said in a very dark voice. Her mind was practically shouting "trouble."

"Will we need assistance?" he asked her, estimating how many empathic Talents might be needed to control a crowd this size.

Sally didn't answer. She was looking around the enormous open area which was filling rapidly. It didn't require Talent to appreciate the aura of excited anticipation that emanated from the audience. The hall was by no means full yet; half the tables were still empty, but most of the couches of the inner circles were occupied. Daffyd had never seen such an assortment of styles, ages and conditions of furnishings.

"They must have been scouring the Sector," Sally said. Then she indicated a table on the outer rim: a table, Daffyd noticed, which was convenient to one of the luminescent exit doors.

They were barely seated, Daffyd on Queen Anne, Sally on Swedish tubular, before a waiter inquired their pleasure.

"What's available?" Sally asked, simulating bored indifference. Daffyd was surprised that she felt the need to dissemble.

"You name it," replied the concessionaire, impatient. His tables were filling up.

Sally "told" Daffyd that this, too, was an innovation.

"Try something simple, schatzie," Daffyd said, managing the verbal slurs of their assumed roles. "The Medboard warned you and I'm not copting you to the drainbrain again this month."

Sally affected petulance, then with dutiful resignation, asked for a mild caffeine. Daffyd, in character, asked for an esoteric blend.

"Nor am I copting you!"

"Make it two milds and bring the pot."

As the conman left, Daffyd leaned towards Sally. "Is this area disaffected?"

She wrinkled her nose. "We get a lot of hopefuls from this Sector."

Sound had come on, more frequency drone than actual note. The dim lights on the girders were beginning to fade completely, and ground spots lit up, adding their eerie moiety to the ambience. Sally looked toward the half-circle of stage which had remained semi-lit. The aura of expectation, of voracious emotional appetite increased perceptibly. Sally shivered and folded her arms across her breasts but Daffyd sensed that the created atmosphere irritated more than distressed her.

She shifted in her chair nervously when the waiter appeared with cups and the pot. He served them disdainfully—he didn't make as much commission from the milder brews—and hurried off, grimacing thanks for the carefully generous gratuity.

The auditorium was almost full now and the conversational murmur impinged on Daffyd's senses as the snarl of the unfed. Yes, the climate of the city was very uncertain indeed. He could feel the tension building rapidly now, with so many feeding it. He noticed the muscle boys spreading through the tables and couches, and he worried harder. The psychology of a crowd was theoretically understood but there was always that gap between theory and reality—that dangerous gap which could be bridged by the most insignificant event—when crowd exploded into Riot. Daffyd and Sally were far too familiar with the "tone" of Riot to be very comfortable in a pregnant situation.

In fact, Daffyd was leaning across the table to warn Sally that they might have to leave when the lighting of the stage area altered and a girl stepped into the center. She wore a white caftan-type unadorned robe and carried an old-fashioned twelve-string guitar. It had no umbilical amplifier which surprised Daffyd as much as the girl's regal poise and simple appearance.

A camouflaged hand deposited a three-legged stool and the girl took her place on it without a backward glance.

Daffyd frowned at the darkness above the stage, wondering where the sound amplification was hidden. She couldn't possibly hope to reach and hold this crowd without electronic boosting of some kind.

Then Daffyd saw the relieved and pleased smile on Sally's face.

The girl settled herself, tossed back her mane of tawny hair and, without taking any notice of the audience, began to play softly. There was no need for mechanical amplification of that delicate sound. For the first note fell into a voracious silence, the most effective conductor.

No—and Daffyd sat up straight—every nerve in his body aware of a subtle, incredible pulse that picked up the gentle melody and expanded it—telepathically!

And this, too, was what Sally had hoped he'd feel, what she'd brought him here to confirm. He saw the happy triumph in her eyes. The girl's voice, a warm lyric soprano, intensified the pulse, "sounded" off the echo as she fed the multitude with a tender ethnic admonition to love one another. And . . . everyone did.

Daffyd listened and "listened," stunned physically and emotionally by the unusual experience: unusual even for a man whose life had been dedicated to the concept of unusual mental powers. On an intellectual plane, he was incredulous. He couldn't deduce how she was effecting this total rapport, this augmented pulse. It was not mechanical, of that he was certain. Why this sensation of "echo"?

The girl would have to be a broadcasting empath: an intelligent empath, unlike poor Harold Orley who hadn't any intellect at all. This young woman was consciously choosing and directing the emotion she broadcast . . . Wait! That was it . . . she was consciously directing the emotions . . . at whom? Not the individual minds of the listeners: they were responding but they could not account for the "generation" of emotion that enveloped everyone. There had to be sensitive minds to generate emotion like that and these people were parapsychically dead. Yet she was manipulating them in some way, using some method that was non-electrical and non-sonic.

The girl continued with a more complicated tune from some early nineteenth-century religious minority which had settled in the eastern United States. And the "message" of the song was a soothing statement of acceptance.

She was deliberately taking the audience out of the technocratic trap, transferring them to less complex days, lulling them into a mood of even greater receptivity. Nor was Daffyd immune to the charged atmosphere . . . except for that part of his brain which could not perceive how she was effecting this deft, mass control.

The singer finished that song and plucked the strings idly, chording into a different key. The third song, while no more intense than the first two, was a rollicking happy ballad, a spirit-lifter, a work doer.

She was preparing her audience, Daffyd realized, deftly and carefully. He began to relax, or rather, the intellect which had been alerted, responded to the beguiling charm of her performance.

Daffyd was suddenly frightened. A deep pang, covered in a flash, overladen with worry that was lyric-inspired. Only it wasn't. Sally had felt the pang, too, glancing nervously around her. The rest of the audience didn't seem to catch alarm: they were in the young singer's complete thrall, caught up in the illusion of unpressured times and ways.

The fear was the singer's and it was not part of her song, Daffyd concluded, because he could detect no other influence, no newcomer in the hall, no change of lighting or aura. Sally was concentrating on the girl, too.

Why would she be frightened? She had the audience in the palm of her hand. She could turn them in any direction she chose to: she could . . .

Her song ended and, in a fluid movement, she rose, propped her guitar against the stool and casually disappeared into the shadowy rear of the stage.

Sally turned anxious eyes to Daffyd, and they shared the same knowledge. *She's the one who's frightened. She's leaving.*

And that's the most dangerous thing she could do, Daffyd "told" Sally.

No one in the audience moved and Daffyd didn't dare. The lighting altered subtly, brighter now, and people began to shake off the deep entrancement, reaching for cigarettes or drinks, starting soft conversation.

"They don't know she's not coming back. When they do . . ."

Daffyd signalled to Sally. It was imperative they leave: they couldn't risk the psychic distortion of a riot and, once this crowd discovered that the singer wasn't returning, their contentment would turn to sour savage resentment. Caution governed Daffyd. They couldn't just leave. But they had to . . .

He reached across the table casually and deftly tipped the caffeine pot over.

"Of all the stupid jerks," Sally cried, irritably, getting to her feet and holding her flared skirt from her.

Daffyd rose, too, with many apologies. They received mildly irritated glances from nearby couples whose pleasant mood was disrupted. As Daffyd and Sally moved toward the main door, Sally kept up a running diatribe as to her escort's awkwardnesses and failings. They reached the sliding doors. The aura generated by the singer was fainter in the lobby and the close knot of men by the box office window interrupted their discussion to stare suspiciously at Daffyd and Sally.

"I can't sit around in this damp dress," Sally said in a nasal whine. "It'll stain and you know it's only this week's issue."

"Hon-love, it'll dry in a few moments. It was only . . ."

"You would be clumsy and right now . . ."

"Let's just stand outside a bit. It's warmer. You'll dry off and we won't miss any of the singing."

"If you make me miss any of Amalda's songs, I'll never, never forgive you . . ."

With such drivel they got out the main entrance. But not before Daffyd experienced a wash of such frightful lewd thoughts that he hastily closed off all awareness.

"Sally, how many minorities did you notice represented there?"

"Too many, in view of your memorandum this morning. Daffyd, I'm scared. And it's not Amalda's fear this time!"

"I'm calling Frank Gillings."

Sally pulled from him. "I'll find the girl. She's got to have protection . . ."

"Can you find her?"

"I'm not sure. But I've got to try. Once that crowd realizes she's left . . ."

Sally turned to the right, toward the rear of the factory, slipping past the little city crawlers until she was out of Daffyd's sight. He made for his copter and opened the emergency channel to the Center.

Charlie Moorfield was on duty and he instantly patched Daffyd through to the office of Law Enforcement and Order as he was rousing the Center's riot control people. If they could get enough telepaths to the site in time, they might dampen the incipient riot before LEO needed to resort to the unpopular expedient of gas control.

"Tell Frank Gillings that Roznine is here, too," Daffyd told the officer on the line.

"Roznine? What'n hell would he be doing listening to a singer?" the man asked.

"If you'd heard the effect this singer has on people, you'd understand."

The officer swore, at a loss for other words. Daffyd wished that swearing were as therapeutic for him.

"Keep the band open, Charlie . . ."

"Dave, you can't stay there . . ." Charlie's voice reached Daffyd's ears even several yards from the copter. Daffyd wished he'd be quiet. He had to concentrate on "listening" for the girl. He could sense Sally's direction but he was used to Sally's mind; he could have "found" her at a far greater distance. But the singer was unknown: alarmingly unknown, Daffyd realized, because he ought to be able to "find" her. He'd been in her presence, in "touch" with her for over half an hour, long enough for him to identify most minds and contact them again within a mile radius. She couldn't have got very far away in such a short time.

The beat of heavy duty copters was audible now: coming in without lights and sirens. Daffyd looked east, willing the Center's fast transports to get here before the riot control squads. It was generally impossible to get enough telepaths during the day to quell an imminent riot unless there'd been a precog of trouble. But, of an evening, there was the entire Center's telepathic population . . . Now, if . . .

He heard the beginning of a subdued murmur from the building. The customers were getting restless. He hoped they hadn't yet realized that the singer wasn't taking a short break.

Someone opened a section of the big main doors, stood framed in the rectangle of light for a moment, peering out. Daffyd identified the stocky figure as Roznine's. Suddenly the figure of the ethnic leader froze. He stepped out, into the night, head up. The man's curses floated toward Daffyd as he slammed back into the building. Daffyd hurried in search of Sally, wondering what Roznine would do now he knew a LEO squad was on the way. Only . . . and Daffyd faltered midstride, how *could* Roznine know, if he did, that the big copters were LEO. Cargo firms used the same type. Yet op Owen knew with unarguable certainty that Roznine had properly identified the aircraft.

Daffyd came round the corner of the old factory just as the personnel hatch in the huge rear door opened. He counted five of the muscle boys, each taking off in a different direction. Then a sixth man, Roznine, whose harsh urgent voice ordered them to find those effing copouts or they'd be subsistence livers for the rest of their breathing days.

'Copouts.' Plural, thought Daffyd. Who beside Amalda? No time now for speculation. Daffyd sent a quick warning to Sally to leave off the search and get back to the copter. She was there when he returned, easily eluding the searching muscle men who were as noisy mentally as they were physically.

"That audience is losing patience fast," Sally said, staring at the ominous black bulk of the building. She was hugging herself against shivers of fear.

Daffyd looked eastward, saw the running lights of the slim Center transports.

"Not long now."

But too far away. Disappointment and whetted appetite rocketed to explosive heights. All along their side of the factory, exits burst open as part of the audience swarmed out, in futile search of the singer. Inside the furnishings were being thrown about and broken, people were slugging and slugged, trampled and hurt as uncertain tempers erupted.

Daffyd wasted no time. He half-threw Sally into the copter, jammed in the rocket-lift, warning Sally to hang on. The head LEO copter blared its summons before he could turn on his distinctive identity lights. As it was, he only just got out of stun range.

Once clear of the busy altitudes, Daffyd hovered, calling an "abort" to the Center transports. The situation had gone beyond their capabilities. He'd only completed one circle before he saw that the LEO copters were laying gas. It was all they could do with such a mob starting to rampage. Sally was weeping softly as he veered eastwards toward the Center.

"I wasn't honestly certain, Daffyd," Sally said, curled in a small contrite ball on the suspended couch in his quarters. She kept examining her glass as if the amber liqueur were fascinating. She'd the appearance of a small girl trying to get out of a scold. Actually her public mind was wide open to Daffyd's, permitting him a review of her initial impressions of the singer. "I mean, while I couldn't think what else she might be, there was the possibility that it was all sonic amplification. You know what a skilled operator can do."

"All the more reason you should have reported it, Sally. That kind of manipulation is why mechanical amplification is strictly licensed to reputable and reliable technicians."

"And not a clue about the girl?"

"Not yet." The licensed owners of the Factory were among those drowsily helpless inside the office in the lobby of the building. They'd be questioned, of course, by Gillings's men. Perpetrators of riots could expect scant mercy from the LEO office.

"We've got to get to the girl first, Sally."

"If only I'd told you sooner . . ." Sally was floating in chagrin.

"I keep telling you, and every other member of my staff, I don't mind being bothered with so called 'trivia.' Because it isn't always as trivial as *you* might believe."

"I know. I know. I simply wasn't thinking clearly." That was what she said, but what Sally was thinking, also for him to see, was that she hadn't wanted to disappoint him, or herself, in case her initial impression about the singer had been wrong. The girl had been almost too good to be true.

"Was she afraid of that crowd, Daffyd? It was three times the size of the one the other night. In fact, the size alone put me off."

"You first heard her . . ."

"Just two days ago. I tried to get backstage to see her . . ." Sally shrugged her failure.

"Muscle boys?"

"No." Sally was astonished. "Everyone else wanted to get next to her. I'd never have had a chance to find out for sure with so much interference, much less suggest she come to the Center."

Daffyd began to stroll about, his arms crossed over his chest, his head down.

"We both sensed her fright?"

Sally nodded.

"We are both agreed that she is a broadcasting empath?"

Sally nodded again, more emphatically. "Could she also receive? I mean, that would account for that 'echo' phenomenon, wouldn't it? She throws the emotions out and then magnifies them on retrieval?"

"That's one explanation."

"Hmm, but you don't subscribe to it with any enthusiasm."

Daffyd grinned at Sally. "It doesn't fit all the circumstances. Besides, Roznine used a plural . . . 'those effing copouts.' "

Sally's eyes rounded with surprise. "She links. That would account for the amplification and the echo." Daffyd nodded. "Then who's the other empath, or empaths?" Daffyd shrugged. "Doesn't she realize what she is?"

"Probably not. We shall have to inform her."

"And how do you plan to do that?"

"I think we ask for Frank Gillings's help . . ."

"But . . . but . . . she started the riot. You know what happens to riot provokers."

"Yes, but I also know that Frank wants all Talented people registered, trained and controllable. So when he's had a chance to question the sleeping beauties . . ."

"We can trace Cinderella and fit her out with glass slippers . . ." Sally grinned saucily as she picked up the analogy.

"Before Pegasus flies away with her."

"Pegasus? He's a myth, not a fairy tale. That's not fair, Daffyd!"

"But the analogy is most apt," and op Owen was grimly serious. "And we've got to put a bridle on her Pegasus or she'll end up with singed wings."

Although the LEO Commissioner and the Director of Eastern American Parapsychic Center were on good working terms, the Commissioner avoided coming to the Center. Respecting this whimsy, Daffyd called through to Gillings's office the next morning, asking for an appointment and specifying his business as the Fact riot.

"How did you happen to be there, Dave?" Gillings greeted him, rising from his chair as op Owen was ushered into his tower office.

Daffyd spent a moment admiring the 360° view of the sprawling hazed metropolis.

"Tracking a rather unique Talent."

"That singer?" And Gillings swore when Daffyd nodded. "Do you know the toll on that caper?"

"No, but it's one helluva lot cheaper than it would have been if we hadn't alerted riot control."

Gillings frowned. "She shouldn't be allowed a public performer's license."

"I wanted to find out if she had one."

Glaring, Gillings icily banged at his desk comset and demanded to be put through to ID. No license had been issued to anyone answering the description of the singer, Amalda: nor had there been a license issued to the Fact for solo entertaining. There were, however, specifications on record as to what mechanical amplification was permitted the management of the Fact, the frequency of the programming and the nights on which public gatherings could be held and the maximum number of people permitted to gather. Last night's performance, it transpired, was completely illegal. Gillings issued a summons for the owners, brothers named Dick and Harry Ditts, who had told an entirely different tale the previous evening when they had recovered from sleepy gas. Five minutes later, Gillings was informed that neither Dick nor Harry Ditts could be located at their residences on record.

"Have they any known connection with Roznine?"

"Roznine?" Gillings regarded Daffyd with a combination of disgusted annoyance and startled concern which faded into deep reflection. "You saw him there?"

"Yes, he was at the Fact. When we were withdrawing from the scene of the imminent riot, he was deep in conversation with several types in the lobby. Later he spotted the LEO copters on their way in and made his way out. Funny he didn't suggest to the Ditts brothers that they leave with him."

"Don't be naive. Roznine looks after Roznine, first, last and always or I'd've had him cooled long ago. But Sector K is far from his bailiwick . . ." Gillings stared out across the city with narrowed eyes. "He's been getting too damned powerful in the City and not just with the Slavs. A megalomaniac is what he is and they operate with a curious ability to avoid minor disasters . . . until they get overconfident. Roznine hasn't made that mistake . . . yet . . ."

"I shouldn't wonder that there's some Talent in a megalomaniac, apart from his madness."

"Talent?" Gillings erupted as Daffyd had known he would. "Christ, that's all I need is a Talented pan-ethnic leader. Goddammit, why don't you people get on the ball and round up all these goddamn freaking Talents before they go haywire. We've got enough problems keeping that . . ." and his blunt-fingered hand described a circle at the panoramic metropolis outside the plexi-glass, ". . . from exploding as it is without unnatural hazards like latent Talents . . ."

". . . Then help us find Amalda. She can be immensely useful . . ."

"She's a riot provoker . . ." Gillings's eyes narrowed with a flash of vindictiveness.

"Are you going to help me, or hinder me, Frank? The girl is valuable to both of us but not in your cooler as an RP. She's an intelligent broadcasting empath of tremendous range and power. I don't think she realizes what she is . . . or didn't until possibly last night. Something frightened her out of her wits halfway through her third song. She ran! I don't know what it was nor do I know exactly how she can broadcast the way she does, but it's imperative that the Center find and protect her."

Gillings's eyebrows rose in ironic surprise. "You and Iselin were there. Why didn't you get her then? What happened?"

"Among other things, a riot. Some people shield automatically, Frank, and if you can't trace the mind, you can't catch the body."

"All right, all right," Gillings said, irritably waving aside Daffyd's mild reproval. "But how come she doesn't know what she is? All right, all right. I know the answer to that, too. All right, what do I do?"

"I want a tracer on any young singer of her description applying for a performer's license anywhere in the country. And I want to know where she has sung, where she trained, where she came from. She's gone to cover and she won't find easy. In the first place, she's terrified of whatever hit her last night. And secondly, she'll have a good idea what happened when the audience found out she wasn't going to sing again. She has two very good reasons for being scarce. I also don't want her frightened out of her wits so let me handle the actual search with my people. I'll get my propaganda team to alter some of the public info broadcasts subliminally. We might get her to seek us out spontaneously which would be preferable," Daffyd added, rising.

"Okay, you handle it but I want that girl found and trained or whatever it is you do with them. And quick. I'll shunt the report on her to your computer. Shouldn't take long to trace her."

It took two days to trace the girl known as Amalda. And the print-out had many gaps.

She'd been born and reared in a small Appalachian commune: educated to her sixteenth year in the County School system which she quit to "travel" . . . a not uncommon pattern for an undirected or unmotivated youngster. There was no record of formal music instruction but music was a feature in her environment: no official record of her for several years until she took work in a Florida food control complex. Two applications for performer's license in Florida were denied by the Audition Board there. The third application was provisionally granted and lapsed without formal request for an extension, but several short term engagements were on record for her as an unamplified, string-instrumented folk singer. A new application as apprentice, non-singer, had been filed in Washington, D. C. four months before: one engagement was listed without a termination date. Then Daffyd had a check made on the play in which she had appeared. Amalda, who had started as a walk-on, had been abruptly promoted to an important supporting role. The play was scheduled for a metropolitan opening in three weeks.

Although Daffyd had only a superficial acquaintance with the mechanics of the Performing Arts, there were several glaring contradictions in this report. And no explanation for Amalda's sudden appearance as a self-accompanied soloist in a minority entertainment hall of dubious reputation.

In the meantime, he and Sally worked with the propaganda department to include in the public information broadcasts a subliminal appeal for someone in Amalda's situation. Daffyd also got in touch with the play's producer.

"I've had enough trouble with that flitting bird," Norman Kabilov told op Owen. "If she does show up, I'll tell her straight: she gets no more contracts and she shouldn't ever hope to get a PP license approved. Not if I have any connection in the PA."

"What kind of trouble did you have with Amalda?" Daffyd asked, injecting placatory thoughts at the irritated little man.

"Troubles, plural, not trouble singular," and Norman Kabilov glowered at op Owen.

Daffyd knew the man was considerably perplexed by the Center's interest in his ex-actress.

"First, she latches on to my stage manager, Red Vaden . . . good man, Vaden. Solid. Dependable. Only this little twit has him hopping to her tune like he'd never tried to brush off a stage-struck tail before. Red doesn't ask many favors so when he wants this bird in the cast . . . so when the show travels, he's not lacking what he's been having regular . . . I say, yes. What harm? Suddenly I got Red begging me to give her an audition for one of the secondary leads. I already got a good PA picked out for the part . . ." Kabilov's expression told Daffyd that his choice had been personal rather than professional. " . . . but I gotta keep 'em happy so I audition the girl." The little producer frowned now, his thoughts vivid to Daffyd. The man had been surprised out of boredom at the quality of the audition and immediately signed Amalda for the role, despite the fact that he'd known he'd be in for a heavy time with the disappointed candidate. "Mind you, it wasn't that great a part until that kid reads it." Another headshake of perplexity. "I dunno how she did it because she sure had no theatre arts credits but I couldn't *not* give her the part. And then the author comes to rehearsal and hell, he's rewriting the part to give her more. I damn near have a jeopardy action from Carla Jacobs who's the name in the play. Only Red goes to work on *her* and she quiets down like a lily. And you gotta believe that Jacobs don't handle that easy. She's pushing fifty, y'see, and any new bird is a threat. Funny thing," and Kabilov stared off above Daffyd's head, his mind taking up and discarding a hundred different glimpses of Carla Jacobs in high tantrum, Carla Jacobs soothed and very few snatches of Amalda. The man was unconsciously censoring those recollections. "Once La Jacobs got to working with the kid, things were okay. Wanta see the reviews we got?"

Daffyd hastily assented but he was given no chance to do more than glance at the commendatory headlines in the fasc sheets.

"As long as we were in Washington, it was okay. But the minute we got to Jerhattan, troubles! La Jacobs storms in here with her lawyers and her current man and she won't play with that creature anymore. In fact, she gets so absolutely violent we gotta trank her. Now I can't lose La Jacobs or I lose the theatre *and* the play since that's the contract. So I tell Red to find his bird another nest. I can't afford trouble. And they both walk!" He was indignant. "Just like that. He walks. A guy I'd sworn was 100% dependable walks out of the show two weeks before opening. On account of a scrawny bird!"

If Norman Kabilov looked the picture of outraged innocence, he "sounded" like a man reprieved from an unknown ordeal. However, he did have publicity shots of Amalda and Red Vaden, which he appeared relieved to give Daffyd: as if by getting rid of everything reminding him of this unsettling episode he could erase it from his memory.

Daffyd op Owen had his best finders scan the pictures, he sent copies to the LEO office and, on an off-chance, gave a final print to his best precog.

"You better find that girl," Gillings told op Owen, "or I'll find her and make her answer—officially—for that riot."

"Frank, don't provoke another Maggie O."

Though the comset was not color, Daffyd was certain that Gillings' face changed shade.

"We're doing all we can," he went on soothingly, "to find her but there's no way of forcing her to come to us."

Gillings growled something dire as he broke the connection.

There were days when Gillings was not Daffyd's only cross. He and Sally had spent most of the morning trying to figure out a way to attract Amalda to them. Lester Welch walked in, listened a few minutes and then snorted in disgust.

"Why don't you just find out where this Red Vaden lives? If he was so gone on the girl he'd leave a successful show, he's probably tied up tight with her. And if he's at leisure," and Lester grinned as he used the performing arts' euphemism, "he's surely checked into the PA Casting Agency."

Op Owen closed his eyes briefly before he thanked Lester with a good grace.

"I'm not sure what we'd ever do without your common sense, Les."

"Oh, someone else'd tell you your nose is on your face." And Les left.

"This is one time I wish I were a kinetic," Daffyd said with a wistful sigh, thinking all kinds of disasters, of a minor sort, to befall the dour New Englander on his way down the aisle to his own office. Then he caught Sally grinning at him, her eyes sparkling. "And if you repeat any of what I was thinking . . ."

She composed her face into solemnity, raising one hand. "Dai, you know I can't 'path that accurately." But in her mind was a vivid picture of Lester stuffed into one of his wastepaper baskets.

Daffyd placed a call to the Casting Agency. Bruce Vaden had reported his availability and a new address. However, the Agency informed him, the address was naturally restricted. Daffyd explained who he was and that he urgently needed to get in touch with Vaden and was informed that Performing Artist Vaden would be contacted and would return his call if he were interested.

" 'If he were interested' indeed," Daffyd repeated, breaking the connection with uncharacteristic irritability.

"Shall we think Lesterish, and perhaps drop a word in the omnipotent ear of our local lion?" asked Sally.

Her suggestion elicited the needed address in five minutes and in less than half an hour, they were on their way by copter to an isolated area of the Coast. The small sea-silvered cottage was tightly locked and obviously untenanted. Rather depressed, Sally and Daffyd returned to the Center. Lester met them at the roof stairs.

"You're covered with canary feathers," said Sally.

"I thought you couldn't read my mind," Lester replied, startled.

"With your expression I don't need to."

But Sally hesitated at the door of Daffyd's office. Rather more aggravated with circumstance than Sally, Daffyd took her firmly by the arm and pushed her into the room. He was instantly overwhelmed by several devastating impressions: contact with Sally informing him that her emotions were highly unstable; there were intense love-hate auras swirling in the room and among them the sure knowledge that the chestnut-haired girl seated facing the door was a powerful and violently agitated empath; that the red-bearded man standing by the window was linked to her in a desperate, despairing bond.

"I'm Daffyd op Owen," he said, "and this is Sally Iselin, head of our Clinic Recruiting Team. We've been looking for you." Daffyd poured out waves of sympathy/ reassurance/overt love and respect.

"*We* found you," replied the man. "I'm Bruce Vaden."

"We tried to locate you at the Fact last night," Daffyd said, turning to Amalda. His second impression was that the girl was about to implode.

At that point, Sally gasped and made a movement towards Amalda as the impact of fear/confusion/hatred/ love/horror/revulsion/affection lapped over the two Talents.

"That's just a sample of what I can do." Despite a southern softness, the girl's voice grated in their ears and was echoed by an intense mental shout that caused both Daffyd and Sally to shake their heads. "I don't want this. It doesn't matter any more if Red is in or out of the room. It works anywhere now." She was drenched in bitterness, but there was pity as well as satisfaction to be read from her glance as she watched Sally beginning to shake with reaction.

Daffyd curtly gestured Sally from the room. She resisted until he reinforced the order mentally, telling her to get Jerry Frames over here on the double. He duly noted that she was rebellious and not bothering to hide the fact in her public mind or her expression. Daffyd winced slightly as Sally slammed the door behind her.

"You're an empath," Daffyd told Amalda, trying to reach through her broadcast to soothe her stampeding emotions.

"I don't care what I am. I want you to stop it. Now!"

"I can't stop it, my dear," he said in his kindest voice, but he had a vision of a bridleless winged horse bolting across the heavens.

Amalda rose, in a single fluid movement, her eyes blazing. "Then I will!" Her words rose to the edge of a scream as she launched herself at the window. Daffyd moved to intercept her, physically and mentally, but not as swiftly as Red Vaden. Not that she could have achieved her end, since the window was unbreakable. So she hit the plastic hard and crumpled into the arms of the redhead, sobbing hysterically and broadcasting such conflicting and powerful emotions that, out of pity, Daffyd reached for the trank gun in his desk and shot her.

There was absolute silence on every level in the room as the two men stared down at the limp figure in Vaden's arms.

"I suppose that was necessary," the man said in a bleak voice as he swung her up in his arms.

Daffyd could read the relief in the man's mind which had been bruised by confusion, fear and an unquestioning devotion to the girl. Op Owen gestured towards the couch.

"All right, op Owen, what now?" Vaden asked after he had arranged Amalda gently in a comfortable position. The man's eyes were a cold, troubled blue.

Daffyd returned the gaze, probing deftly and finding in Vaden's outer thoughts that their visit here had been his suggestion, a last possibility of assistance, since Amalda had been determined to end her Talent even if it meant taking her life.

"First we have the Center's doctor prescribe sedation," and Daffyd nodded towards the painfully thin arm of the unconscious girl, "and a decent diet."

Vaden snorted as if practical advice was the last thing he'd expected from op Owen but he took the chair Daffyd indicated to him.

"Then the Center teaches her to control this Talent."

"Talent?" Vaden exploded. "Talent? It's an effing curse! After the other night, she's scared to go out of the house. She'll never perform again . . . She won't even . . ." and he clenched his teeth over what he'd been about to add but not before the thought, "audible" to Daffyd, made him pity the two more.

"Any Talent is a two-edged sword, Vaden," op Owen said, swinging his chair a little, a soothing motion.

"What kind of a freak is she?"

"She's by no means a freak," Daffyd answered in rather severe tones. "She's a broadcasting telempath . . ."

"And I'm the booster station?"

"I think that would be a good analogy."

"Look, op Owen, I've read a good bit about you Talents and nothing was said about what Amalda does . . ."

"Quite likely. We're just beginning to appreciate the mutations possible in the parapsychic. We have only one true telempath here. He unfortunately has no more mind than a rabbit and he only receives. Amalda can apparently transmit exactly what she chooses. I gather the phenomenon only began when she met you?"

On the top of Vaden's mind was the actual first meeting: a sort of dazed comprehension that they were "meant for each other." Their first love-making had been a revelation to the blasé, sex-wearied Vaden and each succeeding day had strengthened their inter-dependence.

"She was down and out," Vaden said aloud in an expressionless voice. What he wasn't saying was vividly and pictorially flashing across his mind, elaborating with every shade of the emotional spectrum a dry recital of fact. "Thank God it was me she approached . . ." and beyond the flashes of memories, Daffyd saw that Vaden had never allowed himself the luxury of loving or caring for anyone for fear of being hurt and used. In a transient profession, constantly beseiged by stage-struck youngsters who thought a PA license was "all" they needed to achieve fame, he had been invulnerable to physical charms and ordinary ploys. But he had absolutely no defense against the impact of Amalda's mind in his. Now he ran nervous fingers through his crisp red hair. "We went everywhere." He'd been haunted with the fear that she'd leave him or be taken from him. "Even to rehearsal. Then the girl who was to play Charmian was late so I asked Amalda to fill in and read it 'til she came. I've never heard a better first reading. She even lost every trace of her regional accent and became the hard-voiced trollop. We all loathed her. It was such a total characterization! I've never seen such a thing in all the years I've been a PA. I'd expect such expertise from someone like Mathes or Crusada, but a novice? An ex-canary?" Vaden looked toward the unconscious girl and gave a sort of incredulous shrug. "She was so pleased to think she did have ability. She'd tried often enough to qualify as a vocalist." Vaden made an exasperated noise in his throat. "The first time she sang for me I couldn't credit that she'd been refused a license." He turned back to Daffyd. "It just didn't make sense."

"I'd hazard that you were the missing factor."

"A modern Svengali?" Vaden was bitter.

"Not exactly. But the brain generates electrical currents. And in the same way that a receiver must be tuned to a certain wave-length to get a message broad-cast on that same wave-length, minds must be broad-casting on the same frequency. Yours and Amalda's are. Were either of you ever parapsychically tested?"

"Not that I know of."

"Well, we can sort out the pure mechanics later during testing but there is one other pressing question I must ask."

Vaden did have Talent, whether it had blossomed through contact with Amalda or not was immaterial, for he instantly perceived what was on Daffyd's mind and stiffened. Daffyd continued, feeling it wiser not to let Vaden realize that he was in the presence of a strong telepath . . . at least not yet.

"Granted you serve in the capacity of an amplifier for whatever mood Amalda creates, what happened the other night at the Fact? What terrified her so that she fled from what obviously was a smash-success? She had that audience in the palm of her hand."

An expression akin to terror crossed Vaden's face, ruthlessly suppressed in a second.

"You were in the audience?" Vaden asked, temporizing.

"Yes, Sally Iselin had heard Amalda two nights before and wanted me to confirm her suspicion that Amalda was a high-gain empathist. What scared Amalda off that stage? And sent both of you into hiding?"

There was nothing helpful in Vaden's mind except a repetition of what Daffyd and Sally had felt in Amalda's projection. Instead, Vaden's thoughts became despairing.

"That's why you've got to help us, op Owen. Turn Amalda off!"

Vaden didn't attempt to disguise his fear now. And he didn't strike op Owen as easily frightened. He was tough, able to take care of himself from the look of his bearlike build. And had taken care of himself, to judge by the scars on his knuckles and face.

"Fortunately, no one can turn Amalda off. Nor do I yet see the necessity." Only a nebulous but overwhelming fear in both Vaden and Amalda.

"You'd better see," Vaden cried, leaning urgently toward op Owen. His eyes were blazing with anger, fear and a sense of impotence which would be more frightening and humiliating to a man of Vaden's temperament. "You'd better see that it's crushing Amalda to the point where she was willing to commit suicide rather than live with what she's become!"

"You haven't told me *what* frightened her and what, if I may speak candidly, is bothering you as well."

Vaden got a grip on his fear and anger. "There was someone else in that audience," he said in a harsh controlled voice, "who suddenly linked up with us. Someone who was trying to dominate. Who was determined to control what Amalda can do. She got the brunt of it, of course, then I caught it."

Op Owen was certain then, with an awful instinct, that Roznine was the third person. And the ramifications of that premise were decidedly unsettling. He managed to smile reassuringly at Bruce Vaden. He swung his chair idly from side to side with counterfeit unconcern. He had lost Solange Boshe but he wouldn't lose Amalda . . . and Vaden . . . *and* Roznine.

"That's very interesting," he told Vaden. "Does Amalda have any idea of the man's identity?"

"How could she?" Red Vaden asked scornfully. He was making a notable effort to cover his inner perturbations. He couldn't bear even the notion of sharing Amalda with anyone. "The minute she realized what was happening, how strong the guy was, and what he wanted her to do, she made as if she was taking a short break. And told me to follow. But she won't ever sing again. You don't know what it does to you . . ."

"I probably more than any man," Daffyd said with a slight smile.

Vaden discredited the statement with a cutting sweep of his hand.

"You've got to understand that Amalda must be turned off."

There was an edge in his voice now: he was hitting an emotional high, too. Daffyd reached surreptitiously for the trank gun.

"Don't you dare!" Vaden moved with surprising speed and grabbed op Owen's hand.

"I thought you'd understand, op Owen. Whoever that guy is is double dangerous!"

"You'll have every bit of protection the Center and every other Center in the world can offer you, Vaden," Daffyd replied, allowing his voice to take on strength without volume. "Which is not inconsiderable, I assure you. What *you* don't understand, Vaden, is that Amalda's main problem is simply lack of control of her rather breath-taking ability."

"*You* don't understand." Vaden was desperate. "She can control masses of people. Those subbies in the Fact . . . she could have made them do anything. That's what's terrifying her. And me. And that other freaked-out mind . . . *he* wanted to *use* her to control that kind of a dangerous mob. God, man, I know what riot is. I've seen them. I've been caught in them. I know what happens. She could *cause* one. She even started one by not being there. She could incite the entire goddamned Jerhattan complex . . ."

"How?" asked Daffyd blandly.

"By . . . by . . . doing what that mind wanted her to do the other night."

"But," and Daffyd matched Red Vaden's urgency with his own, "she didn't! And she couldn't! And nothing on this world, not even some freaked-out mind with a megalomaniacal bent could make her. And once she's learned to control this . . . winged horse of hers, I think you'll all find this not so cursed a Talent."

"I don't believe you."

"How old is Amalda?"

"What? What has that got to do?"

"How old?"

"She's twenty-two. . . ."

"Twenty-two. And rather young for twenty-two, I should imagine. That's still a tender age." Daffyd could've wished for some of Amalda's empathic strength but he was getting through to Vaden's basic reasonableness. "And she has become emotionally involved with you . . . No offense, please, Mr. Vaden. From a rather humdrum frustrating existence, she has erupted onto the stage, into prominence . . . Even a mature personality could be dazzled. Then she is thrown into a highly charged situation—the concert at the Fact—it was unnerving for me as an observer, and I'm well in command of my emotional responses. She is frightened and runs! For which I don't blame her at all. In short, Amalda has been operating on high for some time. We are still frail masters of our powers, Mr. Vaden. And that receiver/broadcaster unit which is Amalda is overcharged.

"No, Mr. Vaden, we can't turn her off. We don't want to. But we can teach her how to channel her Talent, how to discipline it so it won't run away with her as it has just done. We can also show you how to help her put on the brakes. Oh, yes, you can apply what, to all intents and purposes, are circuit breakers. She will need your strength and aggression, Mr. Vaden. In fact, and this is between us, Amalda is not as important as both of you. So I will consider you a team, because that's what you are."

"Then you can help?" asked Vaden. He didn't quite believe op Owen but the aura of belligerent desperation was fading.

"I just said so."

"No," and Vaden shook his head angrily as if he'd thought Daffyd would "know" his exact referents.

"Emotion is as much a tool as a pen or a pneumatic drill . . ."

Vaden stared at him, and then unexpectedly chuckled. "And Amalda's been swinging the drill?"

Inwardly op Owen cheered. Thank God the man had a sense of humor.

"Exactly. Amalda has all the finesse of a tyro. If you had been the focus instead of this rather impressionable and previously frustrated young woman, I think matters might have progressed more circumspectly. As it was . . ."

"I don't think Amalda's going to believe you, op Owen," Vaden said, looking sadly down at the unconscious girl.

"I don't think she'll have any alternative," Daffyd replied severely. Vaden frowned, his eyes narrowing, but op Owen returned the look, adding a mental reinforcement. "She is exhausted from the look of her, which is what happens when you run an engine on full power for any length of time. We'll sedate her sufficiently to let her body and mind rest. And we'll keep her sedated until she begins to realize that she cannot control everything around her with the grip of a tyrant . . . for that seems to be her main fear. Rather commendable, actually."

"And?" Vaden said in a flat, no-argument voice.

"And, in the meantime, you will have to learn how to aid her. You've been more or less passive. Shall we say," and Daffyd smiled slightly as he bowed to Vaden, "you are both engaged for a long-term contract with no options."

The door burst open to admit Jerry Frames, the Center's physician and Sally Iselin, who glared her way back into the office. Daffyd smiled as he stepped aside to let them through to Amalda.

"What took you so long?" he asked Sally.

"What d'you think I am? A lousy pop Talent?"

"She's able to cover completely now, Daffyd," Sally said with understandable pride.

They were watching through the one-way mirror as Amalda fed Harold Orley. The witless empath was neatly eating, with appetite, and often a small smile of pleasure on his child-like features.

"Never thought we'd use Harold as an instructor," said op Owen. Sally grinned at him, her eyes sparkling. "Harold's a useful old tool."

Daffyd thought fleetingly of Solange Boshe.

"Don't, Dai!" Sally's one word was reinforced by her mental command behind which Daffyd sensed sympathy, pity and, oddly enough, annoyance.

"She's off all tranks now?" he asked, grateful to her.

"Heavens yes. She's got to concentrate on Harold, you know."

"Then let's start them moving about outside."

"I would if I were you. The Red Bear's about to go stir crazy."

"Red Bear?"

Sally wrinkled her nose. "That's what I call Vaden."

"Then Amalda's Goldilocks?"

"Good heavens, no. She's Cinderella, remember?"

"Cinderella and the One Bear?"

"Cinderella, the One Bear and . . . the Wolf!"

Daffyd frowned. "I thought I was a better therapist than that."

"Oh, it's just a back-of-the-mind worry. She's not going to trust herself until she does meet and vanquish the Wolf. And then we can all live happily ever after."

There was a tinge of bitterness in Sally's bright voice that made Daffyd look at her closely. He was tempted to probe but that wasn't ethical, particularly since Sally would be instantly aware of the intrusion. So he observed Amalda for a few more moments before leaving the Clinic.

In the month Amalda had been at the Center, the over-thin, intense girl-child had been replaced by a still slender but composed young woman. Her fears had slowly been eased by Daffyd's adroit therapy and by her own ability to discipline her emotions, to channel the vital energies deftly.

The first sessions with Harold Orley had been conducted with Amalda fairly well sedated. The girl had been revolted by Harold's witlessness. There could have been no clearer mirror for her reaction. Pity for the moronic empath had been quickly suppressed because Harold would disconcertingly burst into tears. At first Amalda had rebelled at being forced to work with Harold but she could not refute the fact that he would react instantly to her emotions and until she could control them in his presence, she couldn't expect to be able to control them sufficiently in public.

In the first days at the Center, she had also demanded, even under heavy sedation, to be lobotomized: an operation which Amalda erroneously supposed would suppress her gratuitous Talent. Then she met Harold and realized that the psionic portion of her brain would not be excised by such an operation. Step Two in Amalda's rehabilitation was her introduction to the Center's star young Talent, two-year old Dorotea Horvath. It didn't take Amalda long to recognize the lesson which was thus demonstrated to her.

Small Dorotea was playing contentedly with six-sided blocks. When they tumbled, her fury exploded . . . to be checked, unconsciously but firmly, by her mother. The young telepath's thoughts were so loud and clear that Amalda couldn't fail to recognize the analogy.

"So I discovered a bright new toy in my mind and it won't play with me, is that it?"

"You have to learn to balance the toy just as Dorotea does . . ." Daffyd said gently.

"So they won't all fall down and go boom?"

"With you underneath," added Sally. "Like the night at the Fact."

Despite sedation, Amalda paled and shuddered.

"He can't find me, can he?"

"Not here, behind shielded walls, my dear," Daffyd reassured her.

Once Amalda could control her emotions, Vaden began to take part in the exercises. It was during these sessions that the phenomenon of the second Fact concert was harnessed. Amalda, with Red, could dominate the emotional atmosphere of any large room, could project, even to the minds of sensitives, any emotion she chose. But the force that Daffyd and Sally had felt at the Fact was absent.

"The team right now is limited," Daffyd said to Sally, somewhat ruefully.

"Limited?" Sally was surprised.

"Yes. As long as there are no dark emotions being counter-broadcast, she can project what she wants of the lighter ones. But I was rather hoping that she and Vaden would be strong enough together to counteract . . ."

"An incipient riot?"

"Yes," and Daffyd leaned forward eagerly. "That would placate Frank Gillings and wipe out that RP he's still got against her. And think what it would mean in riot control techniques: two people instead of twenty sensitives, if we have 'em available when we need 'em, or instead of the gas."

"Well, so that's what you've had in mind."

"As it is, I think we'll let them operate as a team in those gatherings that tend to develop brawls: conventions, fairs, industrial shows."

"And what about the Wolf?"

"Ah, yes, but you see, I want him to come out of the woods.

"And Amalda?" Sally "sounded" furious with him.

"Which would you wager on? A Wolf or a Bear?"

Daffyd op Owen was by no means as callous of Amalda's safety as Sally might think, for he'd circulated

a warning to all sensitives for any inquiry about Amalda
or Bruce Vaden and any unusual activity on Roznine's
part. Ted Lewis, the chief police Talent, gave them their
first hint of interest. A well-known and respected Performer's Agent who just happened to be Polish, asked
for assistance from Central Casting to find a missing PA,
Bruce 'Red' Vaden who was reportedly employed but
who had obviously not appeared with any working company.

"Now that could be legit," Ted Lewis told Daffyd.
"The guy really is forming up a variety show for the
Borscht circuit but for that he doesn't need a stage
director with Vaden's rating."

"What about an unamplified folk singer?"

Ted Lewis shook his head. "Now Roznine may have
found out that Amalda is Vaden's bird but it's also fairly
common knowledge that Gillings is still after the folk-
singer who started the riot at the Fact. Stupid Roznine
isn't. Devious, yes."

It suited Daffyd that Gillings had not yet dropped that
charge, for while Amalda was recovering herself and
learning to control her abilities, the charge would provide
her with a certain protection.

What did puzzle Daffyd was what Roznine intended
doing with Amalda if, as, and when, he got possession
of her. To be sure, the public was informed, in broad
terms, about the capabilities of the Talented but nothing
had ever been released about the more bizarre possibilities of psionic powers. Certainly nothing related to
Amalda's ability for the very good reason that until
Amalda had met Bruce Vaden, such a Talent couldn't
even have been conjectured as possible. Therefore, what
could Roznine's active imagination have suggested to
him? Did he realize that he, Roznine, was Talented? Since
he had domination over his ethnic group, did he plan to
dominate the entire City through Amalda?

"Vsevolod Roznine is no man's fool, boss," Ted Lewis
was saying to Daffyd's further agitation. "He's got every

single employment and patronage plum available for his Slavs. Oh, all very legal; a bit dicey if you're looking at it from some other ethnic corner, but legal. And he's fast moving out of his own bailiwick. He's been getting cooperation where no Pan-Slav has ever got it before. How, why, what he does, we don't know. He may use a common garden variety of blackmail or he may even have a genuine Talent. Though Gillings'll flip if he's got to deal with a Talented ethnic leader!"

"There could be worse things," Daffyd said, though obviously Ted Lewis wouldn't agree. "Have you got the LEO precogs sensitive to both Roznine and Amalda?"

Ted Lewis shot his superior a disgusted look. "They're all sleeping on papered pillows."

"And?"

"Boss, you know you can't force a valid precog."

"No Incidents at all?"

"Nary a one. Only vague feelings of uneasiness." He was evidently repeating a frequent reply, which satisfied him no more than it did Daffyd.

"Keep an open mind on Roznine. And don't let Gillings know we suspect Roznine is Talented. I'm going to start using Amalda and Vaden as a team. Sooner or later Roznine will discover her again."

"You want that?"

"Very much." And in Daffyd's mind, as he left Ted Lewis, was the memory of Solange Boshe's wild demented face before she teleported through a steel door in the parking building.

Gillings was delighted to use Amalda and Bruce Vaden as riot prevention. He even offered to take the charge off the books but Daffyd suggested that it remain a while longer. The team was instantly assigned to a round of rallies, meetings, conferences, and conventions. Such gatherings were encouraged to divert a population with too much unoccupied time but any one of them might explode into a riot, given the proper stimuli. Decibel alarms were legally required in every meeting hall, including churches, but clever agitators could and had sabotaged them so that the suppressant gases were not released when the "noise" level reached the sharp pitch of incipient riot. The professional agitators had also learned how to modulate their voices below the danger level, carefully goading their victims into the spontaneous combustion which neither gas nor water jets could control. And which no precog could be expected to accurately predict until too late for effective action.

Fortuitously, as Amalda learned to control herself, she learned to read Harold with an accuracy and perception that surpassed Sally's. Harold could serve with the team, Daffyd decided, as a gauge for the general atmosphere of a group and as, in an emergency, a body guard for Amalda. (You learned things, even from disasters, Daffyd told himself positively.) Partnered with the empath, Amalda would sit in the center of an audience or circulate through a crowd. Vaden would be on the periphery, ready to "broadcast" if it became necessary. They could also be expected to keep up a running projection of whatever aura the LEO authorities or the sponsors of the occasion requested, if this were not a commercial affair. Subliminal pressures for mercantile purposes were, of course, an illegal and unethical use of Talent.

The team was extraordinarily successful in unexpected ways. The Motorboat show had the lowest incidence of petty pilfering in its history: the Home Show reported no lost children and a remarkably quiet, well-behaved quota of siblings following their parents through the exhibits. Two conventions, noted for the inebriation of their members, had their damage deposits reduced as a result of genial but undestructive behavior.

And Amalda began to gain confidence to the point where Sally remarked that even Bruce Vaden had been seen to smile occasionally.

I was surely right about the menu today, Amalda thought as the waiter plunked down the mock chicken, lumpy reconstituted potatoes and shrivelled snap beans. *Oh, well, all part of Life's Rich Pageant,* she added and started broadcasting recklessly intense delicious taste feelings. Harold began to beam beside her, attacking his food with relish.

She glanced casually around at her table mates, as pompous a crew of convention goers as she'd ever seen and she was now an authority. (Did they always use the same "masks" at conventions? Or could it be the same group of people as the Plastic Container Manufacturers last week, and the Fabric Finishers Association on Tuesday-week?) They responded to her prompting as rapidly as Harold, all grunting with pleasure as they ate their cardboard food. Amalda sighed. Too bad she and Bruce couldn't get a kick-back from the catering staff for "improving" their food beyond the call of duty.

Now there I go again, she thought, *but it does seem that the Talented were letting an awful good thing go the way of Duty and Honor.*

She was rather pleased with her broadcasting today. She had begun to bother with such fine points in their assignments, more to amuse herself at first—like stopping all those kids from whining at the Boat Fair. But it had sounded like home, all her brothers and sisters whining at once, before they'd tied Ma off. If she never heard another child whine it would be soon enough. And making food at least "seem" tasty was in defense of her poor abused digestion. According to specifications, all the nutrients and vitamins were in the food and would be absorbed by her system. But she'd come to prefer "tasting" things. It made these convention luncheons bearable. What a way to earn a living!

And yet, Amalda reluctantly admitted, she didn't dislike it. If only . . . She wouldn't think about that. It'd ruin her appetite. After all, now she'd got the hang of this trick mind of hers, she could make whole bunches of people feel what she wanted them to. When the time came, she could control *him*, too. Bruce was never far from her. She smiled, the warmth of his infinite love a presence to counteract any nibble of fear. Sometimes when Bruce made love to her, she wanted to embrace the whole world with its beauty, but that sort of broadcasting wasn't even moral: that was private between her and Bruce and . . . *He'd* thought things at her that night . . . Things she didn't even dare to think about . . .

Harold was getting restless. She curbed her reminiscences.

And then, the jab. So sharp she gasped, so hard it was physical yet the prod was in her mind . . . and all too familiar. *He* was here.

Harold whimpered, empathizing with her. She hastily damped down her shock of fearful surprise. *He* was as abruptly gone from her mind. She shivered, unable to suppress the lingering sense of revulsion that that recognition touch evoked in her. She overcame the feeling, smiling inanely around at her table mates. She patted Harold soothingly on the arm. He grinned, restored to equilibrium. Good, she must keep this to herself.

But she couldn't keep from glancing around for Bruce: he was at table 4, near the dignitaries. He glanced up, nodded at her, and was then required to make some answer to his partner, a female who simpered up at him.

Sometimes, Amalda thought, *Red has the harder role to play.*

Part of her mind wanted to search for *him*, but her strongest desire was never to be touched by *him* again, ever. She scanned the room now, certain she'd be able to locate his evil self. She'd certainly studied his IDs long enough to spot him physically anywhere. Waiters were coming and going from the kitchens. He wasn't one of them. He wouldn't be one of the conventioneers. She'd've identified him long before now. She opened her mind, making it, as Dave had suggested, like the lens of a

camera, slowly widening. She didn't really want to: too
much of an appalling and revolting nature seeped in.
She wondered how Dave, who was a full telepath and
"heard" actual thoughts, not just emotions as she did,
could bear it. She wondered how much he had "conditioned" her mind to accept her Talent. She knew he had:
he'd told her so. She didn't mind . . . probably Dave
had done that, too. But he was so kind. Now if only
he'd . . .

No, she told herself sternly, *these thoughts you may
not have. Sally loves Daffyd op Owen.* She grimaced.
*For a perceptive Talent, Dave could be awfully dense.
For the Lord's sake, you didn't even have to be a
telepath to see Sally Iselin was madly in love with him.
Or maybe Dave knew and couldn't do anything about it?
Couldn't someone condition Dave? Hmmm. Maybe I'll
get to work on it. No,* and Amalda gave her head a
little regretful shake, *that would be tampering and that's
not ethical.*

She sighed. Being a Talent imposed certain rules and
regulations which absolutely couldn't be broken. In the
first place, you got found out too fast. Not much of a
bridle on that winged horse Dave's always talking about
but it kept you from falling off . . . morally . . .

The waiter was bending over her. Amalda leaned toward Harold to permit the waiter to remove her plate.
Instead he mumbled something.

"I'm sorry. I didn't hear you," she said, smiling up at
him.

He gave her a stare and said something in the same
unintelligible mumble. She could, however, sense his urgency. He had something she must do?

"I'm really very sorry, but would you repeat your
question?" She gestured at the chattering diners by way
of explanation.

The little man looked angry. In a clear voice, he
asked the waiter at the next table to join him.

"I ask her a simple question and she gives me this

so-sorry routine," he said. But he was incensed about something. And his urgency intensified.

"Really, there's so much noise," Amalda said.

The second waiter, a burly man, gave her a fierce scowl.

"What's your problem, miss? You got delusions? Ain't you conventioneers satisfied with nothing? Do like he says and there'll be no trouble."

"I certainly don't want to cause trouble." And Amalda began to broadcast soothing thoughts.

Suddenly a third man was pulling her chair from under her and the first two had her by the arms.

"You just come with us, miss. You just come with us."

They were scared: they were prompted by an urgency which was unnatural and artificially induced. *He* had instigated their actions.

She got Harold to his feet. The poor witless fool was momentarily as confused as she was. She felt Bruce reacting. But she was being physically manhandled away from the table by the two waiters. If they did get her out of the hall—it wasn't that far to the kitchen entrance —Amalda tried to keep from panicking. The next thing she knew Harold reached out and grabbed the waiters by the shoulders, had torn their hands from her arms, and banged their heads together.

Then Bruce and two officials closed in on the knot of people and somehow the unconscious waiters were being whisked from the banquet hall.

"Calm 'em, Mally," Bruce hissed at her and she began to pour out such sweetness and light that everyone at her table stopped eating to beam at each other. She modified the broadcast, got Harold and herself reseated. She even managed to keep her trembling reaction inward so that none of it boiled over to erase the idiotic smile from Harold Orley's face.

By the time the luncheon ended, however, the effort began to tell on her and was reflected in Harold's nervousness. She felt physically drained. What if *he* had been able

to get her away before Harold could react? Before
Bruce, on the other side of the hall, had been able to
get to her? Supposing *he* had . . .

Bruce was at her side, his face set and determined.
She knew that look. But now she was afraid of leaving
the semi-protection of so many people. If he had actually
tried to kidnap her in the middle of a convention . . .

A plainclothes LEO man was bearing down on them.
She rose, smiling brightly. Harold twitched his hulk to
his feet, but his brow was clouding with childlike anxiety.

Disgust at her spinelessness buoyed Amalda's weaken-
ing knees. The instant Red put his arm around her protect-
ingly, she almost crawled into him.

"Let's get her out of here," Red said and gestured the
LEO man to lead Harold.

"Come this way," the LEO man said, gesturing to the
draperies at the side of the huge banquet hall. A door in
the paneling gave onto a small anteroom. "The Waiters
Union is screaming over those busted skulls. We got to
get you out of here quietly. What'n'hell did happen,
Amalda?"

"I don't quite know," she murmured, aware that exhaustion was overcoming mental resolve. "Is it all right
to leave?" She looked back over her shoulder at the
diners dispersing slowly.

"The hell with them," Bruce said in a savage voice.

"I'm so sorry. So sorry." Amalda had a sense of failure.
The first time she came up against *him* she had fallen
apart. She wanted to cry. She was a failure. After all
Daffyd and the others had done to help her . . . to swoon
like any vapid female . . .

"*I'll get you. I'll get you the next time.*" The voice
was as loud in her ears as Bruce's exclamation.

"*Bruce . . .*"

Charlie Moorfield came through Daffyd's door without bothering to knock.

"They did it," he cried, halting his forward momentum just short of gouging his thighs on the desk edge.

Daffyd picked up the images so vivid in Charlie's mind, and despite the fact that he could also perceive that the emergency was over, he sprang to his feet.

"Who did what?" demanded Sally, excitedly. She wasn't accurate enough to 'path the sequence.

"They tried to snatch Amalda at the Morcam Convention luncheon," Daffyd told her.

"Only she got Harold to bash their skulls in."

Sally gasped.

"Gillings said the attempt and the arrest were handled so quickly that no one at the table with Amalda and Harold knew what happened," Charlie went on. "Waiters Union is screaming over the quote unwarranted unquote arrest of three members. There's hell to pay."

"Not necessarily," said Lester but he was glowering as he walked into the room and carefully closed the door behind him. "This is a clear case of professional immunity."

"How do you construe that?" Daffyd asked.

Lester sighed as he regarded his boss with a tolerant expression.

"Amalda is a registered Talent, right? She was present at the Luncheon in a professional capacity. Therefore no one, not anybody, has the right to interfere. The waiters did, by trying to remove her from the hall. They broke the law. Amalda hasn't. Neither has Harold. Even if he was a little overzealous, he is now protected from the consequences of his Talent."

"Wait a minute, Lester," Charlie said, "that Immunity Law only means that you can't get sued when . . ."

"It also means," and Lester waggled a bony finger at Charlie and Daffyd in turn, "according to the way Senator Joel Andres and our legal eagles interpreted it to *me,* that any citizen attempting to interfere with a registered Talent's performance of his duty is violating that law."

"This would be the first time we've had to invoke the law," Daffyd said.

Lester raised his eyebrows in surprised alarm. "So what's wrong with that? Or did you break your . . ." he glanced abruptly at Sally who stifled her laugh . . . "your bones arranging protection *not* to use it?"

Op Owen made a cut-off gesture with one hand. Lester Welch muttered in disgust.

"I thought by this time you'd've learned the cost of idealism, Dave. We sweated out that Bill: it damned near cost us Joel Andres's life; we have a clear case of an infraction and by God's little chickens, you're going to invoke it. If Gillings hasn't already."

The comset on Daffyd's desk lit up, flashing red. He pushed the toggle down.

"Commissioner Gillings, sir, urgently."

Daffyd nodded acceptance.

"Op Owen, we're getting a lot of static from the Waiters Union, about Amalda, false arrest and all that crap," Gillings stated with no preamble. "So far I've played it that their member was pushing a lust act and got told to bug off: that the lady-in-question is sufficiently upset to invoke female citizen's rights. Then we got the honest-employees, good union men with clean sex records and she's a pervert-after-the-damages claim." Gillings sighed with heavy disgust. "You know, the usual convention static. Now, we can clear all this up by invoking the Professional Immunity Act but . . ." and Gillings waggled a thick finger at Daffyd. "I'm not all that eager to break the team's cover. Bruce Vaden told my men that something had scared Amalda and the only thing I know she's scared about is what happened at the Fact. Was there a repeat at the Morcam?"

"I haven't talked to Amalda yet, Frank," Daffyd said. "I assume she's on her way back here with Vaden?" Gillings nodded. "Give me a little time."

"Don't take too much. That Waiters Union packs quite a wallop."

As soon as the Commissioner's face had faded from the screen, Daffyd asked for Ted Lewis in the LEO Block.

"Ted, you heard about the snatch attempt on Amalda?"

"It's all over the place. Say, why don't you just invoke the Immunity Act . . . No?" Ted was as perplexed as Lester.

"Is Roznine involved in any way in the Waiters Union?"

"Hell yes. There isn't one Union he isn't involved with right now."

"Any chance of finding out if he was at the Morcam Convention Hotel this afternoon?"

Ted Lewis held up a hand, flicked on another switch, his words and the reply indistinct, being off the receiver limit of the comscreen. He looked more confused.

"We've had Croner sort of keeping him under the eye/ear. Croner says he's at a TRI-D on Market and Hall. Huh, how's that, Croner? Hey, boss, Roznine has been watching a lot of TRI-D lately."

"Then he suspects he's been under surveillance and is ducking out the other exit of the TRI-D. Fine." This was an unsettling development because it could mean that Roznine was developing as a Talent. If he got pushed too hard. . . . op Owen shuddered. "Let's go see Amalda."

"It was *him*," Amalda told Daffyd. She looked white, shaken and small as she huddled against Red Vaden on the couch in the living room of their suite.

"How close to you?"

She shook her head. "He wasn't in the room. I'd've seen him. But he was near enough to recognize me. My mind, I mean." She gave a delicate shudder. Had he recognized her because she'd been thinking those thoughts about him? She wanted to ask Daffyd but she didn't dare. She'd let him down enough already.

"Were you aware of anything, Red?" Daffyd asked.

"Not at first. Then only Amalda's surprise. I looked up and saw the waiters grabbing her. But before I could get across the room, Harold had acted." There was admiration on Vaden's face for the maneuver. "I should apologize to the guy. I think we got things quieted down before any of the convention crowd got wise."

"After the attempt, were you aware of Roznine's mind, Amalda?"

"Not until we were leaving the hall." She closed her eyes. "He said 'I'll get you. The next time I'll get you.'"

Daffyd looked questioningly at Red who shook his head.

Had you ever received words before, Amalda? Daffyd asked.

Amalda looked at him startled and then shook her head, smiling shyly. "Only from you. Before now." She was aware of his concern. "That's bad, ain't it?" she asked, her soft southern inflection intensifying her regret.

"Not necessarily. We have a problem," he began, choosing his words carefully. "We know that Roznine would like to . . . get you, Amalda, to accomplish his own ends which, knowing your capability, must be illegal control of men's emotions. We have to assume he's been trying to locate you. We must also assume that he may not realize that Bruce is part of your ability. And that's a link that can and will protect you, Amalda." Daffyd reinforced that notion with a stern telepathic voice. "Roznine couldn't succeed in kidnapping you today, could he? Well, he damned well won't be able to anywhere else either."

"You can't be sure of that, Daffyd," she said in a very small scared voice.

"I don't intend to put it to the test, Amalda," Daffyd continued smoothly, smiling at the apprehensive girl, "but kindly remember that you have successfully eluded him twice now. Once by running away and hiding—successfully. And today by direct action against his agents."

Amalda slowly nodded her head in agreement.

"Now, while Roznine is keen to get his hands on you, we . . . and I include the Commissioner . . . are very anxious to get Roznine."

It was Bruce Vaden who stiffened and looked with an intensity close to hatred at Daffyd op Owen. The telepath returned that look calmly, knowing in that exchange that Vaden understood the implication even if Amalda didn't.

"Roznine is obviously a latent Talent. We know he fits minds with Amalda. We don't know what else he can do, and he is in a peculiarly sensitive position in the ethnic situation of this city: in a position to do a lot of damage or a lot of good. We can't push him too far and we can't let him go. We do want him, preferably on his own initiative as you did, to come to the Center. You know what it's like to have an unmanageable Talent . . ."

Daffyd was speaking more to Bruce Vaden than Amalda but it was the girl who answered.

"It's awful . . . awful lonely, awful wonderful." She gave Daffyd a smile, tremulous, and though she held her chin up in an attitude of confidence, he could see the indecision and fear of her mind.

"Now," he went on briskly, "in using the Waiters Union to snag you, Roznine has put us in a difficult position: we can easily use the Professional Immunity Act to protect you but that would necessitate your appearance in court. And believe me, everyone interested in our cover agents would be there to identify you. Your team usefulness would decrease . . ."

"Does *Amalda* have to appear in court?" asked Red suddenly.

"Well, yes. Oh, I see what you mean," and Daffyd started to grin. He managed to keep his smile normal despite what he had read in Bruce Vaden's mind under the cover of the constructive suggestion. "Very good point. Two ways. Yes, I suppose we could make Amalda up to look different . . . or we could have a stand-in for her. In that case, Amalda would have to be physically present because Roznine would be there and he'd know if she weren't present, which could score against us if an EEG reading is requested by the prosecution. Hmmm. Good notion."

"What can Roznine hope to achieve by forcing us into court?" asked Red. He was trying to cover his earlier thoughts before they became apparent to Daffyd. Present now was a thread of hopelessness, a presentiment that the intense happiness and rapport that Bruce Vaden had enjoyed with Amalda was to be sundered: too good to last. Daffyd could only answer the spoken question.

"Now that has me stumped," he said, and meant it on several levels.

"Stand-in?" Gillings appeared to reject the stratagem instantly and just as abruptly, he frowned thoughtfully. "Why? You don't think anyone would be crazy enough to try and snatch Amalda in court, do you? Although . . ." he glanced over at the windows, "the atmosphere is damned unstable . . ."

"I know," Daffyd agreed. Even during the short copter flight to the LEO Block, he'd been aware of the pervasive "darkness" of the city's emotional aura. The weather had been miserable, which didn't help; general employment was down; there'd been the usual complaints about the subsistence-level foods; gripes about the TRI-D programming; nothing out of the ordinary . . . yet. There might indeed be the makings of a major blow-up.

It would take two weeks for an improvement in the food to have a perceptible effect: TRI-D programming was undoubtedly being altered but even the most perceptive Talents could be fooled over what the public really wanted on the boob tubes. The variety of "circuses" available was almost as infinite as food-tastes and yet one never knew precisely what would satiate the public appetite. Op Owen made a mental note to check all precog rumblings. Strange there hadn't been any definite Incident by anyone when such a large population unit was involved.

"Look, op Owen," Gillings was saying, "I've got to have the team available for riot spotting. Particularly right now. And I can't have them identifiable."

"Then we send Amalda to the hearing made-up."

Gillings muttered under his breath about fancy dress and sow's ears and then suddenly swung round to fix op Owen with a startled glare. Daffyd hadn't expected to keep Gillings in the dark long.

"Okay, op Owen, what's behind all this pussy-footing? Who was trying to snatch Amalda at the Morcam Luncheon? Was it the same guy who was at the Fact? Because if it was, let's get him and cool him. I need that team operating. And there's that open charge of riot provocation . . ."

Op Owen took a deep breath. "I don't think it would be advisable to cool Roznine."

"*Roznine?*" Gillings exploded from his chair with all the frustrated astonished exasperated impotence of the strong man suddenly discovering himself in an untenable position. "Roznine! Christ, op Owen, do you know what would happen to this city, in the present mood, if I arrested the Pan-Slavic leader?" He fumed on, in much the same vein, for moments more until either Daffyd's placatory thoughts or his own lack of breath brought a stop to the flow of recriminations.

"I haven't suggested you arrest Roznine. In fact, that would not only be impolitic but dangerous."

Gillings glared at him, snapping out one short explosive word. "How?"

"Because Roznine is a latent Talent. That's what scared Amalda."

Gillings erupted again, thoroughly enraged. This time the shield of his public mind slipped sufficiently for Daffyd to see past the anger to the panic his confession evoked.

"*No!*" Daffyd's negative, forcible mental as well as audible, carried weight on every level and blocked those avenues of action which he could perceive Gillings already plotting. "Roznine is contained . . . at the moment. But—this time we don't force a latent into a position where he can become dangerous to an entire city. I want to avoid another Maggie O far, far more than you do!"

Gillings had no escape from Daffyd's mind, so op Owen did not relent in the pressure until he was certain of Gillings's uneasy and resentful cooperation.

"Roznine is no threat to us . . . yet. But he does threaten Amalda," Daffyd went on. "That threat is real. It would be stupid," and he paused to let that word be absorbed, for Gillings was not a stupid man, "to get Roznine so frustrated that additional facets of his Talent —whatever it is—are stimulated."

Gillings's face was a study of frustration. He gave vent to a stream of profanity which so delighted and enlightened op Owen that he could ignore the fact that he was the victim of the spiel. But, with the avalanche, Gillings recovered his mental equilibrium.

"I told you a couple of months ago that what you guys really need is a law that makes it illegal to conceal Talent."

Daffyd laughed wryly. "Roznine may be unaware that what he uses is Talent!"

"Unaware? My effing foot. With all the publicity you guys have been larding the TRI-Ds with, he's got to know what he is—especially if he's been playing mental patty-cakes with that Amalda. Op Owen, I don't need a Roznine in this city! You Talents put him where he belongs and bridle him or lobotomize him or something. Or I'll invoke whatever law on the books suits me and cool him permanently. I can't have this city turned into a battlefield. Or have you forgotten Belfast?"

His buzzer winked the urgent red. Gillings raised one fist as if to squash the unit and then, swearing viciously, slapped the toggle open.

"Well?"

There was a moment's hesitation. Daffyd could almost

see the caller swallowing hastily, probably wishing he didn't have to continue.

"Commissioner, the lawyers for the WU are here with bail for their members. Do we release them?"

"I want to scan them," Daffyd said in a swift undertone.

"Delay 'em. Someone's on the way down from this office. Then permit bail."

Gillings tossed an oddly designed coat button to op Owen.

"This'll get you anywhere in the building. And keep it."

Daffyd thanked the Commissioner, and left. Prowling the LEO offices would not be a frequent pastime: the "neural" noise level was more than a telepath of Daffyd's sensitivity could bear.

The Waiters Union had sent a battery of lawyers to procure the release of their incarcerated members. They had been shown into a waiting room, just off the main admissions hall of the retention section of the LEO Complex.

Daffyd sauntered by, scanning each man's mind quickly. What he "heard" he didn't like, but it confirmed the fact that Roznine was organizing the proceedings. None of these men knew more than his own assignment. But each was moved by an intense desire to complete it expeditiously and successfully or . . . The "or else" held dark, dire and fearful consequences.

Daffyd returned as quickly as possible to the shielded calm of Gillings's private eyrie. The Commissioner was absent. Daffyd used the few moments' respite for some solid thinking.

There were times, he finally concluded, when a man had to operate on the "feel" of things alone. He was not, God forfend, a precog, but there were also times when a man simply had to dispense with rational thought and its consequences. Particularly when faced by a free agent

like Roznine who could not be expected to have predictable responses to stimuli and pressures.

The similarities between Roznine and Maggie O were
inescapable, but this time Daffyd had a tool and a resolve.

"We've been fighting fire with old-fashioned water,
Frank," he said to the Commissioner when the man
stalked back into his office. "From now on we use modern
methods, foam and tranquilizers."

"What are you jibbering about?"

"I can't explain, but will you trust me?"

Gillings glared back at him, but his tight natural
shield leaked conflicting emotions of desire-to-believe,
distrust, and irritable frustration.

"I goddamn well have to, don't I? But, goddamn it,
Dave, if you Talents don't contain Roznine . . ."

"*We* can," and Daffyd op Owen began to grin with
utter malice for the underhanded, immoral, unethical use
of Talent he was about to invoke. Lester wouldn't ap-
prove either, but then, he didn't plan to tell Lester Welch.

The stratagem did require the invocation of the Immunity Act. What Daffyd didn't count on was the hue
and cry when the news of the hearing was announced
on the media. Suddenly Aaron Greenfield vociferously
supported the Waiters' Union in their outraged cry against
Talent abusing unTalented people and hiding behind
the law. The Morcam Convention Committee tried to
evade any responsibility by claiming that they had not
hired a Talent team for their Luncheon . . . their defense
being that *their* convention members were law-abiding
peaceful people with no record of violence, so a LEO
team was unnecessary and an insult to their good name,
etc. Greenfield made political hay of this as well. He'd
never been in support of the Immunity Law because
"obviously it was a screen for illegal, immoral, unethical
invasion of privacy: one more instance of establish-
mentarianism and totally unwarranted minority privilege."
"Repeal the Immunity Act; no extraordinary privilege

defendant and counsel but that was Amalda's cue and she, and her escort, made their entrance.

There was, of course, the anticipated cry of protest from the prosecuting attorneys. The defendant arrived garbed in voluminous robes, bewigged and made up *à la japonaise,* escorted by two women exactly the same to the last hair and measurement. Even as the prosecution leapt to its collective feet, the three figures shifted in a complicated pattern, making it impossible for any un-Talented person to know which one was which.

However, as this was a preliminary hearing, necessarily conducted in front of the legal computer, the "hearing" judge had no directives about the dress or escort of the defendants and/or attorneys so long as they appeared clad and reasonably clean. Prosecution replied that the defendant was deliberately obstructing justice by appearing with look-alike escorts. One of the Amaldas rose, presented two sets of credentials as legal counselors for the defendant and asked the "hearing judge" if it was programmed to refuse defendant's counsel on the basis of similarity in shape and appearance to defendant. The objection was overruled.

Prosecution instantly demanded EEG readings to prove that the women so attired were in fact the aforesaid attorneys and the defendant.

Defense had no objection and EEG readings were promptly taken, establishing beyond controversy who were the attorneys and who the defendant. At which point, the three women repeated their rapid "shell-act." Daffyd op Owen watched furious anger suffuse the faces at the prosecution table, evidence that the ruse was successful. The audience murmured, half in amusement, the other half totally confused by the antics.

The hearing proceeded with the charge being made of illegal arrest and restraint, countered by the defense invoking the Professional Immunity Act, requiring that the complaint against Amalda, Registered Talent, be dropped.

Rather smug, Daffyd missed the first twinge of Amalda's alarm.

"Daffyd," she said, her mind tone anxious, *"he's after me."*

"Make everyone laugh," Daffyd said and so quickly did she react, with such forcefulness, that Daffyd didn't need to call in the reserve empaths to help.

For a moment Daffyd wondered if fear prompted her outrageous strength, for everyone in the audience, himself and the planted Talents, were struck by an epidemic of giggles. It would appear that the audience was attempting to laugh the complaint out of court.

Daffyd suppressed Amalda's projection sufficiently so that he wasn't doubled with uncontrollable mirth. Roznine had a rictus-like grin across his face: he'd leaned back against the wall in an effort to control his body and he was forcing his head to move so he could scan the audience. Daffyd bent over slightly, counterfeiting excessive mirth, and noticed that Red Vaden and the other Talents were doing the same thing.

Grand! Let Roznine think only Amalda was responsible! But could Amalda—even with Red helping—broadcast so strongly? Could she actually use Roznine without his consent? If so . . .

The hearing judge mechanically sounded the gavel and called for order, its voice getting louder and louder as the giggles continued. It ordered the courtroom cleared of "obstructionists." The paroxyms which had afflicted everyone abruptly ceased and people weakly wiped their eyes and ordered their clothing. Aaron Greenfield looked anxiously around, his face flushed with anger. The man was no fool, Daffyd realized. He'd know that Talent had been responsible and, with his prickly dignity offended, he'd redouble his efforts to get the Talented taxed. Oh, well, you couldn't make an omelette without breaking eggs, thought Daffyd philosophically. He nodded approvingly at Amalda who, with her twins, had sneaked a glance at him.

Prosecution then announced possession of a sworn statement from the Morcam Convention Committee that it had requested no LEO surveillance. Defense replied that all convention situations fell under the Riot-Prevention Act and the LEO Commission was quite within its jurisdiction to use such riot prevention techniques as seemed advisable. The uncertain climate of the city was cited to be in the "unsettled" percentile which permitted the LEO Commission to take such precautions as it deemed necessary to ensure law enforcement and order. The defense counsel reminded the "judge" that any gathering of 200 or more persons (and the Morcam Luncheon had had 525 paid and consumed covers) was liable to auxiliary surveillance whether requested or not when the climate of the city registered in the "uneasy" percentiles. Prosecution demanded to know exactly what riot prevention technique was employed by Amalda. Defense responded that she was a registered empath of a +15 sensitivity and a perceptive rating of +12, and offered to produce positive testimonials from organizations which had employed Amalda in her capacity as a Talent for riot prevention. Prosecution repeated its demand for an explicit description of her crowd control technique and defense invoked the provisions of the Law Enforcement and Order Commission.

Daffyd wasn't certain whether the prosecution wanted to separate Amalda from her look-alikes or discover the exact procedure she used.

Defense again requested that the charge be dropped: she didn't wish to waste the Court's time and public money when the evidence clearly pointed to a *nolle prosequi* situation.

Prosecution insisted vehemently that this was a clear case of personal infringement and misuse of privilege just as the time-limit light came on. There was the rumble as the "hearing judge" searched its programming for precedents. That didn't take long. Moments later the date for a trial appeared on the screen: a date seven weeks hence.

Not bad, thought Daffyd, although he'd half wished that the computer would throw the case out. With no precedents, there'd been slim chance of that.

Amalda's fear was like a knife in his own guts. He tried to get through to Roznine, to fathom what the man was doing. Bruce Vaden jumped to his feet, started down the aisle, his progress blocked by others who were beginning to leave the courtroom.

Daffyd had the sense that every Talent in the audience stiffened suddenly and then Roznine, half rising from his seat, stunned amazement on his face, began to topple slowly over onto the people in the row in front of him.

"Hey, this guy's passed out," someone cried. "Is there a medic around?"

Bruce Vaden kept trying to reach Roznine. Daffyd signalled to two other Talents to assist. If they could bring Roznine to the Center this way . . .

"I'm a physician," a woman said in a firm loud voice, three rows away, holding up her emergency pouch. There was a slight scuffle as Bruce tried to intercept her, but suddenly the Pan-Slavs moved, jumping over seats, knocking people aside in an effort to protect their fallen leader.

Daffyd caught Vaden back, called off the others.

The bailiff scurried from the court, yelling for an ambicopter, as the woman medic and three Slavs lifted the stricken man and carried him to the prosecution's table. The "hearing judge" began to call for order, for the next case, for the obstructionists to be removed from the courtroom. Its voice got louder and louder until it finally called a recess until the court could be humanly cleared.

"All right, all right, we've got him under heavy sedation in the Court Block infirmary," Frank Gillings told Daffyd, "but that took doing. The place is crawling with

Pan-Slavs. We can't arrest a man for collapsing in court . . . and how did you do it?"

"One of the teleports gave him a 'punch,'" Daffyd said with a rueful grimace.

Gillings stared at him with awe and respect.

"One has to be very careful," Daffyd explained almost apologetically, "pressing against the carotid. But he was pressuring Amalda."

"You expected that! But I expected you guys to grab him there. And that goddamned hearing is affecting the entire city. Now don't tell me you expected that!"

Daffyd looked at Gillings and, for a micro-second, hesitated.

"No, not exactly, but we're doing our very best."

"What? What in hell do you mean by that?"

"I mean, we've set the trap and baited it and we simply have to have patience."

"Patience? With this city about to erupt?"

"Curiously enough, Gillings, I don't think the city is going to erupt. Oh, we've recorded some Incidents, minor ones, involving Talents . . ." and Daffyd frowned because the Incidents were distressing and so vague that only a general all-Talent warning could be issued.

Gillings gave one of his disgusted growls. "You guys make me sick. You can't even protect yourselves."

"We'll do what we can," and Daffyd's voice turned steely enough to reprimand Gillings. "What concerns you, Commissioner, is the fact that our precogs have predicted no major Incidents. Your city is going to be safe!"

"Prove it!" demanded Gillings but Daffyd op Owen made no reply as he left the Commissioner's office.

It took the telepath the entire trip back to the Center to get control of his inner perturbation. Of course, Gillings had to be ruthless and consider only the larger aspect, the safety of the City, but it galled Daffyd to think that Gillings could so offhandedly dismiss the personal trials of the Talented. It grieved Daffyd that there would be more precedents on the newly-programmed Immunity Law after the next few days. The fact that Talents would now have redress for the precogged personal assaults on them was no satisfaction. He'd really have preferred never to have had to invoke that Law.

It would serve Gillings proper notice if Roznine did burst out of bounds . . . And how in hell were they to promulgate a law that made it illegal to conceal Talent? Latent Talents were always cropping up when the right connections were made . . .

And not a single Incident connected with Amalda or Red or Vsevolod Roznine. And he'd had every precog in the Center sensitized to that unholy trio. How could that possibly be?

Daffyd's state of mind was grim as he landed the copter on the roof of the main administration building of the Center. He tried to drain the poisons of bitterness and anger from his mind as he descended the stairs. He paused at his office door but swung away. He had to calm himself. This excessive reaction was self-defeating. Gillings might be a latent Talent himself but he remained obdurately impervious to the problems of the Talented, especially when they interfered with the law enforcement and order of his precious city.

While Roznine was unconscious in the Court Block infirmary, Daffyd had managed to implant a suggestion that Roznine seek Amalda out at the Center. It was the only feasible practicable method . . . make the mountain come to Mahomet. And the mountain must apparently come of its own volition. Now, if he could just get Mahomet to do a Lorelei . . . it would speed matters up, and maybe so many Talents wouldn't get hurt.

That brought Daffyd back to the point of anger he'd reached in Gillings's office and the whole thought sequence started again.

His path led him past the play-yard where he could hear the children yelling and screaming, arguing over some violently important triviality. Triviality? To him, perhaps, yet they were as devoted to their separate sides of the argument as he was to . . .

"Well?" Sally Iselin stood in his way, her fists planted on her hips, a mock-ferocious expression on her pert pretty face. "Aren't you pleased with the outcome of the hearing?" She frowned, sensing his uncertainty. "But you were able to plant a suggestion in Roznine's mind? Oh, that Gillings. What is it about a cop that sours the man?"

It was Daffyd's turn to be surprised. "That's pretty good reading, Sally."

As suddenly he felt her mind tighten and the contact that had begun to lift his depression was taken away.

"What does Gillings expect of us anyway?" she asked.

"A happy ending!"

Sally eyed him speculatively and then fell in step with him, grinning.

"There has to be a happy ending to every fairy tale, after all. Though I shouldn't have expected it of Gillings, fer gawd's sake."

Her switch of mood, while it obscured her thoughts from him, lifted his spirits. Nonetheless, he said rather gloomily that there hadn't been a precog of any happy ending for Cinderella.

"Oh, you . . . honestly!" Sally sounded peeved and her eyes flashed at him irritably. "Your trouble, Daffyd op Owen, is that you don't really believe in Talent."

"I beg your pardon?" Daffyd stopped and stared down at her.

"Just because no one has precogged a disaster of some monumental proportion resulting from this fairy tale affair, you're down in the doldrums. Does everything Talented *have* to end in disaster? Are you going to be committed to grief for the rest of your born days? Or are you willing to admit that there hasn't been a disaster precog because there isn't going to be a disaster? That things will work out right? All the sensitives are edgy, but *not* miserably so. Good God, do we have to wallow in sorrow all the time? Do we have to run around wondering if we have a right to be happy?"

Daffyd thought he knew Sally Iselin fairly well but this—from a girl characteristically full of puppyish good-nature and exuberance?

She turned on him, her brown eyes flashing with anger as she stamped her foot. "And I am not a good-natured puppy! I can be just as much of a bitch as any other woman!"

In that outraged mood, she forgot to shield her inner thoughts. It was all there, what propriety had kept Daffyd from "perceiving" and her sense of honor had prevented her from showing him more openly.

Abruptly Daffyd reached out and drew her into his arms, savoring the miraculous disclosure. Unaccountably Sally struggled, and courtesy disregarded, Daffyd probed deeply into her mind, past the barriers she had carefully erected, past the pert verbosity with which she masked those inner feelings. With a strangled sob, she relaxed against him and let him perceive the whole of her conflict. The older man/much younger woman, her yearning to be tall/elegant, an appropriate spouse for a man of his status/abilities, the puppy image of herself from his mind, her feeling of inadequacy because she couldn't locate more and more Talents to relieve the burdens on him . . . all the small sins and great vanities that inhabit the soul of any human being. And what he saw in that instant of perception only endeared her to him more.

With one hand he tilted her head back, forcing her to meet his eyes, amused that a telepath required a look. Her mouth lifted slightly in a smile as she shared his thought. He felt a pressing need to articulate the thoughts he was transferring to her mind but all he could say was her name before he kissed her. No more was needed.

The next morning the nebulous anxieties of the sensitives were translated into attacks on the Talented. One of the finders attached to the LEO Block was beaten up on his way to the Center. A Talent mechanic at the big Mid-Town Parking Complex was seriously mauled and shoved into the boot of the car he'd been servicing. Two healers in the General Hospital were raped and shorn of their hair but their assailants were caught because the girls had the ability to "call" for help.

In the clear light of that morning, Daffyd bitterly wondered if indeed he had a right to any personal happiness.

"And if that isn't a piece of outright antediluvian puritanical nonsense, I don't know what is," Sally said, popping out of the bathroom with all the savagery of a miniature . . . " . . . I am not a miniature anything, Dai op Owen."

But she was comical enough in her undressed state, mentally bristling at his thoughts and aggravated by his pessimistic rumination to put the morning's disasters in their proper perspective.

"I'm not sure what good it'll do to have Roznine marching in here now," she went on, pouring out coffee.

"I'd hoped he'd come as soon as he regained consciousness."

Sally's eyebrows flicked up. "You've never failed of your mark before. Unless . . ." She pursed her lips, frowning.

"Amalda's inhibiting him?" Daffyd caught the half-suppressed notion.

"You know she's scared of him. I mean, scared as a woman is of a very domineering man . . . sexually, I mean. Oh, you *know* what I mean and then there's Bruce Vaden and all that."

"Amalda had proof positive yesterday that Roznine couldn't dominate her."

"Perhaps . . . I mean, intellectually, Talent-wise, yes. But it's Bruce that's holding her back. He's already at the top of the Glass mountain and Amalda doesn't dare roll the other apple."

Daffyd caught the unarticulated ramifications of Sally's thinking. Part of Amalda's reluctance to admit Roznine's attractiveness to her stemmed from a fear of losing Bruce Vaden, to whom she was equally attracted but for different reasons.

"She's not one to drop the bone she's got in her mouth for the one she sees in the water," Sally said.

"Now it's fables?"

"Why not? You added myths to my fairy tales so it's my shot."

"That only leaves me proverbs."

"So?"

"So! That leaves us with Amalda inhibiting Roznine?"

"He should've been here otherwise."

Daffyd was turning over this interesting possibility in his mind when the comset beeped.

"Boss, we got pickets out in front," said Lester in a thoroughly disgusted tone of voice. "Pay your fair share. Everyone else is taxed. Why not you? No Minority priviliges."

Daffyd sighed long and deeply.

"Pete's on reception and he says they've got legal political platforms, their IDs are upstate and they're registered party members. Legally, under the Political Platform Act, they can picket the grounds because there *is* legislation concerning our tax status before the State Senate right now."

"Did you inform Gillings?"

"Hah! They informed us about the time the first picketers foregathered on our gatestep. What'n'hell happened to your Machiavellian nonsense of yesterday?"

" 'There's many a slip twixt cup and lip!' " Daffyd replied. Sally gasped and signaled surrender.

"Huh?" Lester wanted an explanation.

"I must ask Gillings if Roznine's had a visit from Aaron Greenfield since the hearing yesterday," was Daffyd's reply.

"Did you goof, boss? Now what do we do?"

"Keep tabs that the on-lookers remain quiescent, and alert riot control."

"Amalda and Red?"

"No, plunk Harold in the gatelodge with Pete. Ask Gillings . . ."

"Ask him yourself: Charlie says he's just called through."

Before Daffyd could request a deferment of that call, Charlie had patched it through and Daffyd hoped his flinching wasn't apparent to the LEO Commissioner.

"You got troubles?" Gillings's face was impassive.

"Nothing we can't handle . . ."

"Oh, the trap's sprung?" Gillings looked almost pleased.

"Hmmmm . . . but I'd like a few of your riotmobiles around."

Gillings's expression changed rapidly to sour discontent.

"Like that, huh? I thought Roznine was supposed to come like a lamb?"

Daffyd shot a glance at Sally who was muttering something about metaphors being illegal. Her levity was not appropriate to the gravity of the present situation and yet . . . it helped.

"Roznine's a strong personality . . ."

"I'm going after him . . ." Gillings now looked like a trap sprung.

"Gillings," and Daffyd's tone of voice was far sterner than people were apt to use in addressing the LEO Commissioner, "don't go after Roznine. We've exerted all the pressure possible under the circumstances. He'll come . . ."

The Commissioner regarded the Director for a long moment.

"You better know what the hell you're doing, op Owen."

"I do."

"Well, you sound as if you do," Sally said when the call was disconnected.

"I really think I do, Sally." Daffyd looked out of his

window toward the building which housed Amalda and
Red. "Two birds in one bush, two baskets with the
same eggs, two minds with the same great thought . . ."

"Spare me! Uncle! I yield!"

"Good, then let's figure out how to unwind Amalda.
I did not suggest to Roznine that he bring Great Birnam
Wood to Dunsinane."

"I should have guessed that Shakespeare would be
next."

"Considering my propensity for quoting Alexander
Pope, I wonder you dared."

"He's coming for me," said Amalda when she and
Red noticed the circling picketers and the gathering of
curious by-standers.

Bruce Vaden threw back his head and roared. He
wasn't counterfeiting the amusement though it had a bitter note. But her woebegone expression was ludicrous
and his laughter was not the sympathy she'd expected.

"My dear child, if Roznine has to salve his Slavic
ego by resorting to that kind of subterfuge . . ."

"What on earth do you mean?"

"I mean that Roznine simply can't walk in here, no
matter what suggestion op Owen planted in his mind when
he was unconscious."

Her irritation was replaced by a shudder. Vaden could
feel the repugnance she experienced when touching
Roznine's mind. But her impression no longer dominated
his reaction to Roznine. Not after seeing the man in
Court yesterday.

"Did you really look at Vsevolod Roznine yesterday?"

Amalda gave him that wide-eyed innocent stare and
he felt her going "dead" on him. At first Bruce thought
it was because she was afraid of Roznine and censored
any references to him. Now he knew differently.

"Mally hon," and he took her by the shoulders, forcing

her to look him in the eye. "I looked *at* Roznine. I looked him over good and strangely enough, I liked what I saw." That got her where she lived, and Red took a deep breath, opening his own inner mind so she couldn't fail to see the sincerity of his words. "He's the kind of guy I'd trust and respect even if I could probably take him apart in a fair fight. Oh, I know. I've heard all this static about his sewer-sink mind and his power in the city and I don't know as my public mind would be all that clean and pure. I've learned to do my improper thinking carefully but no one's warned Roznine that there're guys around reading him now and again."

Amalda was staring up at him. Her eyes had gone all big and her lips were parted. He wanted to kiss her, to love and reassure her, but not just then.

"Mind you, I don't think Roznine's a crusading saint but feckitall, Mally, he's up against City Hall and when you're fighting City Hall you use every advantage you can beg, borrow or," he clipped her lightly on the jaw, "kidnap. Not that I blame him for flipping his nut over you." He couldn't keep his voice steady and he knew he was playing-back their initial meeting. "If you affect Roznine the way you do me, I'm damned sorry for the poor guy. It must be hell for him to want you and not get you."

Amalda discarded all restraint and now remorse/love/appreciation / agreement / understanding / pride / loyalty/washed over him.

"Don't do that, Mally. I've got to think."

She bit her lip apologetically and "buttoned" her emotions up.

"Thanks. Now, where was I? Yeah. As of yesterday, I don't think Roznine could use you. Not now. Or only if you let him. And you won't. If that's what's bugging you, forget it. Or don't you remember how easily you knocked him out? You gotta take it easy on the guy, hon. He loves you even if he doesn't know it."

"It's you I'm worried about, Bruce," she said in a very low voice, her eyes wide and full of tears.

So he embraced her, pressing her slender body against him, so she'd "feel" all he couldn't express. His knowledge that you aren't selfish with Talent, whatever kind you possessed: that they had a relationship too strong to be broken or diminished by the acceptance of a third party: that Talent had obligations beyond the personal and this was one of them, for both Amalda and Bruce.

She reached up tenderly to stroke his face, her fingers enjoying the tactile contact with the silky hair of his beard, letting her fingers express what she didn't articulate. As she had learned to accept Bruce's right to decide for them both, she accepted his decision now.

"The stage is set, honey," he said finally. "Extras all milling about, waiting for the director. Are you going to let him come?"

She gave an impatient little shrug, then squared her shoulders and smiled at him, ready to move mountains, from the look of her. He liked that about Amalda, among a thousand other things. He conveyed that approval with a gentle, mind-blown hug. Talent has advantages, too.

Roznine rubbed at his temples, wondering what kind of fake powder the medic had sold him as a headache remedy.

They had done something to him when he was unconscious. Just as he, Vsevolod Roznine, knew that *they* had caused him to black out at the hearing. No, not "they"! *Her!*

The conviction that he had to get to her, be with her, returned with renewed and irresistible force. And Roznine fought it again, fought it as his head throbbed, and his hands clenched into fists of effort to withstand the compulsion.

He flung himself from the table, catching the leg with

his foot and upsetting the untouched meal, half-stumbling against the door and striking his temple on the frame. He hit his head a second, a third time. And clutching the molding, threw back his head in bitter laughter.

"Roznine has to beat his own head, because it feels so good when he stops!"

His fingers dug into the frame until his nails bent against the durable plastic. His head turned slowly, as if he could see straight through concrete and plastic, across the miles to the Center in which direction he unerringly turned.

"*NO!*" This time his fists thudded into plastic. "Roznine does not come at a woman's call. She comes to him!"

How had they done this to him? How could she call him? Once he'd known her name and that she was at the Center, he'd had his people find out all they could. She was registered as a telempath. Roznine had looked that up and the answer had only confirmed what he'd guessed himself: she could transmit emotions and probably receive them.

Roznine pounded the wall viciously, transmitting such hatred and discontent as boiled up in him from the frustration of not having her and the humiliation of being knocked unconscious . . . in full view of his constituents . . . by a slip of a girl he could break in two pieces with one hand.

And who was the redbearded man who worked with her? How close did he work with her?

Jealousy was added to the seething emotions of Vsevolod Roznine. And the skin of his skull pulsed with a surfeit of his angry blood.

The intensity of his desire to see Amalda reached another peak. He fought it. He would not go to her. She must come to him! He could not go to her. She had to come to him. She, who could read his thoughts, let her read that one. Let her read his feelings . . .

"No!"

Roznine stopped. Everything about him stopped, his heart, his lungs, the oxygen molecules in his blood. Then he took a deep breath and exhaled, his wide mouth forming an odd smile in a suddenly calm face.

No wonder she had not come to him, the little one. She *could* read his thoughts. She would be terrified of him, Roznine: terrified of the anger he had felt toward his little bird. He had felt her fear before, felt her spirit fluttering away from him. That was why she had run from the Fact. But she shouldn't fear him, Vsevolod Roznine. Every man, boy and adult she should fear but not Vsevolod Roznine. He would go to her. He would explain.

Chort vozmi! Would his head never stop aching?

His comset buzzed. The noise stabbed piercingly through his skull. He grabbed frantically for the set to stop the noise, answering in a savage tone.

"Everyone's in position, Gospodeen."

"Position?" Roznine shook his battered head, unable to recollect which position and where.

"The picketers have been checked by the Center's guards, who are two old men: nothing to worry about."

Picketers? Pickets? At the Center? Oh, yes. He'd discussed that with the little man from upstate. How could he have forgotten?

"And the riot squad?"

"Parked at or working conveniently nearby. The disposal men . . ."

"Good enough!" His head pounded like a drill press but he remembered. How could he have forgotten? So she was a riot control team, was she? Well, let her control this riot! Men would pour in to the Center's so private, so secluded, so sacrosanct grounds from all over the city: men from many ethnic groups so it couldn't be blamed on his section. It had meant cancelling half the favors he was owed but, just let him get his hands on that little riot controller and . . .

He threw open the illegally unsealed window and slid

down the airshaft on the escape line. He opened the
window in the rear flat, which conveniently belonged
to a relative who was blind anyhow, and exited through
the back door. Found the iron pry-bar and flipped up
the sewer lid, snagging it deftly back over the manhole
when he was within. He walked briskly over the thin
stream which trickled down the pipes at this time of day.
Two rights and a left brought him to a wider section
conduit with a catwalk on one side. Two more rights
and two lefts and he climbed a ladder. The manhole
had been shielded and a Disposal truck was just drawing
up. Swiftly he was within the truck and issuing orders to
the driver.

The sensitive signalled LEO headquarters that Roznine
had left his quarters. Immediately Gillings warned the
Center and circulated the alert to all stations.

Charlie Moorfield rang through to Daffyd's quarters.

"Ring Amalda and tell her I'm on my way over."

Sally was struggling into her coverall, excitement making her fingers fumble so that Daffyd held the collar
until she could find the armholes.

"He is coming. You were too much for him."

"Possibly."

Daffyd could also see another interpretation of Roznine's secret exit, particularly with the picketers outside
and the observers forming a larger and larger ragged
semi-circle beyond the gates to the Center.

"Yes, I see what you mean, Dai."

"Let's reinforce Amalda."

The buzzer sounded again. "Boss, I get no answer from
Amalda."

"Tell Gillings to get all riot units here on the double.
Alert ours."

Daffyd op Owen swore as he grabbed Sally's hand and
pulled her out the door. Short of teleporting, he'd never
been down the stairs so fast. Afterwards Sally told him
her feet had touched the steps only three times.

Amalda and Bruce Vaden had exited through one of the side-gates in the grounds. They'd come up on the picketline from one side, mingling with the onlookers until they were directly opposite the main gates. The picketers were dutifully chanting the slogans they carried, the four LEO men routinely assigned a picket, were almost as bored with the proceedings. A passenger conveyance settled to the public landing some hundred yards from the gates and the occupants, carrying collapsed signs, descended in an orderly fashion.

"Those are bully boys, not bona fide picketers," Bruce told Amalda in a quiet voice.

She nodded for she'd unerringly sighted the one man who was important. *"He's* with them."

"Well, this is the last place he'd be looking for us. Are you shielding tightly?"

Amalda nodded again but she didn't take her eyes from Roznine.

He really was attractive, she thought. There was something proud and fierce in his manner. Bruce was right: she hadn't really seen him before. She'd been just so scared of his mind . . .

She stopped thinking because Roznine was suddenly glancing over his shoulder, at the crowd, frowning slightly. He stood near the copter, to one side of the new shift of pickets. They were milling about . . .

"Warn Dave Amalda, and get set. See how they're maneuvering?" Even as he spoke, Bruce glided to a more advantageous position for teamwork.

The new arrivals, for all their aimless movement, could now be seen aiming for the LEO men and the Center's two guards, mild-appearing gentlemen who were in fact top kineticists and could hold a grown man immobile on the ground without lifting a physical finger.

The old shift broke from their circuit, grounding and collapsing their signs, preparatory to leaving. Some elements of the crowd which had watched pacifically from the footpath began to move toward the grounds.

Amalda began to broadcast, gently at first, the feeling of immense fatigue, utter boredom and a dislike of this activity.

Bruce moved further across the street, picking up and increasing the intensity of her broadcast. But he watched Roznine, saw the man stiffen, his head turn slowly, unerringly towards Amalda. The group in which she had been standing shifted and she was by herself.

The setting of the confrontation was superb, Bruce Vaden told himself with a curious objectivity. As if by magic or common consent, everyone melted from the two principals, leaving a clear path between them.

"Don't get scared, honey baby," Bruce told her under his breath, fighting in his mind to hold the broadcast and disguise the inner reluctance of sharing Amalda with anyone at all.

Suddenly he felt buoyed up, felt the indescribable mental support and touch of Daffyd op Owen, speaking through him to Amalda. And it wasn't just Dave, but something . . . no, *someone* else.

The area was blanketed with silence by Amalda's projection which began to waver slightly. Bruce intensified it, imagining as he'd been taught, that the emotion was something visible which he was manipulating tangibly, as visible and tangible as water falling over a specific area, drenching everything with its cascade.

Everything went at half speed. Roznine pulled first one heavy leg forward, then the other, like a man treading through molasses, sticky, cloying. The man's face was contorted with effort and concentration.

Amalda just stood, her chin slightly raised, looking as regal and poised as she had on the Fact stage, so sure of herself that she almost fooled Vaden.

The action was all slow motion: the picketers, real and bogus, discarding their all too heavy signs, inexorably sinking to the ground, sprawling in poses of utter exhaustion. It affected the LEO men though they tried hard to resist the pressure, falling to their knees and hands, faces down on the ground.

Then only she, Bruce and Roznine were standing. She took a deep breath and looked straight at Roznine's eyes: the first time she had done so.

And Bruce was right that Vascha (she found his nickname easily: though he thought of himself, self-importantly, only as Vsevolod Roznine, the Vascha personality was there, too) was nice looking, with a strong body and sensitive hands. She liked long, well-shaped fingers on a man—she liked to have such hands on her body.

"All right, here I am," she said out loud and dared him in her mind to overpower her.

His eyes seemed to eat her flesh hungrily, as if starved for the essence beneath the covering tissue.

"You're mine. I, Vsevolod Roznine, say you are mine." That was his thought, beating away at her. She wanted to laugh, to sing out because his thought couldn't go any further than her mind. It couldn't reach Bruce, standing not more than five feet away. Not unless she wanted it to go further!

"Well, what are you waiting for?" she asked gently because the knowledge of such total power over another human being humbled her.

Some of his bully boys were getting to their feet for she'd turned off some of her blanketing projection to deal with Vascha. Through Vsevolod Roznine she sent a fleeting thought of nausea that instantly reduced them to retching bodies on the grass. And as abruptly, she deflected the actual illness. Then she turned off the empathetical broadcast completely, knowing its cessation would leave the victims disoriented enough to cause no further trouble.

"I think you'd better come with us, Vsevolod," she said to Roznine and took his hand, turning and leading him toward the Center as if he had no other choice. He didn't because Bruce fell in on the other side, their strides matching.

Roznine was dazed, his lips compressed into a thin line. He glared down at Amalda as she led him, at arm's length, like a mother dragging an errant child home.

The gateman nodded to the trio as they passed into the Center's Grounds.

"What'n'hell has happened to your common sense, op Owen?" Frank Gillings demanded. "Letting not only Amalda and Vaden but Roznine into the City Council? For Chrissake that's what he wanted Amalda for . . ."

"Easy, Frank. The team's on assignment, completely legitimate."

"Council isn't a riot situation . . ."

Daffyd raised his eyebrows in polite surprise. "No? According to Roznine, the tempers get so hot no constructive work is ever done. Each ethnic group insists that its members are being discriminated against with accusations and counter-accusations until the mediator adjourns the hearing with nothing accomplished except exhibitions of parliamentary bad manners. Sorry. The team is going to cool things long enough for common sense to prevail. Roznine's reason for wanting Amalda's Talent in City Hall was valid." Daffyd also neglected to add that that was the bargain he'd struck with Roznine to join the Center. All the man wanted was to be certain the employment allotments were impartially assigned. Well, not all, Daffyd amended to himself, but Roznine had gone about it the wrong way.

Daffyd grinned reassuringly at Gillings's image in the comset. "He's part of the team now and *she* follows orders."

"But does Roznine?" asked Gillings sarcastically.

"As I've explained to you, Frank, Roznine is parapsychically dead to anyone else. Oh, Bruce Vaden empathizes with him to some extent now they've both had training, but Roznine's is a one-way Talent, right to

Amalda. She's the focus of the gestalt. You might say, he's been check-reined."

Frank Gillings grunted, somewhat mollified. Then, jutting out his chin, he glared at the Director. "You going to start lobbying for a rider on that Talent Immunity Law?"

"Immediately. In fact," and Daffyd's smile broadened with sheer malice, "Senator Greenfield is helping us get an interim rider through the State Senate on a Bill he has coming up on the Agenda next session."

"Greenfield?"

"Yes. Roznine invited him here at the Center for a chat. The Senator was most amenable to the suggestion."

The LEO Commissioner's frown was partically perplexity. "What'd you guys do to Greenfield? Blanket him with loving kindness?"

"Good heavens, no. It was merely pointed out to him that the Center is not a minority, but a collection of minorities since all ethnic groups are represented. He took a tour of the grounds and instantly perceived that the housing was by no means as luxurious as he'd been previously led to believe, with swimming pools or wasted space that might house additional families. In fact, he complimented us on our planning and thrifty use of facilities."

Frank Gillings was by no means taken in by Daffyd op Owen's bland manner. He growled something under his breath.

"What did Roznine have on him, Dave?"

"I don't know what you mean, Frank."

The LEO man made a gesture of disgust.

"Dave, don't give me any more problems for a while, will you?"

"Nothing's coming up in the foreseeable future."

The screen went blank on Gillings's incredulous expression.

"Daffyd, that was highly immoral, unethical and downright dirty," said Sally, half scolding as she rose from the couch where she'd been sitting out of line-of-vision of the comset. She walked in under his arm, linking him around the waist. He nuzzled her curls and kissed her forehead.

"Probably. Les is always reminding me that it's bad policy to tell all."

"It's a shame about Vascha though." Sally sighed.

"Why?"

"Oh, it's rather sad, his being a psychic mule, her Pegasus."

"Thank God he is," Daffyd said so fervently she looked up, startled. "With the ambition and drive that young man has, he'd rule the world in half a year if Amalda and Bruce weren't there to stop him."

DEL REY BOOKS

ANNE McCAFFREY